NA[illegible]

"A fun [illegible]
Ameri[illegible] ."

—J[illegible]

"A swe[illegible]
clever protagonist, and creamy fudge—a yummy recipe for a great read."

—**Joanna Campbell Slan**, author of *The Scrap-N-Craft* mysteries

"A delightful mystery delivering suspense and surprise in equal measure. A must-read for all lovers of amateur sleuth classic mysteries."

—**Carole Bugge**, author of the *Claire Rawlings* mysteries

"Indulge your sweet tooth as you settle in and meet Allie McMurphy, Mal the bichon/poodle mix, and the rest of the motley crew in this entertaining series debut."

—**Miranda James**, author of the *Cat in the Stacks* mysteries

"A sweet treat with memorable characters, a charming locale, and satisfying mystery."

—**Barbara Allan**, author of the *Trash 'n' Treasures* mysteries

"The characters are fun and well-developed, the setting is quaint and beautiful, and there are several mouth-watering fudge recipes."

—**RT Book Reviews** (3 stars)

"Enjoyable . . . ALL FUDGED UP is littered with delicious fudge recipes, including alcohol-infused ones. I really enjoyed this cozy mystery and look forward to reading more in this series."

—**Fresh Fiction**

"Cozy mystery lovers who enjoy quirky characters, a great setting and fantastic recipes will love this debut."

—***The Lima News***

"The first Candy-Coated mystery is a fun cozy due to the wonderful location filled with eccentric characters."

—*Midwest Book Review*

To Fudge or Not to Fudge

"*To Fudge or Not to Fudge* was as enticing and tasty as a pan of fudge! The mystery kept me on the edge of the seat, and I love visiting with Allie's friends and family. I know I will be counting down the days until the next mystery with Allie McMurphy."

—*Cozy Mystery Book Reviews*

"*To Fudge or Not to Fudge* is a superbly-crafted, classic, culinary cozy mystery. If you enjoy them as much as I do, you are in for a real treat. The setting of Mackinac Island immediately drew me to the book as it is an amazing location. The only problem I had with the book was reading about all the mouthwatering fudge made me hungry."

—**Examiner.com** (5 stars out of 5)

"We LOVED it! This mystery is a vacation between the pages of a book. If you've never been to Mackinac Island, you will long to visit, and if you have, the story will help you to recall all of your wonderful memories."

—**Melissa's Mochas**, Mysteries and Meows

"A five-star delicious mystery that has great characters, a good plot and a surprise ending. If you like a good mystery with more than one suspect and a surprise ending, then rush out to get this book and read it, but be sure you have the time since once you start you won't want to put it down. I give this 5 Stars and a Wow Factor of 5+. The fudge recipes included in the book all sound wonderful. I am thinking that a gift basket filled with the fudge from the recipes in this book, along with a copy of the book, some hot chocolate mix and/or coffee, and a nice mug would be a great Christmas gift."

—**Mystery Reading Nook**

Also by Nancy Coco

All Fudged Up

To Fudge or Not to Fudge

Oh Say Can You Fudge

Nancy Coco

KENSINGTON PUBLISHING CORP.
http://www.kensingtonbooks.com

KENSINGTON BOOKS are published by

Kensington Publishing Corp.
119 West 40th Street
New York, NY 10018

All Kensington Titles, Imprints, and Distributed Lines are available at special quantity discounts for bulk purchases for sales promotions, premiums, fund-raising, and educational or institutional use. Special book excerpts or customized printings can also be created to fit specific needs. For details, write or phone the office of the Kensington special sales manager: Kensington Publishing Corp., 119 West 40th Street, New York, NY 10018, attn: Special Sales Department, Phone: 1-800-221-2647.

ISBN-13: 978-0-7582-8714-4
ISBN-10: 0-7582-8714-3
First Kensington Mass Market Edition: May 2015

eISBN-13: 978-0-7582-8715-1
eISBN-10: 0-7582-8715-1
First Kensington Electronic Edition: May 2015

10 9 8 7 6 5 4 3 2 1

Printed in the United States of America

This book is for George, the wonder dog,
who brought laughter and joy, protection, and love
into my family's life for twelve wonderful years.

Caramel Apple Pie Fudge

1 14 ounce can of sweetened condensed milk
2½ cups white chocolate
4 tablespoons butter
¾ cup dried apple, finely diced
1 teaspoon vanilla
1 teaspoon cinnamon
½ teaspoon nutmeg
¼ teaspoon allspice
½ cup caramel pieces, melted with 2 tablespoons milk.
½ cup apple cinnamon ice cream topping
1 teaspoon butter to prep pan

Butter 8x8x2-inch pan.

Melt sweetened condensed milk, white chocolate, and butter in the top of a double boiler until smooth. Remove from heat and add apple, vanilla, cinnamon, nutmeg, and allspice. Stir until combined. Pour into pan.

Alternately spoon melted caramel and apple cinnamon topping on the top of the fudge. Take a butter knife and swirl topping throughout. Refrigerate fudge 3 hours or overnight. Cut into 1-inch pieces.

Serve in paper candy cups or on a platter. Store in air tight container.

Enjoy!

Chapter 1

June 25

I was working on a red, white, and blue striped fudge recipe when I got a call from Rodney Rivers. So, of course, I let the call go to voice mail. I mean nothing, but perhaps if the curtains are on fire, interrupted working with hot sugar. I was at the most delicate part of making fudge—the stirring to cool. If you overbeat the fudge while it cools, it sugars. If you under beat the fudge, it's too soft. Therefore, a random phone call from the pyro technician in charge of the Mackinac Island Star Spangled Fourth fireworks celebrations could be answered later. Right?

Except I got caught up in the fudge.

Three hours later, still not happy with the recipe, I noticed the blinking light on my cell phone and figured I'd better call up the voice mail.

"Allie, we've got a problem. Meet me at the fireworks warehouse as soon as possible." Rodney sounded angry. "The entire program is in ruins."

Oh, man, that was not good. I'd had to fight my way onto the Star Spangled Fourth event committee in the first place. It was only because old man Slauser had died in May that I had been able to join the committee and take over the fireworks program. It was all part of my ongoing plan to become an upstanding member of Mackinac Island society.

Message two came up.

"Allie, answer your phone, will you? This is serious and time sensitive." Rodney's tone had gone from angry to desperate. "The entire back row of fireworks has been tampered with— Hey, you. What are you doing here? Are you responsible for—" The phone went eerily dead.

Well, that certainly couldn't be good. I dialed the call-back number, but it went straight to voice mail. I left a message. "Hey, Mr. Rivers, this is Allie McMurphy. I just got your voice mails. I was in the middle of making fudge or I would have answered sooner." I winced at my own rambling message. As the boss, I was never supposed to make excuses or apologize. "I'm headed to the warehouse. Call me if you're no longer there. Otherwise I'm coming down to see what I can do to help." I hung up my phone. There was a third message, but I assumed that it was from Rodney Rivers as well. He sounded insistent. I didn't take the time to listen any further. Instead I stripped out of my chef's jacket, which was stiff from sugar and candy ingredients that tended to float in the air whenever I was inventing something new.

The lobby door to the McMurphy was open to let in the soft, fresh lake air which blew the summer white linen curtains softly.

I called to my reservation manager. "Frances, I need to meet Mr. Rivers at the fireworks warehouse. Can you cover for me until Sandy comes in?"

"Sure can," Frances answered from her perch behind the reservation desk. "What's up?"

I'd inherited Frances along with the Historic McMurphy Hotel and Fudge Shop when my Papa Liam died. She had worked the busy summer seasons for Papa and Grammy Alice for as long as I could remember.

"Mr. Rivers didn't say exactly, but there may be something wrong with some of the fireworks."

"Do you want me to call the fire department?" Frances looked at me over the top of her dark purple reading glasses. It was hard to tell she was in her seventies. She kept her brunette hair immaculate and her skin glowed in a way I hoped mine would at her age.

"No, I think if it were bad enough for the fire department, Mr. Rivers would have called them. He's an expert at that kind of thing and has always stressed safety first."

My bichon-poo puppy, Marshmallow—Mal for short—got up from her comfortable spot in the pink doggie bed beside Frances. She stretched her back legs in a manor I liked to call doggie yoga—it mimicked the downward dog position—and trotted over to me then begged to be picked up. When I ignored the blatant display of cuteness, she poked my black cotton covered leg with her nose—a sign she knew I was going out and she expected me to take her.

"No, Mal. It's too far for you," I said and gathered

up my keys and things in a small bag with shoestring handles that turned it into a backpack.

She sat, sighed loudly, and turned back to her bed.

"I'll call as soon as I find out more." I pulled the bag over my shoulders. "Let Sandy know we're short on the chocolate cherry and the cotton candy fudge."

"Will do." Frances went back to her computer. She had been my Grammy Alice's best friend. She'd worked summers for my grandparents for something fun to do and to make a little extra money. When she retired from teaching, she came to work for Papa Liam full-time. When Papa died in March, Frances had stayed to help me navigate the ins and outs of running the McMurphy.

I counted on her to introduce me to our regular customers. Some had been summering at the McMurphy for generations. Others just a season or two, but Frances remembered them all.

I grabbed my thin blue-jean jacket from a hook near the back door and put it on over the top of my pink McMurphy polo shirt and went out the back door of the hotel. Part of the appeal of Mackinac Island—besides the world famous fudge and the grand, Victorian, painted-lady summer cottages—was the fact that motorized vehicles, with the exception of the ambulance and fire truck, were not allowed on the island. That meant there were only three modes of transportation: horse-drawn carriage, bicycle, and on foot.

Since the fireworks were stored in a cinder block warehouse near the airport, I decided to bike it and unchained my bicycle from the stand in the back alley. Two miles on foot might make my current tardiness even worse. I threw my blue Ked-covered right foot over the bike and took off, thankful for the black slacks that were part of my standard uniform.

It really was a lovely day. I was continually amazed at the laid-back beauty of the island and the large state park in the center that offered good hiking, beautiful views, and fresh air to anyone who'd had enough of the hustle and bustle of the fort and shops of Main Street. I watched the Grand Hotel's Cessna 421C charter plane land as I drew close to the airport.

The airport warehouse had been built to store supplies flown in during the winter months when the ferries quit running. We picked it for the fireworks storage because it was cinder block and away from the crowds.

A handful of tourists stepped out of the charter plane and onto the tarmac. The Grand Hotel was a magnet for the wealthy and offered the charter plane service as a quick and easy way onto the island from Chicago or Detroit.

Three men were perfectly groomed and wore aviator sunglasses, stylish jeans, and immaculately pressed linen shirts. Two women wore what appeared to be designer-cut halter dresses with floral patterns. Their long bare legs were made even longer by the gold toned sandals.

The last to step out of the plane was Sophie Collins, the local pilot. She wore a crisp white shirt with epaulets and tan slacks. Her dark curly hair was pulled back in a low, easy ponytail. I waved at her.

She waved back then turned to escort her clients to the waiting horse-drawn carriage that would take them to the Grand Hotel.

I'd met Sophie at a dinner party Trent Jessop's sister had given for about twenty of the local island folks. Unlike the others, Sophie had been the only one to treat me like an equal. We had a long discussion about the cliquishness of island society. She was in her early thirties, had been a full-time pilot for the Grand Hotel for three years, and still occasionally ran up against people who treated her like an outsider.

I parked my bike in front of the warehouse and took note that two other bikes were nearby. One had the look of a rental bike. Many places on the island rent bikes. Most of the better hotels had bike rental right outside their doors. The second bike was a professional off-roader. It had the used look of a local's.

"Hello?" I said as I opened the door. "Mr. Rivers? It's Allie McMurphy. I came as soon as I got your messages."

The overhead fluorescent lights buzzed and hissed above me.

"Hello?" The first aisle was quiet and while the shelves were filled with boxes large and small there wasn't a human to be found. "Mr. Rivers? It's Allie. You left me a message about a problem?"

The second aisle of shelves was empty. I paused to see if I could hear anyone talking. Two bikes outside besides mine meant someone had to be in the warehouse, didn't they?

Two offices in the back near the bay doors were

big enough to bring in full pallets of supplies—in this case—fireworks. Maybe Rodney Rivers was in one of the offices with whomever else was there. It could be that they had closed the door and couldn't hear me.

A quick glance down the third and last isle didn't reveal anything tragic as his voice mail had stated. Perhaps he'd cleared everything up already. After all, it had been over an hour since the last phone call.

My phone rang and, startled, I jumped what felt like ten feet. Clearly, I was on edge in the warehouse. I pulled my phone out of my pocket and saw that the number belonged to Rex Manning, sexy police officer and now my good friend. "Hello?"

"Allie, are you okay? Frances said there may be trouble at the fireworks warehouse."

"I'm good, except my heart is still racing from being startled by my phone ringing." I walked toward the two offices built with half walls of cinder block and the rest window so that the manager of the warehouse could look out and keep an eye on the workers.

Rex chuckled. "Spooky at the warehouse? Where's Phil Angler? He's usually around there somewhere."

"I have no idea. When I got here two bikes were parked outside. One looked like a rental so I assume it belongs to Rodney Rivers. Maybe the second belongs to Phil."

"Was it a blue off-roader?"

"I think so." I continued toward the darkened offices. "I wasn't paying that much attention. I was in a bit of a hurry."

"Hurry for what?"

"I got two voice messages from Mr. Rivers. He's the pyro technician I hired for the fireworks shows. The first message he left said we had a problem at the warehouse and I was to call him back. The second got interrupted, but I think he said something about sabotage."

"I don't like the sound of that, Allie. Get out of the warehouse." Rex's tone of voice brooked no argument. Not that his tone had any effect on me.

"I'm fine. As far as I can tell no one's here." I put my free hand on the glass to shade my eyes and break the glare from the overhead lights and peered into the first dark office. "The phone calls were an hour or so ago. Maybe he resolved things already."

"Allie, I'm serious. Get the hell out of the warehouse. Do it now."

"But—"

"I swear, Allie, sometimes you are too stubborn for your own good. Get out. The place might be rigged and—"

"Could explode," I finished and pursed my mouth, pushing it to the side as I peered down the aisle. The last office was just a few feet away with only the distance of the bay door between me and it. "I watch TV, too. How often does that happen in real life?"

"Allie—"

"Okay, fine. I'm at the bay door in the back, anyway. I'll just stick my head over and take a peek in the second office and I'll leave."

"I'm nearly there," Rex said. "I need you to leave now."

"But it's only a few feet and I'll be careful." I checked for trip wires or anything like what you see in movies that might cause an explosion as I carefully tiptoed across the bay door. "If anyone sees me doing this, they're going to think I'm crazy."

"Allie, I'm very serious—"

"I'm being careful, really. I promise, I won't open the door or anything. I'm only going to peek inside." I slowly made it across the bay to see a light on in the second office. "The light is on. I'm sure it will be fine. Phil's probably inside unaware that I'm skulking around."

"Darn it, Allie."

I peeked inside the window and stopped cold. "Oh, no."

"What is it? What's going on?"

"There's a man slumped across the desk, faceup." I couldn't help the wince in my voice. "I can see his expression and his eyes have the same look that Joe Jessop's did. I'm pretty sure he's dead. And—"

"And what?!"

"Weird. Little paper chickens are all kind of tethered together. It's like a string of lights or something draped over him. Do you want me to go in and see?" I reached out toward the office doorknob.

"Freeze!" Rex's voice echoed from the phone and the hall behind me.

I screamed a little and wheeled around to see him striding purposefully toward me dressed in full police uniform, his bike helmet still on his head. He had one hand out in the universal sign of *stop* and the other hand on the butt of the gun on his hip.

"Darn it! You scared me half to death." I scowled at him. "How did you get here so fast?"

"Frances called me the minute you left the McMurphy."

"Figures," I muttered. "Why didn't you tell me you were in the building?"

"Get your hand off that doorknob, Allie." Rex was serious and his seriousness got to me.

It was one thing for him to be authoritative on the phone and quite something different to see him face-to-face in full cop mode. I raised both hands slowly in the air. "I'm not touching it."

Just then there was a sharp screaming sound and a little pop coming from the other side of the glass. I whirled to see that the little chickens were tethered together by a fuse. They were fireworks. The screaming sound and pop repeated itself over and over as the chickens lit up.

"What the heck?" he asked beside me.

"Fireworks are going off in there," I said as he looked inside.

"Hang up your phone," Rex ordered. His cop's gaze took in everything at once. "Gosh darn it, you're right. He has the blank stare of a dead man and those are screaming chickens going off. Did you see anyone else in the room?"

"Nope."

"You need to get out of the building." He put his hand on my arm and gently led me to the entrance door beside the bay door. He stopped and carefully inspected the door, running his hand along the edges. "Feels clean." He cautiously opened the door and alarms went off, blaring.

I covered my ears and let him lead me outside

and a few hundred feet from the building. We stood where the surrounding parking lot gave way to woods.

"Charlene," Rex said into the walkie-talkie on his shoulder. "We need the fire department, the EMTs, and call in a bomb squad from Mackinaw City."

"Bomb squad?" I heard Charlene parrot.

"That's right." Rex studied me. "Allie McMurphy reported a phone message that someone tampered with the fireworks. When we arrived some minor fireworks started to go off. I didn't see anyone so they were most likely lit with a slow fuse. I want a bomb squad here to check out the warehouse before anyone goes back in there."

"I've got a call into Mackinaw City," Charlene replied over the crackle of the walkie-talkie. "Do I need to send in Shane?"

"What makes you think we need a crime scene investigator?"

"Allie McMurphy's there, right?"

"Yes."

"Then there's a ninety-eight percent chance she found another dead body."

Rex's mouth went flat, making a thin line of disgust. "Get the fire department out here."

"Yes, sir." Charlene didn't sound the least bit contrite. "That girl is trouble, Officer Manning. Be careful."

"Allie didn't find a dead body," he said sharply. "She called in the bomb threat like a responsible adult."

"I'm sure she did." The communicator went dead as they hung up.

I hugged my arms around my chest. "You're right.

He only looked dead. You should have let me go check on him. What if he needed help?"

"Let me hear your phone messages." Rex held out his big hand.

I called up the voice mail, tapped in my password, and handed the phone to him.

His frown grew darker as he listened. "I'm going to have to keep these. They're evidence."

"What about Mr. Rivers? If you won't let me, shouldn't you at least go and check on him?"

"You recognized the guy in the office?"

"Yes, I think it was Rodney Rivers. He is the lead pyro tech I hired to do the Star Spangled Fourth fireworks shows."

Rex shook his head. "Dead or not, I can't take the chance that the place isn't rigged to blow. That's a warehouse full of fireworks. If it explodes, he really will be dead, along with anyone else inside."

I heard sirens in the distance. The island was anti motor vehicle except for first responders. Then all rules were broken. It only made sense that we had an ambulance and fire truck. There was a limit to charm when people needed help.

"Stay put!" Rex ordered and stepped out to direct the vehicles.

I stuck my tongue out at his back. He whirled around, but I put my hands up and blinked innocently. "I'm staying right here."

Rex was not much taller than me, but he was a big man with shoulders as wide as a mountain, a thick neck, and a shaved head in the fit manner of an action hero. In the last few months, I'd gotten to know him well. He had even asked me out once, but I'd already said yes to my current boyfriend

Trent Jessop. It's not that Rex wasn't attractive, but Trent left me feeling like the luckiest girl alive. Rex was a bit bossy . . . if you haven't already noticed.

Thirty minutes later, I still didn't have my phone and had finally given up and sat down on the curb of the parking area. I watched as Sophie had flown out right after the call and came back with the crew from Mackinaw City. Three guys in thick bomb suits, with helmets in hand, strolled around the corner where the fire truck and ambulance sat.

I was far enough away from the vehicles that I couldn't hear what Rex said to the men, but their expressions were deadly serious as they put on the helmets and carefully entered the building through the door Rex had pushed me out.

"First time I ever had to escort a bomb squad on the island," Sophie said as she walked toward me from the far edge of the parking lot. "It must be serious for Rex to call in trolls."

Some people called anyone from the Lower Peninsula *trolls* because they lived under (south of) the Mackinac Bridge. The suspension bridge is the longest in the western hemisphere and the fifth longest bridge in the world. People around Mackinac were proud that it was nearly twice as long as the Golden Gate Bridge, but the claim to fame ended there as it was not nearly as wide.

"Frances told him I had phone messages about trouble at the fireworks warehouse," I said as she sat down on the curb next to me. "He got all bossy and practically dragged me out of the warehouse."

"If Rex called the troll bomb squad he had good reason to drag you out," Sophie said. "I've known him for years and have never seen him panic."

"In my defense, I didn't see anything to worry about until I peeked into the last office." I hugged my knees to my chest.

"Rumor has it you found yet another dead guy." Sophie stretched her long legs out in front of her. "Kind of have a knack for that, don't you?"

"It's a newfound talent." I sighed. "I'd much rather be making fudge right now."

"I heard you hired Sandy Everheart as your assistant. That was good. She's one of the best chocolatiers I've ever met. And living on the island, I've met more than my fair share."

I turned my gaze from the goings on at the warehouse to Sophie. "Sandy is good. She should have her own shop."

"Well, some of us don't have family businesses to go into."

"Ouch."

Sophie sighed and leaned back onto her hands. "Sorry. That didn't come out right." She straightened. "I'm glad you gave her a chance. No one else would."

"I needed the help and she's good . . . better than me with the chocolate sculpture." I studied the building. "Do you think the warehouse will really blow up?"

"No, not unless the bomb guys come across something they haven't seen before."

I winced. "I hope they don't blow up. I've seen enough death in the last few months."

"I'm sure it's just Rex being overly cautious—"

Sudden motion from the emergency guys caught our attention. They were running and hopping into the vehicles and moving them away from the warehouse.

"Where are they going?" I stood and drew my eyebrows together in concern.

Sophie stood with me. "This does not look good." She took my arm and pulled me back to the woods.

Rex sent a quick shout to the last responder and ran at us. "Get back!" He waved his hands and Sophie linked her arm in mine and ran headfirst into the woods.

Panic had my heart racing and my feet pounding over uneven ground. We jumped over fallen logs. Ferns and scrub and wild raspberries ripped at our pants and tore at our shirts. Rex caught up with us and pushed us even faster until we hit the top of a hill and half ran, half slid at least one hundred feet down.

The loudest explosion I'd ever heard erupted from the trees above us. Rex shoved us into the earth, shielding us with as much of his body as possible as dust and rocks rolled over us. I inhaled dust and dry pine needle bits and coughed, my eyes watering. Pushing to sit up and get some fresh air, I watched in amazement as fireworks whistled into the air, exploding at low angles. Their color and sparkles lost in the daylight, they showered the dry woods.

"Get down!" Rex ordered, dragging me back into the dirt as a second loud explosion rumbled, raining more rocks and dust.

The walkie-talkie on his shoulder squawked. "Rex, what's going on? Are you all right?" Charlene sounded more worried than usual.

"Call everyone you can," he barked into the

communicator. "We've got a potential wildfire at the airport."

"Roger," Charlene said. "I'm calling up the volunteers."

"What about the airport?" Sophie asked. Her blue eyes shone in her dirt-covered face. "What about my plane?"

Another explosion filled the air. We ducked. I covered my head with my hands as rocks and branches rained down. We were lucky the small ridge above us sheltered us from most of the blast.

The scent of smoke and dirt and fireworks filled my senses. Falling ash burned my hand and I shook it off. Rex moved and I looked up to see him stomping out sparks as they threatened the dry pine needles.

Sophie and I got up. She tore off her over shirt, leaving her white athletic T-shirt on and used the shirt to beat out small fires. I kicked dirt over the sparks that fell near me. The fireworks continued to scream overhead. Their whistles and winding patterns drove them to various heights through the air, showering the area in ear-shattering explosions and sparkles of red, white, and blue.

My first Star Spangled Fourth had just become the worst disaster Mackinac Island had ever seen. Considering the War of 1812, that was saying a lot.

Chapter 2

"We were lucky that it rained all last week," Ed Goodfoot said. "The wildfire index was low and kept the fire contained to a quarter mile perimeter." He wore the heavy beige and yellow-trimmed fire-fighter's coat, pants, and boots. He held his fireman's hard hat in his strong, square-palmed, long-fingered hands. He had a thick smudge down the side of his strong, high cheekbones.

I stood with Ed, Rex, and a small crowd of smoke-smudged locals who had come out to stamp out any hot coals or ash left over from the warehouse explosion. In front of us, a large blackened hole gaped out of the cinder blocks in what used to be the roof of the warehouse. Glass was shattered and crumbled on the ground as the explosion had blown out every window and door. The back bay door had come up out of the hole in the roof and folded over the top of the cinder block like the peeled back top of a sardine can.

"We've walked the half-mile perimeter," Luke Archibald reported to Bruce Miller, the acting fire chief. "We're as sure as a person can be that the cinders are out." A small man of average size, Luke wore his balding, blond hair carefully brushed back and held into place by hair gel. He wore a dark green T-shirt underneath a green and white patterned, short sleeved cotton shirt. His shirt and his jeans were soot coated. He wore athletic shoes that had been gray and blue at one point but were now dust-covered brown.

His son Sherman stood beside him. Seventeen, with shaggy blond hair, braces on his teeth, and freckles across a little nose, his hazel eyes took in the sights of explosion and mayhem with a sort of wonder. He was busy snapping pictures with his phone and sending them off to people unknown. He stood a little taller than Luke, but it was difficult to tell because he hunched his shoulders and slouched his way around. That is, when he wasn't sneaking phone pictures.

"Thanks for your help." Bruce was tall with broad shoulders encased in a fireman's coat. He looked to be about forty years old, wore a fireman's hard hat, and his brown eyes seemed to take in all the damage with a knowing eye. "We'll have the public keep an eye out for any fires that pop up, but it's unlikely any more damage will happen." He moved on to another weary group of volunteers emerging from the other side of the airport.

"Those fireworks should have never exploded," Angus MacElroy said. "I know Rodney Rivers. He knew his way around pyrotechnics. There's no way he would have let them be handled or exposed in an unauthorized way." His hazel eyes sparkled with indignation and intelligence.

Angus ran the *Town Crier*, Mackinac Island's local newspaper. He was a senior gentleman who walked with a cane. His head was bald on top, with white hair around the edges and a short, cropped, white beard. He wore a blue knit cardigan over a blue and white striped polo and dark blue cotton slacks with topsider shoes. He was a big man, about six-foot-two if you caught him standing up straight—something that seemed difficult on most days.

Unlike the rest of us, he was free from soot and dirt. His old knees would never have let him search the brush for cinders and ash. Instead, he'd hung a camera around his neck and taken action shots for the paper and notes on the notepad in his breast pocket. Angus was smart as a whip, but still old school when it came to reporting. His granddaughter Liz worked with him. She had told me he even took notes in his own shorthand.

"The place was rigged to blow." Rex wiped his forehead with what used to be a white handkerchief. It was as soot covered as his hands. "Transport and handling of fireworks is strictly regulated, but it's also where most firework accidents happen. This was no accident. One of the guys hit a trip wire. He froze long enough for us to move the trucks back then Charles grabbed him and they hit the ground running." Rex motioned toward the back of the ambulance.

The doors were open and Officer Charles Brown sat on the back. His shirt was off and EMT George Marron was cleaning up the blisters where the shrapnel had burned through Charles's coat and uniform.

A young guy in firefighter gear who looked to be

eighteen years old sat beside Officer Brown. The kid appeared dirty but unharmed. His brown hair stood up in short spikes and his brown eyes glittered as he talked fast and furiously motioned with his hands. He was too far away for us to hear what he was saying but it was obvious from the rise of his shoulders and the action of his hands that he was still very excited.

"Looks like the kid has a story to tell for the rest of his life," Ed said. "Wait until the adrenaline crash. Poor kid is going to pass out cold."

I smiled. "I know what that's like. I've had a little bit of experience with adrenaline myself."

"Thankfully no one was badly hurt. I checked on the planes and there was only minor damage." Sophie looked a little worse for wear with dirt in her hair and soot on her face. Her once spotless uniform was a mess and yet she was still cute. Go figure.

"Every one of you was darn lucky." Angus narrowed his eyes at me. "I still have my rabbit's foot right here in my pocket." He patted his breast pocket where his notepad peeked out. There was a bump at the bottom of the pocket. "So don't get any ideas of finding any dead guys."

"Too late," I said and shrugged.

Angus had this idea that I was bad luck for old men. He'd started carrying a rabbit's foot for luck against what he called my bad juju ever since Joe Jessop was found dead in my hotel. I don't know why Angus was worried. I'd only found two dead old men so far. . . .

"What do you mean, too late?" His eyes narrowed farther.

"There was a dead man in the warehouse." Rex

shook his head and squinted at the burned-out building. "The fire trashed the crime scene."

"Crime scene?" Angus pulled his notepad back out of his pocket. "What kind of crime scene? Messy from a fight? Was there blood from a bullet wound or did you find him hanging?"

"No details at this point." Rex held out his hand in a *stop* fashion. He looked straight at me. "Not a word."

"What?" I shrugged and gave him my best innocent look.

Officer Lasko approached the group, her blond ponytail bouncing as she walked. Kelsey Lasko was petite, thin, and my age. Her blue eyes sent me a thinly veiled look of contempt. "You seem to be at a lot of crime scenes, Ms. McMurphy. Why is that?"

"Just lucky, I guess." I shrugged then put my hands in the pocket of my jacket. Thankfully, my jean jacket had not taken any burning shrapnel and remained in one dirty piece.

"Were they able to retrieve the body?" Rex asked.

Officer Lasko turned her neat, perfectly pressed, uniformed body away from me. "No, sir. It appears the blast threw the body up against the wall. We have a serious burn outline and a pile of bone and ash."

"Now that's interesting." Angus licked the end of his stubby pencil and made a few notes in his pad of paper.

"That had to be more than fireworks," Rex said. "The fireworks were stored in magazines."

"The magazines were tampered with," Ed said. "The fire marshal is investigating."

"So is that arson? Or tampering with a crime scene?" I had worked up a good sweat with all the running and putting out the little coals and such. My hair stuck to my forehead where the sweat had pinned it. Now that we'd been standing for a while, the wind off the lake felt cold. I huddled inside my jacket.

"Could be both," Officer Lasko said. "The two incidents might not even be related."

"I say, use the duck test," Ed said.

"If it looks like a duck, quacks like a duck, it's probably a duck," we all said in unison and then chuckled.

"Fine," Officer Lasko said and held up her small elegant hands. "If it's not a duck, we may have a killer and an arsonist on our hands."

"Let's hope not," Rex said.

"Coffee, anyone?" Frances brought over a tray full of hot coffees.

"Thanks!" I said.

We all dove in and grabbed coffees. I hugged the warm cup to my chest and watched Archie frown as Sherman gulped down the cup as if it were water. Sophie hugged her coffee and sipped it as if it were ambrosia. The look on her face made me smile.

"You should come by the McMurphy," I said. "We have a coffee bar, open twenty four-seven."

"I may just take you up on that," Sophie said.

"Jenn figured you all could use refreshments." Frances pointed to my best friend in the distance.

Jennifer was five-foot-nine and a curvy size six. You couldn't hate her for it because she was so darn nice and smart and loyal. Anyway, she had arrived on her bike with a two wheeled trailer in tow which held coolers and various small portables. Jen set up coffee, lemonade, and water dispensers on a small portable table. Her long black hair was safely pulled into a single braid down her back. She wore khaki shorts and a pink polo with the Historic McMurphy Hotel and Fudge Shop embroidered above the front pocket.

Leave it to Jenn to show up with drinks and sandwiches. The men in the group headed straight for her. I'm going to say it was the food. After all, everyone knew she was dating Shane Carpenter, a local crime scene investigator. I'd like to think I had something to do with that. I was the one who'd introduced them. Of course, it wasn't exactly a social occasion, but they seemed to make the best of it.

"I'm going to head out, ladies," Sophie said. "I'm beat."

"Thanks for saving me, today," I said. "Seriously, feel free to come by the McMurphy. We have fudge . . . and coffee."

Sophie laughed. "Fudge is the last thing I need." She patted her taut abdomen. "But coffee like this is always welcome."

Frances and I watched her walk toward the runway where the planes were parked until the sound of men laughing caught my attention. I glanced back toward Jenn. She had them eating out of her hand . . . literally. "What kind of sandwiches did she bring?" I asked Frances as the pile disappeared into the hands of tired firefighters.

"Ham with cheddar cheese and turkey with Swiss cheese." Frances tucked the tray under her arm and sipped her cup of coffee. "Are you okay?"

"Sure, why?" I asked, turning my gaze from the group.

"You're shivering and it's seventy-eight degrees out," she stated.

"Stupid adrenaline." I frowned.

"Drink your coffee. Then you should head back to the McMurphy before you fall down from exhaustion."

"Okay, but I'll need to let Rex know I'm leaving." I sipped the warm brew. It tasted sharply bitter. I liked coffee for the bitterness. Some people loved it doctored up with flavors and sugar, but I liked mine with cream at the most, just enough to smooth out and give body to the bitterness. "The coffee is great."

"Jenn made it," Frances said. "Come on, I'll walk you to your bike."

I froze. "My bike! I completely forgot about it. I had parked it next to the warehouse." I handed Frances my coffee and rushed to where my bike was parked. Thankfully, it was still there. Covered in soot and smoke, it appeared unharmed.

"The cinder blocks saved it."

I turned to see Liz MacElroy surveying the damaged building. She stood about my height with black hair pulled back into a no nonsense ponytail, and bright blue eyes. She wore khaki cargo shorts, a baby blue tank, and a plaid, short-sleeved shirt over the tank.

"Hi Liz. When did you get here?"

"I got here as soon as I heard the explosion. The sight of sparkling fireworks in the daytime was like sending up a flare. It caught everyone's attention." She had a smudge on the side of her cheek that I hadn't noticed when I first looked at her. "I spent some time with the volunteers stomping out cinders in the woods."

"Ed Goodfoot said we were lucky it rained all last week. The ground cover isn't too dry."

"The best thing about fireworks is they burn fast," she said as she stepped up to inspect the building's exterior. "You were here when it blew?"

"Yeah," I said then paused. "Are you interviewing me for a story?"

She flashed me a grin. "Maybe."

"She can't talk to the press," Rex interrupted.

We both turned to him at the same time. "Why not?" We asked in unison. "Jinx!" we shouted and laughed.

"Because she is my witness." Rex pulled my bike out from its spot and wiped off the seat. "But I'm not going to question you here and now. The sun is starting to set. Go home, get cleaned up, and get a good supper. I'll come by tonight and take your statement."

"Such service." Liz crossed her arms, her eyes twinkling.

"You'll get your statement along with the rest of the press tomorrow," Rex said and handed me the bike. "For now, we'll say that we've got a suspected arson and a probably homicide. Right, Allie?"

"Yes," I agreed and took my bike from him. The handles were gritty and oily with soot.

"An arson and a murder?" Liz's expression perked up. "What makes you suspect murder?"

"Well, there was a—"

"No," Liz held up her hand in a *stop* sign. "Don't tell me. Let me guess. You found another dead body."

I made a firm line with my mouth.

"Allie," Rex said softly and shook his head. "Go home."

"Fine." I let a shiver run over me. The air was cooling quickly as the sun set. The sound of crickets and night insects were a gentle but welling hum in the distance. "Bye, Liz. I'll talk to you when I can. Bye, Rex. See you tonight."

I walked the bike a few steps before I tested my weight on the tires and then hopped on.

"She's dating Trent Jessop, you know," I overheard Liz tell Rex.

"I know," he answered as I biked away.

I liked Rex. We were good friends, but I was falling for Trent. He was in Ann Arbor on business and notably missing from today's action. It was a story I'd have to tell him when he was on the phone. Or maybe when we were snuggling on the couch. That way, I couldn't see the look on his face when he found out being a fudge shop owner was more dangerous than it seemed.

Coconut Cream No Bake Fudge

8 ounces cream cheese, softened in microwave for 15 seconds
6 cups powdered sugar, sifted if lumpy
¼ cup melted butter plus 1 teaspoon to prep the pan
¼ teaspoon almond extract
½ teaspoon vanilla
1½ cups coconut flakes
1 cup chopped almonds

Butter 8x8x2-inch cake pan.

Mix cream cheese, sifted powdered sugar, butter, almond extract, and vanilla extract until smooth and thick. Hint: the amount of powdered sugar will depend on how thick you want the fudge. Start by adding 4 cups and then the last 2 cups in ½ cup increments until the fudge is smooth and thick.

When the base is smooth and thick, add coconut and almonds until combined. Scoop into buttered pan and pat smooth with wooden spoon.

Score 1-inch pieces with butter knife.

Refrigerate for 2-3 hours. Remove from pan and split into pieces. Serve in individual paper candy holders or on platter. Store leftovers away from heat in covered container.

Enjoy!

Chapter 3

I didn't have to wait long to hear from Trent.

When my phone rang, I was soaking in a tub of bubbles and sloshed around as I reached for it. Technically, I had been banned from answering my phone while in the bathtub for sort of obvious reasons. Okay, I tended to drop my phone, and phones and bathwater don't exactly mix.

Not surprising, I was still recovering from today's fright and didn't think past the fact that my phone was ringing and it could be Rex saying he was downstairs ready to interview me. I held the phone out of the tub, hit ANSWER and SPEAKER and carefully placed it on the stand next to the claw foot tub in my bathroom. "Hello?"

"Allie, are you answering the phone while taking a bath?" Trent's deep warm voice came out of the phone.

"Maybe . . . how—?"

"I heard sloshing and figured it was either the tub or the lake. I prefer to think about you in the tub."

"Oh." I felt the rush of heat from a blush go up

my neck. "Hi, Trent. I answered the phone because I thought maybe you were Rex."

"Okay, I'm going to wait for you to explain that before I get worried. Should I be worried, Allie?"

"No, no." I grabbed the phone as if bringing it closer to me would bring him closer to me. "Rex is stopping by to question me."

"And I repeat, should I be worried?"

I laughed. "No, I'm fine. There was an incident this afternoon, but I'm fine. The fireworks on the other hand are not so fine." I explained what had happened as I sank back into the bubbles and leaned the back of my neck on the curve of the tub. "And so Rex is stopping by to ask some questions. How was your day?"

"Not nearly as eventful as yours," Trent said. "I've picked up a couple new draft horses. I've got two animals that I'm retiring this year and I'm looking at breeding some better carriage stock."

"Sounds interesting."

"You mean boring." He laughed.

"I don't know anything about horses." I sighed at the disappearing bubbles in my bath. "I was in the kitchen when all the other girls were out learning to ride. I sort of look at horses as big dogs—pretty but tough to clean up after."

That made him laugh a deep, rich, belly laugh. "I take it you don't know much about dogs, either."

"Mal is my first," I admitted. "My mom and dad weren't really into pets."

"You missed out," he said softly. "Remind me when I get back to take you around to see the stables. We'll have you riding like a pro in no time."

"I don't think you know me that well," I said in

semi-seriousness. "Coordination is not high on my list."

"That just means you need more practice. I'm looking forward to practicing."

"Oh." I was blushing again. Not that anyone could tell. "When do you come back?"

"I'll be back tomorrow. Can we have dinner?"

"Sure, as long as I'm square with Rex."

"Great. I'll pick you up at eight."

"Should I wear riding boots?" I teased.

"Dress pretty. There are other things I'd like to do with you than put you on top of a horse."

I was left speechless after that comment and let my imagination fill in the blanks. "Okay. Pretty it is."

"Good night, Allie."

"Good night, Trent." I hit the END button on my phone and couldn't stop smiling. The water had grown cold and I leaned over and put the phone back on the stand and stood to grab a towel when the ring startled me. I reached for the phone and it slipped in my hands, barely escaping a drop in the tub. "Hello?" I said as I stepped onto the aqua bath mat and snagged a big white fluffy towel. "Trent?"

"Hi Allie, it's Rex. I'm on my way over. Are you still up for some questions?"

"Oh, sure. I'm getting out of the bath now, so give me about fifteen minutes and I'll be downstairs."

Dead silence on the other end of the phone.

"Rex?"

"Sorry." His voice sounded strange. "You *were* in the bathtub or you *are* in the bathtub?"

"I'm just stepping out. I promise, I'll be down really quick. Jenn made extra coffee and Frances has some cookies she brought over. Help yourself."

"Okay."

"Great. Bye." I hung up the phone and wrapped my hair in a towel. I slipped on panties and a bra and then comfy yoga pants and a soft green T-shirt.

Jenn and Mal were heading into the apartment as I headed out. "Hi guys." I held the door open for Mal who decided she was going to wait and see where I was going before she crossed the threshold and got stuck in the apartment.

"Rex is downstairs waiting for you," Jenn said. "I told him we'd come and get you."

"Yes, he called to let me know he would be here soon." I closed the door so that we were all going down the stairs.

The McMurphy was a boxy square building with four floors. The top floor was the owners apartment—mine now—along with the business office which I shared with Jenn who was my acting hospitality manager. I'd met her in college when I was studying hotel management. She was getting a hospitality degree in hopes of running her own event planning company. She'd given up her dream to spend my first season with me on Mackinac Island and had taken to the island like a duck takes to water.

Two floors of guests rooms were under the apartment. They were serviced by staircases on the end of each hall with two elevators that ran in the middle. We took the stairs because they were faster.

"Oh, Mr. Devaney said that the west elevator needs servicing again," Jenn said as we walked down the second set of stairs that spilled into the wide lobby area. "It's starting to stick. He had to pry the doors open for the Clemons family in three-o-two."

"Ugh. Those elevators are costing me a fortune."

"You can take them out," Jenn suggested. "But I think that limits your guests. Quite a few have difficulty with the stairs."

"I suppose I could put in a really long switched back ramp," I paused and studied the floor space of the lobby from the vantage point of a few stairs up. "No, that's a really bad idea."

"I don't know," Jenn said eyeing the same piece of real estate. "Let me see about bringing an architect in. There might be something we can do."

"It has to be wheelchair accessible," I said. "Papa was firm about being available for persons with disabilities. It was why he made the over-sized bathroom in room two-o-one and insisted on showers for all the bathrooms when we moved from the one bathroom per hallway to all en suite baths. He wanted his older clients to be able to safely walk in and out of the bath."

"What are you two discussing?" Frances asked from the bottom of the steps. "Officer Manning is waiting, Allie."

I continued down the stairs as I answered her. "We were talking about whether or not we could remove the elevators."

"Why? I like them," Frances said.

The elevators in question were actually small boxes, relics from an earlier time. The doors were ornate grates that allowed a view of the lobby before disappearing up the shaft. Once the car stopped at a floor, it was necessary to open the other side of the elevator to step out onto the floor.

"They are quaint," Jenn said, "But in constant need of maintenance. Someday, you will have to put in new ones. There won't be anyone alive who knows how to fix these."

"There isn't much to fix," Mr. Devaney said. "I'd do the work myself, but you need a certified guy to sign off for the safety inspector." He was my cantankerous handyman. About six feet tall, he was a retired teacher with a balding head on top and thick hair on the sides cut very close and gray in color. He always dressed, well . . . like a teacher. He wore brown corduroy slacks and a pale blue dress shirt open at the collar, showing a T-shirt underneath. The sleeves were rolled up to the elbow exposing brawny forearms. On his feet were comfortable brown leather slip-on shoes.

"I'm going to have an architect come in and see what he has to say about it," Jenn said from her perch on the stairs behind me.

Unconcerned about the elevators, Mal had rushed down the stairs and jumped up into Rex's lap as he sat in one of the wingback chairs scattered in the open area between the twin staircases. He had showered and changed into a new uniform.

Come to think of it, he always wore a uniform when he stopped by on police business. It was as if his uniform helped him maintain some distance in his role as an officer and as a neighbor. He lived a ways away, but on an island as small as Mackinac everyone was considered a neighbor.

"Hi Rex. I see Mal has made herself at home," I walked over to him. "Do you want to come up into my office so we have a quiet place to talk?"

"That would be best." Rex stood, carefully putting Mal down on the floor.

I noticed then that she had grown quite fluffy. I

would need to have a fluffy intervention this week and take her to the groomer. Unfortunately, groomers were as dreaded by Mal as hair salons were by me. I could grow my hair out. Mal, on the other hand, had to be groomed. As a non-shed dog, her hair would grow quite long. The longer it got the fluffier she got. I kept her groomed in a short puppy coat. Show Bichons had four-inch long coats. I couldn't imagine the daily grooming that went into that. As it was, I had to brush her every day to keep her short coat from matting.

"Can I bring you up a tray with coffee, tea, and some cookies?" Frances asked as we walked by my small team to head up the stairs.

"Thanks," I said.

"No need to bother," Rex said at the same time. "This won't take long."

"Oh," I said. "Well, we can stay down here then." I sent my crew a look. "They were all heading up to the apartment. Weren't you?"

They agreed. "Sure." "Right."

"Well, there are a few cookies left on the coffee bar." Frances picked up Mal and made sure my puppy went up with the rest of them.

"Do they always gather in your apartment at night?" Rex asked.

"We're a big family," I said with a small shrug. "I like the company." I waved him back over toward two overstuffed chairs that faced each other across the rag rug in the heart of the lobby.

The McMurphy was quiet this time of night. At a certain point, the ferries quit running. The entire Main Street closed up except for a couple bars and the hotel restaurants. Life on Mackinac was intentionally quiet and slow. The bigger hotels had front yards where fire pits were lit and marshmallows toasted. People would sit outside and talk until the cold or the mosquitos drove them back inside.

The coffee bar was on the east side of the lobby near the other set of stairs. The fudge shop area was closed off by glass walls and the work area was separated from the viewing area by a long thick glass counter where the trays of fudge were displayed.

Across from the fudge shop was a small settee, two chairs, and a fireplace. Frances's reception desk was tucked up near the staircase I came down. Behind her large bar-like desk was a wall of slots that held mail or notes for each guest room. People could leave their keys in the cubby knowing that they were never left alone. After nine PM the doors were locked and guests had to carry their keys to access the entrance to the lobby.

"Do you have an identification on the dead guy?" I asked. "Like I said at the warehouse, I'm pretty sure it was Rodney Rivers."

"We are unable to make an official identification at this time. Not much was left of the body. We also suspect it was Rodney. No one has seen or heard from him since this morning. As I recall, you received a couple calls from him." Rex sat, took out a notepad and a pen, and leaned toward me.

"Yes, I've got three calls from him all time stamped." I took my cell phone out of my pocket. "I got caught up in fudge making for the Star-Spangled Fourth celebration and didn't think to check my phone." I put in my password, then flipped through the recent calls section. "He called me three times, see?" I showed Rex my phone. He took down a note. "If you want, I'll play the voice messages for you, again."

"Yes, I'd like that if you are willing to let me listen."

"Sure." I dialed my voice mail box and put the phone on speaker.

"You have two new message and two saved messages," the phone's messaging system said. "First unheard message sent today at five P.M. 'Hi Allie, this is Trent. I was just calling to see how your day was going and to ask what you were wearing."

My eyes grew big and I touch the speaker button to mute the rest of the message. "Sorry." The heat of a blush rushed up my neck and into my cheeks. "Hold on." I put the phone up to my ear and looked away from Rex as Trent's sexy message continued.

Note to self. Check all your messages before you make them public.

I couldn't help the smile that appeared on my face at the rest of the message. Trent Jessop, handsome, wealthy, and overall sexy good guy was leaving me hot messages. That did so much for my poor shabby ego.

"Second unheard message," the phone said. I pulled it away from my ear and hit SPEAKER. "Sent today at one-o-three PM. 'Hi Allie. Rodney again. There is something really wrong going on here at the warehouse. It looks like the padlocks have all been cut and the magazines opened. Call me back. This is important. The fireworks show might be in jeopardy.'

"End of message," the phone droned. "To delete this message press seven. To save it press nine."

"First saved message, sent today at twelve thirty-four PM." 'Allie, we've got a problem. Meet me at the fireworks warehouse as soon as possible. The entire program is in ruins.'

"End of message," the phone droned. "To delete this message press seven. To save it press nine."

I pressed the nine key.

Rex wrote notes, his head down, his gaze on his paper. I assumed it helped him to listen if he wasn't looking at me.

"Next saved message," the phone went on. "Sent today at 1:30 PM. 'Allie, answer your phone, will you? This is serious and time sensitive. The entire back row of fireworks has been tampered with— Hey, you. What are you doing here? Are you responsible for—'

"End of message," the phone droned. "To delete this message press seven. To save it press nine."

I pressed the nine key.

"End of messages," the phone said. "To repeat these messages press five or press pound for more options."

I hit the END button and put my phone down on the end table beside my chair. It suddenly felt a lot heavier. I leaned back in my chair and hugged my waist. "Now that I think about it, the dead guy had the same hair color and cut as Rodney. I know that I didn't know Rodney very well, but I'm certain it was him on that desk. Can you say I identified the body? I mean, sure, it would have been better if he was standing in front of me with his pyro technique plan in his hands, but if it helps his family to know sooner . . ."

"It's okay, Allie." Rex looked at me with his flat cop eyes. "We don't need you. Listen, I'm going to need to ask the phone company for your cell phone records and a copy of those recordings. Do I have your permission to do that?"

"Yes." I was suddenly very tired. "This was the first year Rivers Productions was going to do the three fireworks shows. I pulled some strings to bring Rodney in to the Mackinac Island celebrations. He was the world's best fireworks guy. I don't know how we are going to replace him."

"How did you get him to agree to do the show? If he is the world's best, I have to assume he was quite a bit outside the Mackinac Island Fourth of July budget."

"He was." I nodded in agreement. "But my Mom's cousin did him a couple favors and he owed the family. Mom remembered him and got his name from her cousin. I called and the rest is history. No one here had ever called to use his services until I got on the committee." I ran a hand over my face and sighed. "I wanted to impress everyone so they would see that I'm a valuable part of the community."

"You are valuable," Rex said. "You don't have to prove anything to anyone on this island."

"Yes, well tell Angus that. He still carries his rabbit foot around to ward off my negative juju."

Rex laughed and sat back, settling into his chair. "Angus is just messing with you. He does that with people he likes."

"Oh, okay. That makes me feel a bit better." I curled

my feet up onto the seat of my chair. "If the dead guy is Rodney, then I have two problems. First, I have to try to replace the fireworks that blew up and second, I have to replace Rodney. Neither of those things is going to be easy."

"No," Rex agreed and stood up. "They're not."

I stood with him. "Was that all you needed?"

"Yes, thanks for your help." He put on his police hat and I walked him to the front door of the McMurphy. "If you hear from Rodney, let me know as soon as possible."

"I will. Let me know the moment you get your identification. I'll get started on finding new fireworks."

Rex pushed the door open and held it. His gaze grew serious. "If I were you, I'd hedge my bets and find another pyro technician. I have a feeling Rodney isn't going to show up anywhere any time soon."

I drew my eyebrows together and frowned. My heart was heavy with the loss of a man I barely knew, my hopes for the Fourth of July fireworks display, and my dream of being the best thing that happened to the Mackinac Island Star Spangled Fourth celebration.

Suddenly, a cat zipped in through the crack of the door that Rex held open. It was a streak of calico.

Startled, I said, "Oh!"

"Cat!" Rex closed the door and we stood for a moment, watching the cat run under the settee in the center part of the lobby. "Do you have a cat?" he asked, confused.

I shook my head. "No. How strange is it to just have a cat come in out of the night?"

Rex and I walked together over to the settee. I got down on my hands and knees and peered under the couch. "Hi kitty."

The cat bunched itself up and hissed at me.

Rex knelt down beside me. "I don't recognize the cat. Do you?"

"No."

The cat hissed again.

"Come on kitty, kitty." I made a loud kiss noise with my lips. "Pretty kitty."

The cat backed up farther from me. His eyes were large and wary.

I turned my head toward Rex. "I don't think he likes me."

"I'll get him." Rex reached and swept his hand under the couch to grab the cat, but the cat was having none of that. It shot out the back of the couch and up the staircase.

Rex and I sat back on our knees, looked at each other, and burst out laughing.

"Looks like you might have just inherited a cat," he said, standing up.

"I hope not." I stood up, too. "It's not that I don't like cats, but I have a hotel full of guests and a fudge shop that needs to be maintained under strict food inspector rules. I already have a puppy. Any more animals might be a code violation."

"Then I guess we need to go on a cat hunt." Rex brushed off his hands.

Thankfully, the floors in the lobby were finished wood floors and Frances ensured that they were kept spotless. A quick glance at my hands proved there was nothing to brush off.

Rex pointed upstairs. "You'd better call your crew

down. I've had cats for pets. They are masters at hiding. There have been days that go by without seeing my cat."

I drew my brows together in concern. "Don't they need food and water?"

"Yes," he said with a wry grin. "But they are sneaky suckers. One minute the food will be in the bowl and the next gone without me ever having seen the cat."

"Awesome," I said and pulled out my phone. I dialed Jenn's cell. "What a day. I lost a warehouse full of fireworks and possibly a pyro technician but gained a stray cat."

Rex shook his head. "Some days are like that."

Chapter 4

I discovered that Mal was great at sniffing up dead bodies and rather indifferent to searching out stray cats. She did, however, glory in the fact that she had us all following her around the McMurphy.

Frances was the first to call off the search. "I'll put up notices for the guests tomorrow. We'll find the cat. In the meantime, Allie, go to bed. You have to get up in a few hours to make fudge."

"And you have to be back here to man the reception desk," Jenn pointed out to Frances. "We have a group of ten coming in tomorrow. If they come in early and the rooms aren't ready, we'll have to store their luggage and coordinate the cleaning."

Frances nodded and hid a yawn. "Yes, the Summersets in room three-o-three already tried to extend their stay. I had to tell them we were fully booked, so I suspect they will take their time leaving."

"I'll put a note under their door reminding them that check out is at eleven." Jenn said.

"What will we do with the cat once we find it?" I asked. When they all looked at me as if I was a simpleton, I added, "What? I never had pets growing up. Mal is my first. I wouldn't even know how to pick up a cat, let alone what to do with it after I'd done that."

"Nonsense," Frances said. "Cats are sweet babies. Okay sometimes ornery and always in charge, but sweet."

"We can put the cat in Mal's carrier and take it to the vet for safekeeping," Jenn suggested. "Someone must be missing their baby. I'll take a picture and hang up posters."

"It's a plan," I said.

"Unless you want to keep the cat," Frances suggested as Mr. Devaney held out her windbreaker for her to put on.

"I don't think I can." I furrowed my brow. "There are codes about having animals in places where food is served."

"You could always install a door on the fudge shop," Jenn suggested after we hugged and waved the older couple off into the night.

I glanced at the fudge shop and pursed my lips. "That might work, but it would be very expensive. All to keep a stray cat."

"Stray cats are the best," Jenn said and grinned as we followed Mal up the stairs to the apartment. "There's a song that says so."

The next morning the Summersets had to be ousted out of their rooms. They left begrudgingly, vowing to never stay at the McMurphy again. Jenn handled it with tact and great aplomb.

Still no sign of the cat and I had begun to suspect

my tired mind had made up the entire episode. I don't remember Papa Liam every having a cat just make itself at home in the McMurphy. If one ever had, he wouldn't have kept it a secret. In fact, he'd have created this giant story about it. I smiled at the memory of his wild stories and for the first time in a few weeks tears filled my eyes. I missed Papa. It would have been fun to share the great cat hunt with him.

My cell phone rang and I put the bowl I was washing back into the sink, pulled off the rubber gloves I used when dishwashing, and grabbed the phone. "This is Allie."

"Hi Allie," a female voice said. "This is Mrs. Amerson, the chair of the Star Spangled Fourth planning committee. How are you today?"

"I'm good," I said and headed out of the fudge shop. "How are you?" I waved at Jenn who nodded and moved into the fudge shop to man the sinks and candy sales while I was on the phone.

"I'm not good, Allie. I heard about yesterday's explosion at the warehouse near the airport."

"I know. It was awful, wasn't it?" I walked upstairs toward the office.

"I understand we lost all the fireworks for the Star Spangled Fourth."

"Yes, the warehouse was a complete loss," I said as I hit the third floor. A movement caught my eye and I saw a black and white and orange cat strolling down the hallway. "Cat!" I shouted into Mrs. Amerson's ear. A quick look around told me that my staff was nowhere close enough to hear my shout.

"Excuse me?" Mrs. Amerson sounded angry. "Are you yelling at me?"

"Oh, no. I'm sorry." The cat and I froze and stared at each other. "A stray cat got into the McMurphy last night and we have been unable to find it. Now that I'm on the phone with you, it's out and in the middle of the hallway."

"I see," she said, sounding even angrier. "Allie, the fireworks display is far more important than your stray cat antics. Mackinac Island is proud to have a tradition of three eye-catching and spectacular fireworks shows. I will not allow you to come in and ruin that tradition. Do you understand me?"

"Yes," I said softly and dropped my shoulders.

"Then you will stop your nonsense and tell me how you're going to fix this mess you put us in."

"What do you mean, *I* put us in?"

"This is your first year on the committee and this is the first year the fireworks were stored on the island. You contracted with the Rivers Productions company. Therefore, you are one hundred percent responsible for the poor management that lead to the explosion. Now tell me what you plan to do about it?"

"I'll get us fireworks," I said. "You and the rest of the committee can be assured that the shows will go on and they will be spectacular."

"They'd better be, Allie McMurphy." Mrs. Amerson's tone was stern. "They had better be." The phone went dead in my hand.

I tried not to worry over much about the promise I had just made to the head of the Star Spangled Fourth celebration planning committee. The cat and I were still frozen in place, each one waiting for the other to make a move. I lifted up my phone and hit the CAMERA button. If nothing else, I would have a photo of the cat to show the staff and post on notices.

I slowly lifted the phone with the cat fully visible in the target box. I hit the PHOTO button and in the seconds between the lift of the camera and the shutter going off, the cat streaked past me and down the stairs. "Darn it!" I said as I noted the picture was nothing but a fast blur going down the hallway. I stuffed the phone into the pocket of my chef jacket and headed down the stairs after it.

"Here kitty, kitty," I called and pursed my lips to make kissy sounds. "Good kitty." Yeah, that still wasn't working. I stopped on the second floor landing and studied the hallway. There was no sign of the cat, but then three of the rooms were open. I headed down the hall, the old floor creaking under my feet.

I had replaced the worn, thin, green carpet in the halls when I had the McMurphy remodeled in early May. The carpet was now a soft mix of dark green, rose, and tan. The pattern was a series of swirls. I had asked about carpet that was all one color and had been advised that in high traffic areas such as the McMurphy's hallways I should go with patterned flooring. The swirl pattern was supposed to be similar to a carpet pattern popular in the early 1900s when the McMurphy was first built. The scent of carpet freshener filled the air.

I popped my head into the first open guest room. "Kitty, kitty."

Frances came around with balled up dirty sheets in her arms. "Did you see the cat?"

"Yes. I tried to take a picture, but all I got was a blurred streak, see?" I thumbed through my phone, brought the picture to the front, and raised it for Frances to see with her reading glasses. "It was in the third floor hall. It went down the stairs fast. I think it's on this floor."

"I haven't seen it," she said. "But before I lock up the rooms, I'll check under the beds and in the closets. I don't want guests to check in only to discover they have a cat when the critter starts running around like crazy at three in the morning."

I paused. "They do that?"

"Yes. It's a cat thing." Frances smiled fondly. "I used to have a cat named Tiger. He was orange with brown stripes. We were very creative at naming our pets back then. He lived sixteen years, and then one day just disappeared." She sighed. "But he would come inside at night to sleep with the family. He was famous for the three AM sprints about the house."

"Everyone's had a cat, but me," I said with what I'll admit was a tiny pout. "I have no cat stories."

"Douglas . . . Mr. Devaney"—Frances put the sheets into the soiled linen bin on the housekeepers cart—"had the best idea."

"What was that?"

"Let's put some tuna inside the dog carrier. The cat will get hungry, eventually, and Douglas said he could rig the carrier to shut like a trap whatever critter went inside to eat the tuna."

"Just as long as he doesn't hurt the cat," I warned. "I won't have innocent creatures hurt."

"We won't hurt it." Frances's brown eyes glittered. "We love all critters. You should know that."

I sighed and dropped my shoulders. "I do. I'm just worried about the poor thing getting stuck somewhere where we won't be able to find it or help it."

"We'll be easy with it," Frances said and pulled fresh sheets off the cart. It was her day to make up the second floor and Jenn's to make up the third. I really needed to get at least one maid. But the ad in the *Town Crier* wasn't doing much good. I considered sending an ad to St. Ignace or Mackinaw City.

"Fine. I'll be up in the office. I just got a call from Mrs. Amerson. She is hopping mad that the fireworks shows are ruined. I promised I'd get us more fireworks and the world's next best pyro technic company."

"You know we've never had an issue with storage of the fireworks before. Why is she so mad about this year's? Is it because they exploded? I mean that is always a possibility, isn't it?" Frances asked as she put the sheets on the dresser and opened the bottom sheet and started making the bed.

"I changed things," I admitted and felt the heat of a blush rush over my cheeks. "The usual company stores the fireworks on the Lower Peninsula, then sets them up on barges and shoots them off from the lake. Rodney said he would do better by setting them up on the hillside a little higher than the fort. That's why he had them airlifted in and installed magazines in the warehouse to hold them. It's also why they were stored at the airport—to avoid the ferries and the busy docks. Plus the warehouse was made of concrete and the magazines were all properly locked per regulations."

"And still they got blown up," Frances said as she ran her hands over the tucked in sheet to smooth it.

"It was sabotage. Or murder. I told you I found the dead guy before the fireworks blew."

"Yes, the early edition of the *Town Crier* said they identified the body as Rodney Rivers."

"Oh, no," I said and leaned against the door jamb. "I was afraid that it was him but still held out hope. Did the paper say how he was identified? Rex wouldn't say last night and according to Officer Lasko yesterday the explosion sort of evaporated the body."

"Liz wrote that his identity was confirmed by an unusual ring that Mr. Rivers was known to wear and bridgework found in a partial jawbone."

"That's horrible." I made a face. "I take it Rex contacted Rodney's family and business partner, Henry Schulte."

"You know he had to or he would have never let Liz print the man's name." Frances unfolded the top sheet and floated it in the air so that it came down perfectly square on the bed.

I tapped the edge of my phone against my chin in thought. "I wonder if Henry would know where we can get replacement fireworks. They have to be insured for that kind of thing, right?"

"I don't know," Frances said. "Call him and find out."

Calling Henry Schulte was easy. Getting him to answer was a problem. I had only talked to him once on the phone and had never met him in person. For that matter, I'd only met with Rodney once and therefore, hadn't been able to reliably identify him as the man lying faceup on the desk in the warehouse. I could blame the angle and the lack of light and such, but mostly I really didn't put much stock into appearances and sometimes I had to know someone for a year before I even realized what color their eyes were.

I left several voice messages. An hour later, I called again. The phone message said no one was available at this time, please leave a message. "Hello, Mr. Schulte," I said into the phone. "It's me again, Allie McMurphy on Mackinac Island. I was going over the contract we have with your company. It clearly says here that in the unlikely event of an accident that Rivers Productions will replace all materials needed for the show to go on as planned. I really need to know if you have a backup plan and if so, how you intend to execute it. Please call me back at 906-555-2222."

I hung up the phone and studied the contract that was spread out on the top of my office desk. The contract clearly stated that Rivers Productions was fully bonded and insured in case of accident or loss. We were only days away from the Fourth of July. What if he couldn't get any fireworks in that little time?

I ran my hands over my face and tugged at my dark brown ponytail. I picked up the phone and called my mother in Detroit. The phone rang a few times and I started to drum my fingers on the desktop.

"Hello?"

"Hi, Mom."

"Hi Allie. How are you? Are you able to get down for the Independence Day celebration?"

"No, Mom. I've got to make fudge and ensure the McMurphy is working well, remember? The summer season can get crazy around the festival weeks and the Star Spangled Fourth is one of those weeks."

"Of course," my mother said, her tone clearly disappointed. "That's fine. I understand the business comes before your father and me . . ."

"I love you, Mom." Sometimes those simple words would disarm her before she went too deeply down that path of why did you leave us—even though I'd been living in Chicago for the last five years. I think she somehow thought I'd eventually give up on my "crazy" idea of taking over the family business.

"I love you, too, dear. Your father says that he saw something on the news about an explosion on the island. Did you hear about that?"

"Yes." I ran my hand over my face again. "Someone set fire to the warehouse that stored the fireworks. Rodney Rivers died in the explosion. Well, no. Actually, he may have been dead before the explosion. There is some speculation he was murdered. I can't get into the details until we know more.

"Oh, no, not another murder," My mother's tone turned serious. "That's one a month since you got there. I don't like that kind of trend. Are you safe?"

I nodded, even though she couldn't see me. "I'm safe, Mom. Really, it's simply been a run of unusual things. But I'm in charge of the fireworks and now I have to get us an entirely new show. I have calls in to his business partner. It's just that we don't have a lot of time left and I know that the supply of professional, arsenal-style fireworks can't be so big that we will have our choice of shows now."

"Surely they have insurance to cover any incidents," Mom said. "I'll ask my cousin Helen. She's the one who recommended them. Maybe she can point us in the right direction to get this taken care of."

"Really?" I asked, hope rising in my chest.

"Sure. I'll call her and let you know."

"Great." I slumped with relief. "Could you? Tell her to let them know there are multiple shows. If they go well, we can negotiate a long-term contract."

"I'll tell her," Mom reassured me. "I'll let you know what she says."

"Thanks, Mom."

"You're welcome. Come visit us soon, okay? Before it's fall?"

"I'll do my best," I said. "Bye."

Maybe, just maybe we'd get lucky and my mom's cousin Helen would come through for us. In the meantime, I would Google the world's best pyrotechnic groups and see if I couldn't find someone who was not only really good, but also wasn't under contract to already do a show those nights.

I had a feeling I was going to have to get very, very lucky.

Banana Cream Pie Fudge

½ cup butter, melted plus 1 teaspoon to prep pan (coconut oil is a good nondairy substitute)
¼ cup milk (almond milk is a good nondairy substitute)
1 3.4 ounce package of banana cream instant pudding and pie filling
1 teaspoon vanilla
6 cups powdered sugar, sifted.
1 cup dried banana chips, chopped (I actually crunched them up by pounding the bag. They crumble easily.)

Butter 8x8x2 inch cake pan.

Mix butter, milk, unprepared instant pudding, vanilla. Add powdered sugar 1 cup at a time until you reach the desired thickness. Fold in banana chips.

Scoop into prepared pan. Pat until smooth. Score into 1-inch pieces with butter knife.

Refrigerate for 2-3 hours until set. Break into 1-inch pieces along score. Serve in individual paper candy cups or on a platter. Store leftover in covered container in the refrigerator.

Enjoy!

Chapter 5

Trent showed up at my door with a bouquet of gorgeous flowers in his hand and a bottle of merlot.

"Hi," I said as I opened the door. Simply by looking at him, my heart was all aflutter.

The epitome of tall, dark and handsome, he stood a head taller than me with gorgeous brown eyes that were rimmed with black lashes a woman would envy. He had a long straight nose, a square jaw, and a mouth that made me want to sink my teeth into it. His skin glowed a golden tan.

Tonight, he wore a tan shirt with an open collar, a dark brown velvet suit jacket, and light brown slacks. His brown shoes had square toes.

"You look amazing," he said.

I smiled and did a little twirl, causing the skirt of my sleeveless, red dress to bell out. "You said to dress pretty. Is this pretty enough?"

"Oh, now you're fishing for compliments." His voice had a low tremble that made gooseflesh rise on my arms.

"Yes," I said, owning up to my need for validation. "Yes, I am. So please give it to me."

He stepped into the apartment and handed me the flowers. "You are stunning. Let's stay in and take that off—"

"Wait." I held up my hand in a motion of *stop.* A blush rushed up my cheeks. "I like the sound of that, but it took me an hour to get dressed. So you have to take me out."

He grinned and bussed a kiss on my cheek. "I suppose I can wait."

"Good." I walked over to the galley kitchen separated from the living room area by a breakfast bar. I put the flowers on the counter and reached into the cupboard underneath to pull out a vase. Filling the vase with water, I smiled. "What do you have in mind for tonight?"

"There's a social over at the yacht club. I need to see a couple guys to talk business."

I turned and let my disappointment show on my face. "Oh, and here I thought it was going to be a romantic dinner."

"It will be," he promised and set the bottle of merlot on the counter. "There's no reason I can't mix a little business with pleasure. Besides, I want to show you off."

I picked up the flowers and stuck them in the water without taking the time to trim or arrange them. "Okay, so that last part makes me feel a little bit better."

Trent's expression turned to one of concern. He reached over and took my hand and held it up. "What happened?" he asked as he brought my cut and bruised hands to the light.

"Yesterday's explosion," I explained.

"Explosion? You didn't say anything about an explosion." His eyebrows drew in closer. A muscle on his jawbone ticked and his sensuous mouth went flat. He gently ran his thumb across the back of my hand. "You were in an explosion. Was that what happened with the fireworks?"

"Yes." I felt the color in my face rise. I didn't expect him to look so upset. "You should see the other guy," I teased.

"There was another guy?" His eyes narrowed.

"Oh, boy." I sighed and walked around the bar and drew him to the couch to sit with me. "I had hoped to tell you over dinner. You know, when you ask me about my day."

"I don't think the yacht club is the appropriate place to tell this story." He gathered me against him. "I'm just going to hold on to you while you tell me. Please tell me you were not near the explosion."

"Well, see, now I can't do that." I leaned back against his chest and felt his heart racing under me.

He put his arms around me and took my hands in his. "Then tell me what happened from the beginning."

"I got a call from the pyro technician I'd hired to do the fireworks show for the Fourth of July. Really, I got three calls because I got caught up making fudge and forgot to check my phone."

"You do get caught up in your fudge." He slipped his fingers between mine and rubbed them gently. I could feel him smile as he kissed the top of my head. "Go on."

"The last message Rodney sent asked me to come

to the warehouse as soon as possible. Someone had messed with the fireworks."

"I don't understand. Why didn't he call the police?"

"I don't think he thought it was anything he couldn't handle. He's been working with these things for twenty years. I'm pretty sure he wanted to figure out logistics for bringing in new fireworks or he wanted to discuss what to do about the price of replacement fireworks. Those would be things I would need to handle."

"Okay. So you went up to the warehouse? Which warehouse?"

"The big cinder block one near the airport. Rodney had brought in magazines and stored them in the warehouse. I rode my bike up and left it—" I paused.

"What?"

"There was another bike when I got there." I sat up fast. So fast I narrowly missed hitting Trent's chin with my head. I turned to him, my eyes large with concern. "There were two bikes there when I arrived, but after the explosion one of the bikes was gone." I scrambled up, went over to the breakfast bar, and took my cell phone out of the date-night handbag I'd chosen to take tonight. "I need to call Rex."

"Hey now," Trent said, staying my hand. "I'm sure Rex doesn't need this information tonight."

I paused and looked into his handsome face. "Are you sure?"

"What would he do with the information?"

"He could track down the bike."

"In the dark?" Trent pointed to the windows to

show me that our eight PM date was happening under the dew-tipped stars.

"Right. Okay."

"We have reservations. This sounds like a long and complicated story."

"It is." I made a face to show my regret. "And it's not exactly romantic."

"So before we go, tell me. How badly are you hurt?"

I lifted my cheeks and squinted my eyes. "I've got a few cuts and bruises, but nothing broken."

He took my hand and stepped back at arm's length and twirled me around. "I hadn't noticed the bruising on your legs earlier. I was too busy admiring the dress."

"If you don't want to show me off—"

"Oh, no, I'm showing you off," he said firmly. "As my beautiful and brave date."

"I like the sound of that." I let go of his hand. "I'm ready." I put the cell phone in the night clutch and walked with him to the door. As we passed the wrought iron coatrack and umbrella stand, I snagged my white pashmina scarf and slung it around my shoulders.

Trent opened the door and I walked into the hall with him, turned and locked the door.

"Do you have a cat?" he asked.

I froze for a moment. "Not on purpose. Do you see it?"

"Yeah," he answered and nodded.

I followed his gaze. The cat was at the top of the stairs. It looked for all the world as if it belonged there as it sat and licked its front right paw.

"We need to catch it," I said. "Rex let it in last

night and we have had the devil of a time trying to catch it."

"It's just a cat," Trent said with laugher in his eyes. "You just go get it." He strode toward the cat with confidence. "Hello cat." He leaned down and picked it up.

I swear that the cat let him. It did not run or even mildly protest as he lifted it up and slung it over his arm so he could scratch it behind the ears.

"She's pretty," Trent said.

I approached the two slowly and held out my hand for the cat to sniff first. "Yes, she is. Wait.Is it a she?"

Trent laughed. "I'm pretty sure."

I gave the cat a scratch behind the ear. At that moment, Mal decided to come bounding up the stairs. She barked, startling me. I jumped and the cat leapt out of Trent's hands and onto the ground and the chase was on.

"Mal! No!" I called as we hurried down the stairs after the cat and dog.

Mr. and Mrs. Bertnell were coming up the staircase as the cat and dog hit the second floor and raced passed them.

"Oh!" Mrs. Bertnell cried, her hand going to her mouth, her eyes wide as she stepped to the side to let them by. Thankfully, she was wearing jeans and athletic shoes. Her sweatshirt had WORLD'S BEST GRANDMA printed on it.

"What the—" Mr. Bertnell was just as startled as he high stepped it around the cat and dog as the two raced by. He also wore jeans, white athletic shoes, and a sweatshirt printed with I'M WITH THE WORLD'S GREATEST GRANDMA.

"Sorry," I said as Trent and I brushed by.

"Animals are a hazard in a hotel," Mr. Bertnell shouted behind us.

"I know. Sorry," I shouted to the ceiling, hoping it would carry up.

Trent beat me down the stairs . . . mostly because I was wearing four-inch heels. Sexy heels I might add. The sacrifice in wearing sexy heels was that I was slower. Hurrying kind of hurt my bruised body parts.

"Mal!" I shouted as the dog and cat chased round the chairs and settees in the lobby.

"Cat!" Frances exclaimed from her post behind the reception desk.

"I'll get it," Trent declared. Blocking the animals' path, he swooped down to get the cat, but at the last second it dodged him. He turned to go after them when Mitzy Hanfer opened the front door to enter. She had her hands full with a paper tray filled with four ice cream cones and held the door with her elbow.

"Watch out!" Trent yelled.

But it was too late. The cat escaped out the door.

Fortunately, I had caught up to Mal by then and scooped her up before she hit Mitzy's legs. "Sorry," I said to Mitzy.

She looked startled and frozen to the spot. "What happened?" Her blond hair floated around her head as she glanced from me and Mal to the sidewalk behind the closed door.

"Stray cat," I said.

"Do you have the dog?" Trent asked me.

"Yes." I took her over to her downstairs kennel.

"Bad puppy." I put her inside and closed and locked the kennel door.

Mal's tongue hung out and she looked pleased with herself. In fact, her expression seemed to say that while I put her in jail, she'd do it all over again if she got the chance.

"I'll check to see if the cat's okay." Trent pulled open the door and headed down the street in the direction of the cat.

"Never a dull moment." Shaking her head, Frances laughed.

"I'm sorry I let your cat out." Mitzy was staying the week with her parents. Mackinac was a pretty safe place and the sixteen-year-old had begun a habit of going for a long walk after dark to pick up ice creams and bring them back.

"It's okay," I said, out of breath. I straightened to my full height. "The cat belongs out there."

"Where did Mal find it?" Frances asked me.

"It was up on the fourth floor landing washing itself," I said. "The cat let Trent pick it up. I was about to pet her when Mal came up and startled the cat who leapt out of Trent's arms and, well, the rest you saw."

"Maybe it will think twice before coming back inside the McMurphy." Frances studied me. "You look nice."

I adjusted my pashmina. "Thanks. We have reservations at the yacht club."

Trent came back inside. "Sorry, no cat." He held out his hands. "I'm going to wash up and then we can go to the club. They won't hold our reservations much longer." He escaped into the men's restroom behind the staircase.

"I hope the cat is all right," I said, drawing my eyebrows together.

"Maybe it will go home to its owner." Frances went back to watching her computer, her reading glasses firmly resting on her nose. "Have fun. I'm locking up at nine and heading home early. Last night was a long one."

"No problem," I said. "See you tomorrow."

Trent came out of the bathroom. He'd adjusted his jacket and his black hair was carefully combed back. "Are you ready?"

"Yes," I said and put my arm through his. "After that little excitement, I need a drink."

"That certainly had to be tame compared to the fireworks explosion."

"Yes," I said with a smile. "And certainly less bruising."

Chapter 6

The next morning came early. I went downstairs in my chef's coat to start making fudge at three AM. The ferries started running pretty early but, because most stores didn't open until later, the tourists usually started to show up in bulk between nine and ten. I usually timed my batches so that the candy counter was filled by ten. Sure, I did demonstrations twice a day, but those small batches of fudge would never have kept the customers happy.

Mal followed me down. I gave her a customary biscuit from the glass dog biscuit dish that sat on the receptionist desk. I liked the quiet of the early morning. I made the first two pots of coffee which would eventually fill the self-serve carafes. I liked to keep coffee on hand for my staff's morning arrival and for guests who ventured down early to catch coffee before they went out for a day of island exploring.

The sharp scent of coffee filled the air as Mal finished her treat and snuggled into the dog bed beside the reception area where she would wait for Frances to come in and feed her breakfast.

The thing about Mal was that I'd trained her to never step foot inside the fudge shop. If I had a cat, I was pretty sure there was no training it to stay out of anywhere it didn't want to go.

I poured myself a cup of coffee, added a splash of half and half, and took a sip. The warm brew was a balm to my soul. Then I turned on the lights in the fudge shop and pulled down sugar, butter, milk, and cocoa. The basic ingredients rarely changed. With dark chocolate, milk chocolate, or white chocolate, plus ingredients from dried blueberries to Traverse City cherries to walnuts and pecans, I could vary the flavors, always with the same fudge base.

I measured out ingredients and filled the large copper pot we cooked the fudge in, turned on the flame below and stirred the mixture with a wooden paddle, then left it to cook to a nice soft boil.

I glanced outside to the quiet dark of Main Street. At this time of night, no one was out or about. The bars had closed a few hours prior. All the residents were still asleep. The stores were closed and the carriages not yet lined up, waiting to take tourists on tours or to their hotels.

I liked Main Street best before the ferries deposited the first tourists—when the sky started to lighten with lighter and lighter blues chasing the thick dark night away. The morning star was shining bright in the night. I thought of the cat and wondered if it had a home. Maybe I would ask around town. If I knew that it was somewhere safe, I would feel much better.

Three batches of fudge into my routine, the day had begun to bustle. Frances brought in the morning trays of donuts and Danish and bananas and juice. The first residents had headed down to snag some food before they went down to the docks to catch the ferry home. Sometimes people would check out and have us store their luggage in the big utility closet across from the bathrooms behind the stairs and go spend one more full day on the island, only to return to gather their things and leave on the five o'clock ferry out.

"How was your date last night?" Jenn asked as she bounced down the stairs at ten dressed in black pedal pushers and a white short sleeved top with blue dots. Her long black hair was pulled back into a ponytail. She went straight to the coffee bar and poured herself a cup then checked the pots and brewed some fresh. "You were out late."

"We went to the yacht club for dinner and dancing," I said with a soft smile at the memory.

"Sounds romantic." Jenn leaned against the candy counter and sipped her coffee. She had made herself a latte with caramel and cocoa. I could tell from the delicious scent that emerged with the steam from her cup.

"It was romantic, except for the fact that the dinner was with a couple business associates and their wives."

"That's what happens when you date an important man." Jenn wiggled her fingers at me. "They like to double dip their time."

"It was fine with me," I said and cut thick chunks of caramel pecan fudge from the loaf that I had on the cooling table. Once I'd developed a feel for fudge, I could slice them almost exactly into one quarter pound slices. I transferred the slices to the tray. "There was an ego boasting pride in his eyes when he introduced me and he kept reaching for my hand at odd times. Plus the man can dance."

"Also a perk with a wealthy guy," Jenn said with a sigh. "They usually learn to dance at boarding school."

"He wasn't exactly happy to see my bruises," I mentioned. "He insisted that I tell him the entire story."

"Did you walk back or take a carriage?"

"It's only a few blocks so we walked. We went down by the marina and strolled the walkway there." I couldn't help the secret smile that came with the memory of Trent's kisses.

"Oh, you're smitten," Jenn teased. "Good. It's about time."

'Good morning, Jennifer," Frances said as she came inside with Mal and took the leash and halter off the puppy.

Mal came running up and stopped to slide on the polished wood floor before coming to a stop at the very edge of the floor where it changed to tile for the fudge shop. The puppy had become a master of the slide and rarely, if ever, touched the tile. She knew she would be put in time-out if she did.

"Good morning, Frances," Jenn said and stepped out to hunker down and give Mal a good and thorough rub and pat. "Any juicy gossip today?"

"Besides the fact that you spent the night with a certain crime scene guy?" Frances raised her right eyebrow.

Jenn grinned and shrugged. "We've been dating for two months."

"Sounds pretty serious," Frances said. "I hope you

know what you're doing. You might end up on the island permanently."

"We'll cross that bridge when we come to it. For now, I'm having fun." Jenn stood. "We have an eightieth birthday party in two days. The Koontz are coming in today for a three day family extravaganza. I have the entire third floor booked for the families."

I put the tray of fudge into the candy counter and closed the sliding glass door. "Sandy is coming in this afternoon to make the chocolate sculpture for the tables."

"It's going to be so much fun!" Jenn said. "Phyllis Koontz is turning eighty and she loves hot air balloons. So Sandy is going to cast one for each table of ten. There are fifty guests so five sculptures."

"Parties are such fun," Frances said. "I'm glad you included those types of ideas in the McMurphy website and brochures."

"The cake is coming from All Things Bakery off Market Street," Jenn said. "It's a three tier chocolate and white checkered cake with a hot air balloon on the top. Before the party, they are meeting at Mackinaw City and taking a balloon ride over to the Mackinac Island airport. Then, after the party they will take the ferry back to home."

"I didn't know there was a hot air balloon service," I said.

"There isn't, but I asked Sophie Collins and she put me in touch with a guy who planned the whole thing."

"It's too bad the warehouse is all black and burned. It has to ruin the scenery," Frances said.

"That reminds me." I came around to the lobby.

"Frances, with Jenn making up the third floor rooms, can you watch the fudge shop for an hour or so? I need to go see Rex."

"Sure, but why do you need to see Rex?" Frances asked.

"I remembered something last night when I was telling Trent the story of the explosion."

"What did you remember?" Jenn's eyes sparkled with curiosity.

"There were two bikes parked outside the warehouse when I got there. When I left, mine was the only bike there."

"A clue," Jenn said with a smile.

"I certainly hope so." I took off my chef coat and placed it on the coatrack near the back door. Mal poked me with her nose.

"You can't go, sweetie. You just went out with Frances." I reached down and patted Mal on the head then grabbed my keys and handbag and went out through the alley that ran behind the McMurphy. The day was warm and the scent of flowers filled the air along with the sound of carriages, bikes, and birds.

Locals often walked the alleys when the crowds on the streets swelled. Mr. Beecher, Papa's old card buddy, was on his morning stroll down the alley that ran behind the Main Street buildings. He wore a pair of black slacks, a black and white tweed jacket over a white dress shirt. He had an old golf cap set on top of his head and his cane was black with silver tip and handle.

"Good morning, Allie. Where's your puppy?" Mr. Beecher always reminded me of the snowman from the old stop action Rudolph the Red-nosed Reindeer show.

"Hi, Mr. Beecher. You just missed Frances and Mal. They came back from their walk not five minutes ago."

"My loss," he said with a tip of his hat. "They are two of my favorite people to meet on my walks. You are my third."

"Oh." I felt a blush in my cheeks. "You are always so sweet." I gave him a hug. "I'm on my way to the police station to see Rex. It looks like you're going home."

"I am." He pointed his cane in the opposite direction of the police station. "One of these days we need to take a walk together."

"That would be nice." I straddled my bike. "You take care."

"I will." He gave s short nod of his head. "You do the same, young lady."

"I will." I took off down the alley, rounded the end of it, and turned right toward Market Street and the police station. Liz was on the sidewalk when I emerged from the alley and I quickly braked to a stop. "Hi."

"Hey, Allie. Are you going to the police station?" Liz wore cargo shorts, a light green tank top, and a green and white blouse. Her bare legs were long and ended in socks and hiking boots.

I drew my brows together. "Yes, how did you know?"

"There's been another fire. I figured you heard about it and—like me—were headed to see Rex and try to get the details out of him."

I laughed. "Yeah, like he'd give up details."

"To you, he might," she said, her expression sober. "Seriously."

"Right and Papa Liam is really alive and living in my attic."

"Whatever." She shrugged.

"I'm sorry." I put my hand on her arm. "That was rude. I hadn't heard about the fire. I was going to see Rex because I remembered something from the day of the explosion."

She stopped short. "What did you remember?" She reached for a small notepad she kept in her breast pocket just like her grandfather did.

"It has to do with where I parked my bike." I paused. "You know what? I need to let Rex know first. Okay?

"Sure." She put away her notebook. "Let's go hear what the man has to say about the fire and whatever you remembered. I'll meet you there, since you have your bike."

"Now that's a plan I can stick with," I said.

Liz arrived as I was locking my bike on the rack and we walked in tandem toward the big white building that housed the administration and police and fire stations. Ed Goodfoot was outside wiping down the fire truck. When it came to an ambulance and a fire truck, the island had state of the art vehicles. It looked so odd to see them parked next to bicycles and horse-drawn carriages, but when it came to essential equipment the island was ready.

"Hi Ed." Liz waved.

"Hi Liz, hi Allie." He stopped cleaning. "Nice day."

"It is," I agreed.

Liz steered us over to him. "I heard there was another fire."

"Yes," Ed said, his mouth flat. "That makes two this week."

"Is that unusual?" I asked.

"For Mackinac Island?" he asked. "Yes, there are maybe one or two a year."

"If you count today's fire there have been five fires this year," Liz said. "That is, if you don't include the explosion. The first was an untended campfire." She ticked them off on her fingers. "Next was at the edge of Great Turtle Park that appeared to be from an unextinguished cigarette. The third was a trash barrel on Luke Archibald's property. He was burning brush and the fire got too close to his shed and set it on fire. I always thought that was stupid, but then Luke isn't known for being the brightest."

"What does Luke do again?" I asked. "I've seen him and his wife Clara and his son Sherman around, but I don't know what they do."

"Luke's a painter—and not the artistic kind. He's the house and room kind. In the spring, many of the summer cottages need to be touched up for the season. Luke is always one of the first painters on the island to start the rush to the season," Liz said. "Clara teaches school in St. Ignace. Her family has owned a cabin on Mackinac Island for eighty years. They come out on the weekends and keep it up."

"Oh. Huh, my general contractor Benny didn't hire Luke to do the subcontract work when we did our remodel."

"Benny and Luke don't really get along," Liz explained. "It happens when you're competitors." She waved her hands dismissively. "Let's get back to the fires. There was one more before the warehouse. Trash and bicycle tires started on fire. It was a slow burn because the trash and tires were damp. When it took off, the fire was difficult to stop. Ed, are you telling me that all of those fires might be arson? If so, do you suspect one specific arsonist?"

"I'm not saying," Ed answered carefully. "Not on the record."

"Is there a pattern to the fires?" I asked. "On television, if one person is setting fires, they tend to have a pattern."

"No real pattern," Ed said, "Unless you count the shed near each fire."

"But the first fire was a bonfire, right?" I asked. "No shed involved."

"No shed involved," Ed agreed. "That's what I was saying. If you look at the fires one by one, they all have reasonable explanations and don't appear to be an arson pattern. They all seemed small and there was always a ready reason for the fire."

"And the newest fire? Does it have an easy explanation?" Liz asked.

"No. Today's fire was set under the front porch of the Fogarty B & B."

"It was a porch fire?" I asked.

"Yes," Ed said. "It didn't get far before it was spotted. The owners had fire extinguishers and it was mostly out by the time we got there. I had the guys tear the porch off the house in case anything was smoldering that might reignite."

"How do you know it was arson?" Liz asked.

"An accelerant was used," Rex said behind us. We both turned toward the sound.

As usual, he was dressed in a perfectly pressed

uniform. His hat sat squarely on his head, his baby blue eyes shaded by the brim.

As he walked up, Liz asked, "What kind of accelerant?"

"Lighter fluid," Rex said.

"That's got to be hard to trace," I said. "I mean everyone has lighter fluid somewhere near their house. We all grill."

"It is hard to trace," Ed agreed.

"Correct me if I'm wrong, but the fires seem to be coming closer together," Liz said.

"It certainly appears that way." Ed glanced at the clear blue sky. "Let's hope the humid weather holds. We've never had a fire sweep the island. I don't want to have one now."

"I don't like the sound of that." I looked back at the barely visible roof of the McMurphy. "Too many people's livelihoods would be ruined. Not to mention over a century of historical buildings and such."

"Whoever is setting the fires isn't thinking about history," Rex said, his expression stern.

"No, arsonists that escalate like that are usually addicted to seeing the fire burn," Liz said. "Some describe fire as an animal and arsonists tend to have a love-hate relationship with it."

"How do you know this?" I asked.

Liz smiled. "I watch television."

"Life is not like television," Rex said carefully.

"Okay. So, there have been random fires over the last three months and they may or may not have been arson with a consistent accelerant of lighter fluid," Liz said. "That's all on the record."

"What about Rodney Rivers?" I asked. "Was his

death caused by arson or was the arson used to cover up his death?"

"We're still investigating," Rex said, his expression like a stone wall.

"Okay." I raised both hands in innocence. "I'm not investigating. I was coming to see you, actually."

Rex put his hands on his hips and scowled. "Why?"

"I remembered something about the day of the explosion."

He glanced at Liz's eager expression and Ed's curious looks. "Let's take this into my office."

"You don't have to keep it secret," Liz said. "She already told me it has to do with where her bike was parked."

"Liz," I said and sent her a look of dismay.

She shrugged. "I'm an investigative journalist."

Rex tilted his head, lowered his shoulders, and sent me a look of disappointment. "Allie, I thought I asked you to let me know first if you remembered anything."

I winced. "I know. I'm sorry. All I told her was that it had to do with my bike."

"Fine." Rex pulled out his notebook. "Since you've already told the press, who can't print this because it may hinder my investigation—"

Liz held up her hands in an innocent gesture.

"Tell me what you remembered."

"It really might not be anything important," I said. "But when I arrived at the warehouse, I parked my bike at the bike rack outside the door."

He frowned. "Yes, I know. I helped dig out your bike so you could ride it back home."

"Well, when I parked it, there were two bikes in the slots beside it."

"I remember you telling me about the bikes when you were on the phone." Rex narrowed his eyes. "Wait—yours was the only bike left after the fire."

"Exactly."

"Did you see anyone ride away from the warehouse?"

"No." I frowned. "I've been trying to remember. Once you forced me out, I sat on the curb and watched the firemen come and then waited for the bomb squad. There were a lot of guys coming and going."

"That's true," Ed said as his dark brown eyes narrowed. "I don't remember seeing anyone on a bike, but I was concentrating on the potential hazards."

"I'll ask around," Rex said. "A lot of people were there. Someone might have seen something. I'm glad you remembered that, Allie."

I smiled. "I'm happy to be of help. By the way, the cat ran back out the door."

"What?" Liz cocked her head. "Is that code for something?"

I laughed. "No, Rex let a stray cat into the McMurphy the other night. We spent hours trying to find it but finally gave up. Rex went home and I went to bed. Then I spotted it once or twice before Mal got involved and chased it for a while until someone walked in and it went out the door."

"Mal didn't follow, did she?" Liz looked horrified.

"No, I caught her before she could. Trent went out looking for the cat, but it was long gone."

"Weird."

"Right." I said. "It was a very pretty black and

orange and white calico. So if you see it or hear of one missing . . ."

"I'll keep my eyes and ears open," Liz said.

"She's got all the gossip in town," Ed teased.

"Hey." Liz smacked him in the arm. "I'm a reporter. It's my job to be nosey."

"It was a pretty cat," I said. "I might have never seen it if Rex hadn't let it in."

"It wasn't intentional," he said. "I held the door open to leave and the darn thing just slid right in faster than lightning."

"Well, this might be a story for the society page," Liz said with a grin. "Police officer invites strays to live in the Historic McMurphy Hotel and Fudge Shop." She splashed the words across an imaginary headline. "Do you have a picture of the cat?"

I pulled out my phone. "All I've got is this sort of orange streak." I flipped through my pictures and pulled up the blurred one.

"Huh. Well, that sort of looks like a cat," Liz said, studying the image on my phone. "Maybe we can call in a sketch artist to do a rendering. We can put up the picture as part of a wanted poster."

"Okay, now you're just being silly," I said and everyone laughed. "So, Rex, that was all I had. I'll let you know if I remember anything else, but I think that was pretty much it."

"Okay. I suppose it's something."

"What about the arsons?" Liz asked, wanting to get back to the topic. "Doing the math from the first fire, they are escalating. That can't be good."

"I don't think the arson and the murder are connected," Rex said. "Rodney Rivers was only on the island for two weeks."

"I agree," Ed said.

"So as Officer Lasko originally thought, we might have two problems," I said. "A murderer and a fire starter. Which one is more important?"

"Both," Rex said, his expression suddenly grim. "There isn't a lot of crime on Mackinac Island and I aim to keep it that way."

"All of us would like that," Liz said. "I'll do what I can to keep specific facts out of the paper for now. But if things don't get solved soon, I'm going to have to post something. Seriously Rex, someone might know something. This is a small island. Murder doesn't happen without someone knowing something."

"Have you been able to get ahold of Rodney's partner?" I asked. "Because I've left several phone messages and he's not answering."

"Henry is scheduled to come in tomorrow. I'll let him know to stop by the McMurphy."

"Please do," I said. "We have a contract with his company and he needs to help us get replacement fireworks."

"That may not be possible at this late date," Liz said.

I frowned. "I know, but I have to try."

"Good luck with that," Liz said.

I knew I was going to need it.

White Chocolate Blueberry Cream Pie Fudge

2 cups white chocolate
1 14 ounce can sweetened condensed milk
1 teaspoon vanilla
¼ teaspoon orange extract
1 cup blanched almonds, chopped
1 cup dried blueberries
1 tablespoon grated orange zest
1 teaspoon butter to prep pan

Butter 8x8x2-inch pan.

In a double boiler melt white chocolate and sweetened condensed milk. Stir until smooth. Remove from heat.

Beat in vanilla and orange extract.

In a medium size bowl, mix orange zest, blueberries, and almonds. Pour chocolate mixture into bowl and combine thoroughly.

Pour into prepared pan and refrigerate for 3 hours or overnight.

Cut into 1-inch pieces. Serve in paper candy cups or on a platter. Store in air tight container.

Enjoy!

Chapter 7

The next day, I was working on my red, white, and blue fudges for the Star Spangled Fourth celebration. I had three suggestions for the red—Traverse City cherry, red velvet, or raspberry. I lined up all three on a table at the entrance to the McMurphy. People were allowed to taste test and then vote for their favorite.

The white was simple. It would be white chocolate with almonds and coconut. What had me stuck was the blue. Blueberry was kind of a tradition for the blue part of any Independence Day celebration. But I wasn't certain I wanted to go with something so expected.

"What other foods are blue?" Jenn asked as she arranged flowers for the lobby.

"I Googled blue foods," I said as I stared at my cell phone's browser. "They suggest blue cheese, blueberries, bilberries, blue corn, blue potatoes, and some cabbages that give off a blue color. Who wants potato or cabbage fudge?"

Jenn made a face. "I know I don't."

"I suppose blue cheese fudge might be interesting," I mused.

"Oh, but not with cherry," Jenn said. "Plus blue cheese isn't really all that blue. I mean, it's mostly white, right?"

"So, blue corn or blueberries?"

"I think you're stuck with blueberries. There's nothing wrong with that, you know. They are a traditional Michigan fruit. They would go well no matter which red fudge wins the contest."

I rested my elbows on the registration desk and placed my chin in my hands. Frances was off on her lunch break and I was hanging out near the room keys. I liked the fact that the McMurphy used actual keys and that we hung them from a hook above a small mailbox for each room. It seemed so quaint and cool.

But guarding over the keys should be a twenty-four hour a day, seven days a week kind of job. But who had the money to staff that much? So I'd decided to have a contractor put a sliding Plexiglas door in front of the keys and cubbies. That way, one lock would keep everything in place for those times when the front desk wasn't manned. Like when I was making fudge and Jenn was planning an event and Frances was out running errands. The only problem was the contractor wasn't due to start working on it until after the Fourth of July.

That left me in front of the room keys debating on what kind of blue fudge would be best.

"Hello. I'm looking for Allie McMurphy."

I glanced up to see a guy who appeared to be in his mid-thirties approaching the desk. He was about five foot ten with a round face, spiked hair with blue tips, and wore a grunge T-shirt and jeans.

I stood. "I'm Allie. How can I help you?"

"Henry Schulte," he said and shoved his hand in his pockets. "Officer Manning said you were looking for me."

"Oh, hi." I came around the desk and stuck out my hand.

He ignored it.

I was not put off by his lack of social graces. Rodney had also struggled with social niceties. I guess one had to be a bit of a nerd to want to own a fireworks company. "Yes, first off, my condolences on the loss of your partner. Rodney seemed like a great guy."

"He was the world's best pyro artist," Henry said. "He's going to be hard to replace. That is, if I can replace him."

"And that is why I need to speak to you. Do you have replacement fireworks for the ones that were lost in the explosion? The Star Spangled Fourth committee is very concerned. The island is known for our three fireworks shows and it's important that we continue on with that tradition."

"Yeah, well, fireworks themselves are pretty scarce this time of year."

"That's what I thought." My shoulders slumped. "You have insurance, right?"

"Yeah, but we have to wait for an adjuster to come out and compare the list of fireworks purchased for the show with the lost inventory. Then it's mainly a money thing. They pay us. We pay you."

That did not get my hopes up. "I'm not concerned

with the money. I'm really concerned about having a show this year."

"Yeah, well, I've got a lot of crap to do now that Rodney bit the bullet. So good luck with the show." Henry turned to leave.

"Wait!" I rushed around him to stand between him and the door. "I don't need luck. I need you to come through per our contract."

"The contract was pretty much void the minute Rodney bit it. Insurance will pay me for the loss of revenue, but the show is your gig."

"Wait! No— What am I supposed to do now?"

Henry shrugged. "Who'd you use last year? Call them." He walked around me and out the door.

"Well, that wasn't helpful at all," Jenn said as she stood beside me to watch my hope of having a fireworks show walk across the street.

"I don't know what I'm going to do. I am not exactly on the best side of last year's guys. They were pretty ticked off that I went with someone new."

"Ticked off enough to kill him?" Jenn asked.

"Well, I hadn't thought about that." I frowned. "I doubt it. I mean the business is kind of cutthroat, but not really worth killing someone over."

"I don't know. I don't like that partner guy. He seemed to not care at all about Rodney or his customers."

"I know, right? Do you know any good pyro companies?"

"I might have some strings," Jenn said. "Let me make some phone calls."

"Great. I'll do the same. And I haven't heard back from my mom, yet. There has to be someone who can fill in the gap."

"I'm sure there is," Jenn agreed. "We'll find them."

* * *

The afternoon was busy with two fudge making demonstrations. The crowds had begun to swell in anticipation of the Star Spangled Fourth celebration. I tried not to panic as I searched for a new pyro technic company. The fudge contest was going well and from the looks of things the red velvet fudge was going to be the ultimate winner. That still left me with trying to figure out a blue fudge. The idea was to layer the three flavors so that it was not only attractive and relevant but also tasty.

My cell phone rang. "This is Allie McMurphy. How can I help you?"

"Allie, it's Mrs. Amerson again. I heard that Rodney Rivers partner was in the McMurphy speaking with you. What's going on with the show?"

I sat down on the stool behind the candy counter. My feet hurt from standing and thankfully there was a lull in the crowd at the moment. "Hello, Mrs. Amerson. The good news is that the fireworks are covered by insurance. The bad news is that the insurance won't replace them in time for the Fourth."

"I see." She sounded very unhappy. "What are you going to do about this? We have never missed a Fourth of July show. Our Fudgies are counting on it."

Fudgie was a happy term for the tourists who came to the island. Mackinac was the fudge capital of the world. A lot of people came strictly for the fudge and nothing else. The fudge lovers earned the name of *Fudgie.*

"I've got some calls in to other companies," I said. "I'm going to make the firework shows happen."

"You'd better," she said. "You were the one who pushed for a new company. Now make it happen."

"Yes, ma'am." I stood.

She hung up on me.

I sighed and called Trent.

"Trent Jessop." Hc sounded busy.

"Hi Trent. It's Allie. Do you have a minute?"

"Sure, Allie. What's up?"

"Your family has been part of the island community for generations, right?"

"Yes, we were one of the founding families."

"So someone in your family, at some point had to be part of the Fourth of July celebrations."

"Sure."

I could hear the smile in his voice. "Do you have any connections when it comes to fireworks shows?" I had my fingers crossed.

"No, not that I'm aware of." His tone was serious business. "But I can put some calls out if you need me to."

"I think I need you to. Rodney's partner says we're covered for losses of the fireworks and may get some return on our deposit, but that's it. Mrs. Amerson is on me to fix this problem. We can't not have a show this year."

"I'll make some calls."

"Thanks, Trent. I owe you."

"No, that's what friends are for."

I hung up and realized that I was making friends on Mackinac Island. I had slowly but surely moved away from knowing only Papa Liam and Grammy Alice's friends to building my own relationships. It would be nice if I could keep people from reaching for good luck symbols and get them all to trust that I would follow through on a commitment, no matter how difficult.

Finding replacement fireworks would help.

Chapter 8

"Happy news. I've found a company with fireworks," Jenn said as she hustled into the fudge shop kitchen where I was in the process of cooking a batch of Maple Walnut Fudge.

"Great!" I stirred the sugar and cream as it cooked. "What's the cost?"

"It's in line with your budget and they can get them to us on the dates we need them."

"Sounds perfect," I said as I removed the syrupy base from the heat and added butter and maple flavoring.

"There's just one catch," Jenn added hesitantly.

"Well, I figured. What is it? Are they brand new? Will the fireworks show times be less?"

"No, the company has been in business for fifteen years and have loads of references." Jenn leaned against the counter, watching me pour the hot candy onto the cooling table. The metal frame caught the liquid like a dam around the edges.

I paused before scraping the pan and studied my friend. "What's the catch?"

"They have only fireworks. All their technicians are booked. They don't have a good technician to put the show together and light the fireworks."

I grabbed a handheld spatula and scrapped the pan clean then put it back into its holder. I set the timer for ten minutes. The fudge had to cool to a certain consistence before I began to stir it. "Fireworks don't do us much good if there's no one to fire them."

"I know." Jenn went on. "The person to fire them has to be certified. I can't find anyone who fits the bill who isn't busy already."

I drew my eyebrows together and frowned as I poured soap and water into the pot. "I wonder if Rodney's partner is certified to run the show. I mean, he is Rodney's partner. That means he has to have some kind of license. Right?"

"He must," Jenn agreed. "Do you still have his number?"

"I do. I'll call as soon as I finish this batch."

"Do you think he'll do it?" Jenn asked, her eyebrows drawn together.

"I'm betting he can't say no. We do have a contract. I'll pull it out and see what it says. If we have fireworks, then he has to do the show, right?"

"That would be ideal."

"Thanks, Jenn." I finished washing and drying the pot in time for the timer to go off.

"You're welcome. I love watching you make fudge. It never gets old," Jenn said as I removed the frame from around the fudge and it set in place, slipping only slightly toward the edge of the table.

"I know what you mean." I grabbed a long-handled

spatula and started to flip the fudge. "Where are the fireworks? Can we get them here in time?"

"Yes, if we expedite the shipping."

"Do it. I'll call Henry and send him a copy of the contract if he needs to see it. We paid them fifty percent down. I think that entitles us to someone to run the show, don't you?" I switched from the long handle to the short-handled scraper and turned the fudge into a long loaf. Then made short work of cutting quarter-pound pieces and placing them on a tray.

"Sure do," Jenn said with a grin.

"Thanks for tracking them down."

"That's my job." She curtsied and bowed.

"Remind me to give you a raise someday."

"I'm counting on it."

A few minutes later, I was upstairs in my office with the Rivers Productions contract in my hands. I dialed the phone and put it on speaker.

"Rivers Productions. This is Henry Schulte. I'm unable to get the phone. Leave your name and number and reason for calling and I'll get back to you as soon as I can."

The phone beeped and I frowned. "Hi, Mr. Schulte. This is Allie McMurphy. We were able to find enough fireworks to do the shows we contracted Rodney to do. What we need now is someone to light them and do the show. I've got a contract in my hand that says Rivers Productions will supply the personnel to do the show. I know Rodney is dead, but you are still alive. Please call me back. The show must go on."

I left my number and hit END, scowling at my

phone and willing it to ring. Henry Schulte had been the most difficult person to get ahold of. If he didn't call back by this time tomorrow, I'd go see Rex. He had somehow gotten Henry to come down to the station. Maybe he could help me track him down again.

You know, maybe if I hurried I could find Henry still at the police station. I yanked off my sticky chef coat, tossed it on the back of my desk chair, grabbed my copy of the contract, and headed down the hall to the apartment. I'd take the fire escape down to the alley. It would keep me from running into too many people. It sometimes took an hour to get out of the McMurphy. People always wanted to know about fudge making, or they had an issue in their room, or they needed directions.

It wasn't that I minded so much talking with them and helping them out. But I had a feeling if I didn't hurry, I might miss Henry altogether. And that was not something I was going to take a chance on.

I stuffed the contract in my purse and opened the kitchen door and stepped out onto the fire escape to find the beautiful black, white, and orange kitten sitting on the stoop, licking its paw as if he belonged there.

"Hello. So you're back." I paused, careful to ensure the door was closed tightly behind me. The last thing I needed was another episode of loose cat in the McMurphy. "Do you live nearby?"

The cat didn't answer. In fact, he barely paid me any mind at all. If it was a he. Or was it a she? I couldn't remember what Trent had told me he thought the sex was. Not that it mattered. I like boys and girls.

I squatted down and held out my hand. "Pretty kitty."

The cat continued to ignore me.

I studied its shiny fur and bright eyes. It looked to be of medium size and didn't have any of the awkwardness of a kitten. "Are you an alley cat? Or does someone nearby love you?"

Slowly, I reached into my pocket and took out my cell phone. Then I aimed the camera at the cat and snapped a nice picture. I sent the picture to Jenn in a text. Look who is outside on the fire escape.

She texted back immediately. Pretty!

Do you think I should bring him out some tuna?

If you feed it, it will keep coming back.

I laughed. Some guys I know are like that.

She texted, *snicker*.

Can you create a flyer? That way if the cat has an owner we can let them know not to worry.

Sure thing was her texted reply.

I stood and studied the cat who continued to act as if I didn't exist. "If you're still here when I get back, I'll bring out some tuna and water," I promised.

The cat seemed to expect me to do just that. I sighed and climbed down the metal stairs. I was supposed to be going to find Henry Schulte. A glance at the time told me I'd be lucky to catch him still at the police station. It was growing later in the evening and Rex would have no real reason to keep Henry.

That is, if he hadn't left the island right after he walked out of my shop this morning.

I pushed open the door to the white administration building and went straight to thc police department. "Hello," I said to the officer on desk duty.

He looked up and I realized it was Officer Brown. He was about my age with dark green eyes and caramel colored hair. He had nice broad shoulders and wore the uniform crisply pressed.

"Oh, hi, Charles."

"Hey, Allie, what brings you by?" He put down his pen and gave me his full attention.

"I was looking for Henry Schulte. I know that he was here earlier to see Rex. Is he still around?"

"Rex or this Schulte?" Charles asked with a twinkle in his eye.

"Schulte, actually." I scrounged around in my purse until I came up with the contract. "I've located replacement fireworks for the shows, but I need a tech to light them. Since we still have a contract with Rivers Productions I want to see if Henry will run the show in Rodney Rivers' place."

"That's smart," Charles said. "Where did you find replacement fireworks at this late date?"

"Jenn found them. She is amazing at scrounging up stuff."

"I'll give Rex a ring and see if he knows where Schulte is. Why don't you have a seat?" Charles pointed at the four plastic chairs across from the desk.

"Sure." I sat down and watched him pick up the phone and place the call.

"Hey, Rex. Allie McMurphy's here looking for Henry Schulte. Is he still around?"

I could hear Charles' deep voice over the top of

the wooden reception desk. The floor between him and the chairs where I sat was tiled and polished to a deep shine. A five-by-seven foot rug filled up most of the space so that it was difficult to slip or fall on all that shine.

"I see. Okay. I'll let her know." He hung up the phone.

I stood. "Is he here?"

"Rex asked him to stay on the island for a few days. He got a room over at the Hamilton B & B. You can try him there."

"Thanks. Have a great day."

"You, too."

"Oh, wait." I turned on my heel and pulled out my phone. "You wouldn't happen to know if anyone is missing this cat, would you?" I showed him the picture on my phone.

He studied it carefully then shook his head. "No. Nice cat, though. Is that the one Rex let into the McMurphy?"

I couldn't help but match the grin on Charles' face. "Yes. This time it was sitting on the fire escape. I was careful not to let it inside."

"Don't feed it," he warned. "It will never go away if you do."

"I'm having Jenn put up signs. It's a pretty cat. Someone must be missing it."

"I'll let you know if anyone calls. Usually they call animal control, but sometimes they call here, too."

"Thanks," I said. "Is the shelter here on the island?"

"No, Mackinac County Animal Shelter is in St. Ignace."

"Okay." St. Ignace was the closest town on the Upper Peninsula side of the island. Several ferries went to and from there daily. "I'll have Jenn fax them a picture."

"Good luck," Charles said with a grin.

"Thanks." I texted Jenn about the animal shelter. I wanted her to let them know we had the cat if anyone was looking, but I didn't want them to get the cat. I had no idea if they were a no-kill shelter or not. I couldn't live with the idea that that beautiful cat might be no more.

The Hamilton B & B was just off Market Street less than a mile from the police station and two blocks behind the McMurphy on Main. It was a lovely old cottage that had been turned into rooms. I walked up the sidewalk and enjoyed the fresh air and the cool flutter of the leaves on the tree-lined street.

The Hamilton was deep sage green with orange and white painted trim. It had a wide front porch that overlooked a deep front lawn. It was times like this I wished the McMurphy had a wide front lawn or any lawn for that matter, but my family had given up the lawn for prime real estate on Main Street. The Hamilton had a fire pit in the center of its lawn and several comfy looking metal Adirondack chairs. Two big oaks framed the four-story house. It had pitched roofs and gingerbread trim in all the corners.

The porch held several rocking chairs. Two chairs were currently filled by a middle-aged man in denim shorts and a navy T-shirt and a middle-aged woman in shorts and a white tee with a big flower print.

"Hello," I said as I reached for the brass handle on the door.

"Hello," they said, revealing their Chicago accents. "Nice day, isn't it?"

"It sure is." I opened the door.

The inside smelled of beeswax and old wood. The house had a central foyer and hall. To the right of the door was a large wrought iron coatrack. To the left was a mirrored, oak foyer bench and coatrack.

"Hello?" I called.

A woman with short gray hair and oversized black glasses stepped out from the far left doorway. "Hello. I'm Susan Hamilton. How can I help you?"

"Hi Susan." I stuck out my hand. "I'm Allie McMurphy. We're neighbors, sort of. . . ."

"Ah, the McMurphy girl," Susan said, her pale blue eyes sparkling behind her glasses. "Nice to meet you, dear." She shook my hand. "I knew your grandparents well. I'm so sorry for your loss. Liam was a gentleman through and through."

"Thank-you."

Mrs. H was about five foot six inches tall and wore a sweatshirt with a Michigan State logo on it over jeans and athletic shoes. "What brings you to the Hamilton?"

"I suppose you heard about the fireworks explosion," I said.

"Oh, dear, me, yes. I was in the kitchen when it happened. I could hear the booms and see the smoke. What a ruckus." She shook her head. "I understand you were there."

"Yes," I said with a nod. "It was not fun. We lost all the fireworks for the Star Spangled Fourth."

"Oh, dear." She pushed her glasses farther up on her nose and blinked at me. "That won't do. That won't do at all. What is the committee doing about it?"

"That's why I'm here. I'm the person in charge

of the fireworks. I've been lucky enough to find replacements. All we need now is someone qualified to fire them."

"I see." She frowned. "I don't know what that has to do with me. I'm certainly not qualified."

"Oh, no." I touched her forearm in reassurance. "I'm here to see your latest guest, Henry Schulte. He's the partner of Rodney Rivers, the technician we lost in the explosion."

"Oh, dear, someone died?" Mrs. H asked. "Why did I not hear about that?"

"The death is still under investigation, but I'm pretty sure it was reported in the *Town Crier*. I know that Liz was at the scene."

"Well, that's the reason. I've been in Petoskey visiting my sister. She lives on a farm and when we get together we do so much chin wagging that we don't even turn on the television, let alone read a paper."

"That makes sense," I said. "Can you tell me if Mr. Schulte is in?"

"I saw him about an hour ago when he checked in." Mrs. H went to a small desk on the wall across from the staircase. "I can't give out his room number, but you can leave him a message." She handed me a notepad and a pen.

"Wow, that is old-fashioned." I laughed.

"You'd be surprised at how many people pay attention to a handwritten note over a text message."

"Okay." I wrote out a small note asking Henry to call me and gave my number. "I don't think he'll follow up, but it's worth a try." I tore off the note, folded it, and put his name on the underside then gave her the note. "It was nice to meet you, Susan."

"You, too, Allie," she said and took the note. "I'll give this to him right away. Best of luck with your search for the fireworks technician. We really count on the shows."

"I know you do. I certainly know you do."

Chapter 9

"I heard that Rodney Rivers was getting death threats," Jenn said as we gathered for our nightly staff meeting in my apartment.

I poured sangria for myself, Jenn, Frances, and Mr. Devaney. Sandy Everheart, my part-time chocolatier, had ducked out to spend time with her family. The apartment windows were all wide open and the cool breeze off the lake made the curtains flutter.

"Where'd you hear that?" I asked as I curled up in my favorite chair. "Oh, no, wait—" I held up my hand. "Was it your inside source?" I grinned.

"Yes." Jenn tried to hide a secret smile by taking a sip of her drink.

"How does Shane know?" Frances asked.

"It's a small department," Mr. Devaney said. "I imagine there is some water cooler talk."

"Actually, Rex sent Rodney's smartphone out to be forensically searched. Shane is interested in the process for electronic evidence and was chatting the guys up who did the work. They told him that usually there isn't much to be found on a victim's phone, but Rodney did most of his business on his phone so there were all kinds of receipts, e-mails, and documents."

"And they found threats? What kind of threats, viruses?" I asked.

Mal jumped up onto the chair beside me and with a comfortable turn she settled into my lap.

"He was getting e-mail messages from collectors about unpaid bills. There were also phone messages that were quite explicit."

"Yikes. That's scary," I said.

"I imagine Rex is looking into Rivers' finances," Mr. Devaney said.

"Unpaid bills aren't exactly a motive for murder," Frances said. "If that were the case, there would be a lot of dead people in this world."

"I suppose that's true." I tilted my head. "Were the threats only from collectors?"

"No." Jenn's blue eyes sparkled with interest. "There were a couple unidentified e-mail threats."

"I thought all e-mails could be identified these days." Mr. Devaney pulled his left ankle up to rest on his right knee exposing argyle socks and dark brown shoes. His slouchy corduroy pants were dusty from today's work. His dress shirt was checkered red, cream, and brown and protected by the deep brown cardigan he wore over the top.

"It's true most can be eventually traced to an IP address, but sometimes that takes time and a whole lot of effort." Jenn sipped her drink. "The police would have to be really convinced that those threats were worth the time and effort to dig up the source. Even then, it might be a library or Internet café used by multiple people during the day."

"You sound like you know a lot about cyber stalking." Frances waggled her eyebrows. Her short brown hair shone in the lamplight.

"I love to watch those television crime shows," Jenn said. "Shane tells me things are so much different in real life. There are labs full of evidence waiting to be looked at, but there isn't time, money, or good equipment always available. So they make you think that bad guys will be caught, but that's not always the case."

"Poor Rodney," I said. "His threats turned out to be real."

"Or they may not have been related to the murder at all," Jenn said. "Shane was telling me of this case in Ann Arbor where some woman had a stalker, but as we all know there isn't much the police can do unless some harm comes to a person. Well, she was shot and in a coma for a week. The Ann Arbor police pulled in her known stalker, but couldn't connect him to the gun or the alley where she was shot."

"What happened?" Frances asked as she settled slowly into the couch until she rested ever so carefully, nonchalantly touching Mr. Devaney. Seriously, we all knew about those two, so why did she continue to pretend nothing was going on?

"Oh, the woman woke up and, once the doctors intubated her, the police listened to her story and discovered she could identify her attacker and it wasn't the stalker. It turns out it was a random mugging that had nothing to do with the fact that she had a stalker. The stalker was let go because the woman was able to identify her mugger as a different man in a lineup."

"Wow," I said. "Poor gal. To have a stalker is scary enough, but then to get mugged in a separate incident. Terrible."

"Speaking of terrible, did you find out if Rodney's partner will conduct the fireworks show with our new fireworks?" Jenn asked.

"No." I pursed my lips and drew my eyebrows. "I found out he was staying at the Hamilton B & B. I went over to talk to him, but Mrs. H wouldn't give me his room number. All I could do was leave a message for him to call me."

"And we all know how good he is at calling you back," Jenn said.

"Yeah." I sighed. "Before I went to the B & B, I'd left four messages on his phone at the office and he hasn't called back once. If he hadn't stopped in this morning, I would have to think he was purposely avoiding me."

"What did he say when he stopped in?" Mr. Devaney asked. "I was up in three-ten repairing the stuck window."

"He basically said that the insurance would cover the cost of the fireworks, but, since we only made a down payment he wasn't obligated to continue on with the shows."

"That doesn't sound right," Mr. Devaney said.

"It's not. I checked the contract. That's what I wanted to talk to him about. Jenn found replacement fireworks so he needs to either be our technician or find us a replacement."

"Did you let Rex know that this guy was dodging your calls?" Frances asked.

"No." I patted Mal, giving her a good scratch behind the ears. "He has his hands full with the murder investigation. It's not appropriate for me to use Rex's time to track down a guy about a contract agreement."

"You should call your lawyer," Mr. Devaney said. "It might take some finagling if this guy doesn't want to keep his part of the contract and it sounds like he doesn't."

"I suppose you are right. I'll try to get ahold of Mr. Schulte again tomorrow. If I can't, I'll call Frances's cousin William. He's a criminal lawyer, but he might know someone who can help with a civil case."

"I'm sure William would be happy to help," Frances said. "This isn't just your fireworks show. This affects the entire community. Maybe if you explain that to Mr. Schulte he will understand how important this is to us."

"I certainly hope so."

Later that night, Mal wanted to go out for her end of the day walk. I slipped on her pink harness with the reflective white stars and snapped on her pink leash. We went out the back door of the apartment.

It was one of those cool nights where the sky was clear and filled with stars. The breeze off the lakefront rustled the leaves on the trees. The sounds of night insects filled the air. We moved quickly down the metal fire escape.

When I'd first moved into the apartment, the last rung of stairs was a ladder that could be pulled up to keep others from coming up the fire escape. But after I got Mal, I realized that it would be advantageous to be able to use the back fire escape so I had

Mr. Devaney install permanent black medal steps all the way down. Mal was used to hopping on down them and often beat me to the bottom.

The alley was quiet. A single street light illuminated the walkway between the McMurphy and the Oakton Bed and Breakfast behind us. Well, actually it was the pool house to the Oakton. At one point, Papa Liam and Mr. Thompson had an agreement that both hotels would share the expense and the use of the pool house, but they had a falling out and since then, the pool house was exclusively for the use of the Oakton guests.

A small patch of grass at the edge of the alley and a fence separated us from the pool house which sat up on a hill. The pool house shutters were open, leaving the wind to blow through the screened-in windows that surrounded the pool. It was quiet, but a light was on inside.

Mal used the patch of grass for her business and I wondered if the pool house was in use by guests or if Mr. Thompson had simply forgotten to turn off the light.

The light seemed to be getting brighter and I noticed the strong acid scent of burning wood. I scowled and stepped closer to the fence. It wasn't like the Oakton to have a bonfire near the pool house.

Mal barked and pushed her way under a hole in the fence, yanking her leash from me.

"Mal!" I shouted. "Come back here."

She was gone.

I climbed the fence and noticed a figure moving toward the shadows. "Hey, excuse me. Can you help me get my dog?"

The person turned and I recognized the familiar slouch of Sherman Archibald. He was wearing a T-shirt and baggy jeans and his shaggy hair was greasy.

"Sherman?" I called. "Did you see my dog, Mal? She's a white bichon-poo."

"Naw," he said and shrugged his thin shoulders.

Mal barked in the distance.

"Okay," I muttered and took off to the pool house. "Mal! Come here puppy." I ran around the corner to find the edge of the pool house engulfed in flames. I gasped and stopped short. Mal was barking at the flames that licked up the side of the building.

I grabbed my puppy and ran back out of the way of the flames. "Fire!" I shouted. Earlier this month when I'd shouted "*fire*" in the alleyway, no one had heard me so I wasn't banking on it working this time. I grabbed my phone out of my pocket and dialed 9-1-1.

"9-1-1. What is your emergency." Charlene's voice was clear and confident.

"Hi, there is a fire at the Oakton pool house. Send help fast."

"The pool house is on fire?" Charlene asked.

"Yes, the Oakton pool house between the Oakton B & B and the McMurphy."

"Is this Allie McMurphy?" Charlene asked.

"Yes, Charlene. Hi. There's a fire and it's getting closer to the pool house roof."

"I'm sending the fire department. Is anyone hurt?"

I glanced around. "I don't see anyone."

"Are you inside or outside the pool house?"

"I'm outside. The shutters are open and the windows are screened."

"Can you get a fire extinguisher?"

I held tight to Mal who was squirming and barking. "I don't know." I walked around to the door of the pool house and tried to open it. It was locked. I glanced inside and saw the faint glow of a nightlight, but no one was inside. "No, the place is locked up tight."

The sound of sirens filled the air as the fire truck left the administration building.

"The guys are on their way. Step back and stay safe," Charlene advised.

"Will do." I hung up my phone as the truck pulled up. Four firemen in full gear jumped out of the truck and hauled the hose out, hooking it up to the fire hydrant in the street above the pool house and then rushing down the slope of the hill to spray the roof and smother the fire.

Mal squirmed in my arms, but I held on to her tight. "Oh, no you don't." I was a few feet back and firmly out of the guys way as I watched them do the work quickly and efficiently.

"Another fire," Liz said as she strode up with her camera in hand and took pictures. Her hair was down and loose over her shoulders. She wore a simple T-shirt, shorts, and socks with her hiking books untied and flapping. "I heard the dispatch call and came right out." She snapped action pictures of the firemen hosing down the smoldering side of the building. "Did you call it in?"

"Yes. Mal got loose and started barking. I climbed over the fence to find her in front of the fire."

Liz smiled. "That pup of yours is getting to be a regular hero."

The fire was put out fairly quickly and Ed Goodfoot came over. "Hello, Allie."

"Hi." I put Mal down. Now that the excitement was over, she was happy to sniff around.

"Thanks for calling in the fire. We were able to catch it before it got too far."

"Oh, you're welcome. I was out walking Mal when she escaped and came to bark at the fire. It really is all her doing." I pointed at my dog. "Do you know what caused it?"

"Not certain yet. I'm glad we caught it early. With tonight's winds it could have traveled through several nearby buildings."

"Funny, but you would think a pool house would not be something that would catch on fire easily."

"Was it another arson?" Liz asked.

"Hey, Allie, what's going on?"

I glanced over to see Jenn heading toward us.

"The pool house was on fire."

"Oh, that's not good," Jenn said as she climbed over the fence and hopped down.

"What's going on?" Pete Thompson asked as he puffed around the corner of the pool house. My backdoor neighbor wasn't on the best of speaking terms with me since Papa Liam died. It hadn't helped that I had planned a party in the pool house and we'd found a dead man floating facedown. "Ms. McMurphy, what are you doing on my property?"

"My dog slipped under the fence. When I got to her, I noticed the pool house was on fire so I called the fire department."

"She saved your pool house," Ed said. "You're

lucky. If she hadn't called in when she did, the fire would have hit the roof and burned down the entire structure. We're lucky, too. With tonight's wind, the fire could have easily jumped from building to building."

"Why would the pool house be on fire?" Pete rubbed his heavy jowls with his pudgy hand. He wore a pair of dark sweatpants and a T-shirt. His chubby body looked squeezed into his clothes.

"Did you have a bonfire tonight?" Ed asked.

"No, we cancelled the fire pit due to the wind," Pete said. "It had to be sabotage." He scowled at me. "Maybe we should ask Miss McMurphy here what she was doing when the fire started."

"I was walking my dog," I said.

"A likely excuse." He crossed his arms over his wide chest and glared at me.

"Don't be ridiculous." Jenn patted his arm. "Allie wouldn't start a fire on a property so close to the McMurphy. Maybe it was electrical." She wore a silk kimono top over soft pajama pants and looked like a Hollywood starlet.

Pete softened his stance at the sight of her. "I just had the electricity checked after the murder. The insurance company insisted that I check so that there would be no further accidents around the pool."

"It's too dark to tell if it was deliberately set," Ed said. "Stay away from it and we'll come back in the morning and investigate."

"Is it safe to leave it over night?" I asked. "I mean, what if whoever started the fire decides to come back and tamper with the evidence? Or worse, what if they try to finish the job?"

"We'll have round the clock surveillance," Rex said. "I've got Officer Brown coming down for the night."

"Thank-you." Ed turned to me. "I just wanted to thank you for your quick thinking, Allie." He touched the brim of his fireman's hat. "Good night."

"Bye," I said at the same time Jenn did.

"I'll be glad for the surveillance," Pete said, his forehead breaking out in a sweat. "I'll have cameras installed as soon as possible." He looked at me pointedly. "I don't want to see you on my property again. Is that clear?"

"Crystal," I replied and refrained from sticking my tongue out at him.

"We'll be glad for the cameras," Jenn said trying to be diplomatic. "The alley hasn't been that safe and cameras will really help. In fact, it might not hurt to install our own on the back of the McMurphy."

I frowned. "I'll get Mr. Devaney to check into the pricing. If it's not too expensive, we should do it."

"You may save on insurance," Rex said. "I'd do it."

"What is the world coming to?" Liz said. "This is the fifth fire this year. Do you have any idea who is doing this? Or if the fires are even related?"

"I can't talk about an ongoing investigation," Rex replied and crossed his arms. "I do need to talk to Allie about what she saw."

Jenn and Pete just looked at Rex.

He scowled. "Alone."

"Oh," Jenn said. "Sure thing. Here, Allie. Let me take Mal."

"Okay." I handed her Mal's leash.

"Come on, baby. Let's go home." Jenn picked Mal up and climbed back over the fence with her.

"I need to get a taller fence," Pete muttered.

"There are building codes," Rex reminded him.

"Right. Fine. Just keep one of your guys on my property," Pete groused and turned on his heel. "I don't want to have to wait for another fire to find out I was right to blame my neighbor."

"I didn't set the fire," I said.

"At least you didn't blow it up like you did the warehouse," Pete said as he walked away.

I opened my mouth to tell him I didn't blow anything up, but shut it when I realized I couldn't reason with an unreasonable person.

"Are you okay?" Rex asked me.

"Sure." I shrugged. "Why are people crazy?"

He scowled. "There's no knowing what is going on in some people's heads. Want to tell me about the fire?"

I shoved my hands in my pockets. "I took Mal out for her late walk. I noticed what I thought was a light on in the pool house. It's kind of unusual for this time of night."

Rex took notes on his small notepad. "I'll have to check to see how late the pool is open."

"It used to be until nine PM," I said. "But he may have changed that. Mal did her business and then sniffed the fence. I figured she smelled something interesting like she does on a regular basis, but then she took a quick tug of her leash and slipped under the fence. She was fast. Faster than I could catch her and suddenly she was barking and out of sight."

"So then what happened?"

"I climbed the fence and went after her. I noticed a teenager between me and her and asked him if he saw my dog. He didn't. So I hurried off. When I rounded the corner, I realized it was the pool house on fire, not a light inside the pool house. I called Charlene right away."

"Who was the kid?" Rex asked. His eyebrows were drawn in concern.

"Sherman Archibald, Luke's boy. I remember him from their help with putting out embers at the warehouse."

"Right," Rex said.

"Wait. You don't think he had anything to do with the fire, do you?"

"I don't know." Rex stuffed his notepad into the breast pocket of his uniform. "I hope not. Luke's a nice guy. Sherman seems like a great kid."

"I know."

"Listen, don't fret. We don't even know if the fire was arson at this point. It could simply be electrical in nature."

"Okay." I nodded. "You said you'd have someone guard the site."

"Yeah, I called Officer Brown. He was working the night shift. He'll keep an eye on things."

"Good. This fire was close. I don't want to have to sleep with one eye open."

"Go home, Allie," Rex said. "We've got this."

"Thanks, Rex. You're great."

"Just doing my job," he said, his voice gruff. "Take care of that dog of yours. She helps out a lot around here."

I smiled. "I will."

Easy Strawberry Cream Pie Fudge

2½ cups white chocolate chips, melted
1 3 ounce package strawberry flavored gelatin dissolved in ¼ cup hot water to reduce graininess
1 16 ounce can vanilla frosting
1 cup dried strawberries, chopped into tiny pieces.
1 teaspoon butter for pan prep

Butter 8x8x2-inch pan.

Carefully melt white chocolate chips and dissolved gelatin in the top of a double boiler. Hint: White chocolate burns faster than regular chocolate. Melt slowly and stir constantly.

In a medium bowl, mix can of frosting, melted chocolate-gelatin mixture and chopped strawberries. Stir until combined.

Pat into pan. Score into 1-inch pieces with butter knife and refrigerate for 3 hours. Remove and cut into 1-inch pieces following the score marks.

Serve in individual paper cups or on platter. Cover leftovers in air tight container and store in refrigerator.

Enjoy!

Chapter 10

The next morning, the cat was back on the fire escape. When I exited to take Mal out for her morning walk, the cat leapt up on the rail and pretended not to notice us. Mal jumped up and tried to reach it, her doggie tail wagging a hello.

"So you're back," I said to the cat. "Well, if you are going to visit us, then you must be properly introduced. This is Mal. She is very smart and loves everyone so if she chases you, it's all in fun."

The cat did not respond and instead, lifted its front paw for a good lick.

"I see you don't have a collar. I figure you might be hungry so after we get back from our walk, I'll get you some food and water. That is, if you are still here." Mal and I went down the stairs and out across the alley to her favorite potty patch of grass.

I noticed that the hole under the fence seemed bigger this morning. I stepped up and was able to put my foot through it. I frowned. I'd have to tell Pete about it in case he wanted to fix it. Or maybe I'd fix it myself so that Mal couldn't get away from me so quickly again. That might be the neighborly thing to do, anyway.

Mal jumped up on me and gave my face a good lick as I squatted down and tried to bend the chain link to fill the hole. It didn't budge.

"Good morning, Allie," Mr. Beecher said as he strolled down the alley. Today he wore black slacks, a checkered vest over a pale blue shirt, and finished the entire ensemble with a black sports jacket.

"Hello, Mr. Beecher." I rose.

"Problem with the fence?"

"Yes, it got pulled up somehow. Last night, Mal snuck right under and went racing off toward the Oakton's pool house."

"I heard there was a fire," the old man said as he stopped next to me.

"Yes, apparently the pool house caught fire. Last I heard they didn't know what caused it."

"I saw the pictures in this morning's *Town Crier.*" He eyed the yard up to the pool house. "My guess is it was a bonfire that got out of control."

"I hope so. Or an electrical fire."

He drew his eyebrows together. "What else could it be?"

"Arson," I said with a frown. "Liz thinks there has been a string of arsons on the island since January."

"What a strange time for arsons to start." Mr. Beecher frowned, too. "These sorts of things don't just start out of the blue. For them to start when most of the inhabitants are locals seems odd. I don't know. Something isn't adding up."

"I agree. I was going to ask Pete to fix his fence,

but I'm not exactly on speaking terms with him. It might be easier to fix it myself."

"Good fences make good neighbors," Mr. Beecher said with a twinkle in his eye. "Or so I've heard."

I smiled. "There is some truth in that, I think."

"Well, have a good morning." He patted Mal on the head.

"Wait." I stopped him. "Do you know Luke Archibald and his son Sherman?"

"Sure, why?"

"I saw Sherman last night cutting through the Oakton yard about the time the fire started. I wondered if he might have seen anything."

"Sherman is a good kid," Mr. Beecher said. "Luke has painted some trim for me. Sherman always comes to the site where his father is working. He has a strong interest in becoming a painter or so Luke tells me. I'm sure if Sherman saw anything, he'd let the police know."

"Thanks. Rex most likely already checked that out. I was just wondering."

"Well, if you ever need exterior paint work done on the McMurphy, I'd recommend Luke any day."

"I'll remember that." Mal and I started down the alley in the opposite direction of Mr. Beecher. Our walk would take us by the grocery store. I wanted to pick up cat food and a fence repair kit.

The ferries had come in with their first run of tourists. The crowds spilled out of the docks like children entering wonderland. The air was soft and filled with the sounds of waves crashing, boat engines churning, and gulls squawking. The fudge shops had yet to open their doors, but the nearest

T-shirt shop and the welcome center were open. People could buy their tickets to get into Fort Mackinac or the art museum. The horse-drawn taxis were lined up along the north side of Main Street.

Mal hurried along. She liked to sniff out all the smells left on the sidewalks from the night before. We stopped outside into the grocery store to look at the produce on display.

Mary Emry was working the counter and stepped out when she saw us. "Good morning. Hi Mal." She came around the counter to give Mal a good pet. "How's my favorite puppy today?"

"She's good," I said.

"I heard she spotted a fire at the Oakton Pool house," Mary said as she scratched Mal behind the ears.

"Yes. She slipped under the fence. I was wondering if you had anything to fix it."

"There is some chicken wire in the back corner with the hardware stuff. I would recommend you get that and then bury the bottom and attach the rest to the fence. That way she can't do any more digging."

"I'm pretty sure she didn't dig the hole under the fence." I frowned. "I've never seen her dig, anyway. But burying the chicken wire sounds like a good idea. Can you watch Mal a minute?" When Mary nodded her agreement, I handed her Mal and headed inside, down the aisle toward the back of the store, picked up a roll of fencing, and went quickly down the pet food aisle to pick up a couple cans of cat food.

I placed my purchases on the checkout counter,

and stuck my head out to ask, "Did anyone recognize the cat?"

"Cat?" Mary echoed.

"Yes, the one in the FOUND posters that Jenn put up. The cat is a beautiful stray. She seems to like the McMurphy and has been hanging around my fire escape."

"Are you sure it's a girl?"

"I don't know for sure. I haven't gotten close enough to find out. Trent picked her up and thought she was a girl." I shrugged. "It's a beautiful cat, though. Someone has to be missing it."

Mary gave me Mal's leash, stepped inside and rang up my items. The counter was a few steps from the door which was open and so we were able to continue our conversation. "I haven't heard anyone say that it was their cat. It might have stowed away on the ferry and decided it likes island living." She noted the cans of food. "You do realize that if you feed it, it will be your cat."

"I can't not feed it," I said with a sigh. "It's been out there for three days now."

"Well, if you decide to keep it, you'll need to catch it and take it to the vet. Make sure it has all its shots and gets spayed or neutered just like Mal or the island will be overrun with feral cats."

I made a face at the idea of that beautiful cat causing the island to be overrun. It was ridiculous. Nonetheless, having the cat looked at by a vet wasn't a bad idea. "Maybe I can get Mr. Devaney to catch it for me."

"Do that," Mary advised as she held out her hand

and I gave her my debit card to swipe. "In the long run, it's best for the cat and you."

"Thanks," I said and picked up my bagged purchases, tucking the bundle of wire under my arm. As Mal and I stepped toward the street, Sophie came through.

"Hi Allie," Sophie said. "Is this your puppy?" She bent down to pat Mal's head.

"Yes, this is Marshmallow. Mal for short."

"Well, hello Mal. Aren't you cute?" She straightened. "So, Allie, do you know any more about the dead man in the warehouse or who set the explosion?"

I sighed. "It was Rodney Rivers, my pyro technician who died. As far as I know, the police still don't know who set the explosion."

"Oh, no. You lost all your fireworks and the guy who can do the show? What are you going to do now?"

"We've found replacement fireworks, but I need to get someone to fire them."

"Isn't the dead guy's partner talking to Rex?" Sophie asked.

"He is," I said. "But that doesn't mean he has to talk to me. In fact, he came into the McMurphy to tell me that the insurance company would send us a check to pay for the fireworks but that was it. We were on our own."

"That doesn't seem right." Sophie crossed her arms. She wore her pilot uniform of white shirt with epaulets and black slacks stylish with black boots polished to a high sheen. They had squared toes and a stacked heel that was about an inch tall.

"It's not right," I said. "I checked the contract and he's obligated to shoot the shows for us. But he isn't getting in contact with me."

"That seems lousy," Sophie said. "Get Oscar Osborn on it. He'll send him a certified legal notice."

"Who's Oscar Osborn?" I asked.

Sophie laughed. "I forget you are so new to the island. Oscar is the town lawyer. He's pretty much retired now, but he is active in the chamber of commerce. He handles legal issues that come up, especially ones that threaten something as important to the community as the Star Spangled Fourth celebration."

"Great, thanks. I'll call him." Mal and I took a step to toward the fudge shop.

"Hold on a second," Sophie said. "I want to grab a soda. Let me do that and then I'll walk back to the McMurphy with you."

"Okay."

Mal sniffed around my feet while I waited for Sophie to get her drink, pay for it, and leave with us.

"Did you have an early flight?" I asked as we stepped into the slowly crowding streets.

"Yes, I brought in the Bailey's for the week. They own a summer cottage near the library." Sophie twisted the top off her drink and took a sip. "Theodore Bailey is a principal investor for the group that owns the Grand Hotel and a few other places."

"I imagine that's a nice investment property," I said.

"I wouldn't know," Sophie said with a grin. "I'm not much into real estate. I prefer the air to the earth."

"If you don't mind my asking, how did you get

into flying?" We stepped around the block to cut into the alley that ran behind the Main Street shops.

"My Dad was a pilot. Mom says he took me flying the first day I left the hospital." She shrugged. "I grew up with it. In fact, I flew my first solo when I was twelve. They had to issue me a junior license. My Dad was pretty proud."

"Did you grow up on Mackinac?" My tone sounded as wistful as I felt. The freedom to fly anywhere sounded so romantic.

She shook her head. "No, I grew up in Green Bay, Wisconsin. My Dad flew for a couple regional companies with small jets. He heard that the Grand was looking for a new pilot and told me to apply. I did and got the job about three years ago."

"You seem like such a regular fixture around here," I said. "I had no idea you were also new."

Sophie laughed. "Yeah, I'm a foreigner here, too. Only other foreigners think I'm not."

"Great. I keep giving myself away," I said and sighed. Mal trotted along in front of us.

"What's the chicken wire for?" Sophie asked.

"There's a hole in the fence between the McMurphy and the Oakton. I don't want Mal running over there like she did last night."

"Tell lazy Pete Thompson to fix it," Sophie said.

"He's not talking to me. Mal discovered a fire at his pool house last night and he blames me for the damages."

"That's just wrong." Sophie drew her eyebrows together. "Seriously, that guy is better at making enemies than friends."

"I take it you know him pretty well?"

"Well enough to have flown him a couple times. The guy complains the entire time. The last time I flew him, he wouldn't shut up so I did a few barrel rolls. He was too busy being sick to complain anymore."

I laughed. "That's one way to shut him up, I guess."

"I see you have cat food." Sophie pointed at the cans in the clear plastic bag. "You have a cat and a dog?"

"No, just a dog. A few days ago, Rex let this beautiful cat into the McMurphy. He opened the door to leave and it just walked right in and disappeared up the stairs."

"Oh, no. Really?"

"Really," I said with a smile at the memory. "By the next day, Trent Jessop coaxed it out of hiding."

"Yeah, I could see that," Sophie said with a twinkle in her eye. "That man is gorgeous. He could coax me out of hiding."

"I know. We're kind of dating."

"Kind of dating? A man like that you do not *kind of date*," Sophie said, her eyes twinkling.

I winced. "It's still pretty new."

"I heard the rumors," she teased.

"Anyway, the cat leapt from his arms and Mal chased it out the door."

"Oh." Sophie looked confused. "Then why the cat food?"

"It's been hanging around the alley. We took pictures and have signs up, but so far, no one has come to claim it."

"You bought the food so that it won't go hungry."

I felt the heat of a blush rush over my cheeks. "Yes

and yes. I've been told if you feed a stray cat, it's your cat."

"Cats are great to have around," Sophie said, "as long as they are spayed or neutered."

"If no one claims it by the Fourth of July, I'll see if I can't get Trent to catch it again and I'll take it to the vet in St. Ignace and get it taken care of."

"You are a big softy," Sophie said.

I grinned. "Yeah. I suppose there are worse things to be."

"I suppose that's true."

"Do you have time to come up?" I asked as we hit the back of the McMurphy. "Jenn made some beignets this morning."

"Sounds lovely. We foreigners need to stick together."

I laughed. "I agree. We can call ourselves the Foreign Legion."

"Small in number but mighty in presence."

As we walked toward the back of the McMurphy, I noticed Luke walking toward the Oakton pool house. "Hey, Luke," I called and waved.

He stopped. "Good morning, ladies."

"Hi Luke," Sophie said.

Mal pulled us toward the hole in the fence as he walked over to us from the other side.

"What brings you to the Oakton?" I asked. "Did Pete call you to repair the fire damage?"

"No. Actually, I'm putting the finishing touches on the trim of the lower level of the B & B." Luke wore white painter's jeans, a T-shirt, and a white shirt over that with his name embroidered over the pocket and had a plastic bucket with various paint brushes inside it in his right hand. "Pete turned the formal parlor into a business center. He needed the room painted and the trim painted white to match the rest of the interior trim. He also wants me to come back this fall and paint his hallways."

"Wait. Pete put in a business office? What's in it?"

"A few computers and a printer," Luke said.

"Really? Does he get much call for a business office?" I asked.

Mal tugged on her leash. She wanted to go under the fence so badly and greet Luke.

"I think he is trying to compete with the new Grander Hotel," Luke said.

"Crazy about the fire," Sophie said. "Were you here when it happened?"

"No, I'd gone home about half an hour before it broke out. I hear your puppy discovered it." He glanced at Mal who had given up on the hole and jumped on the fence begging for him to reach over and pet her.

"Yes, she got under the fence through this hole," I said. "It's why I bought supplies to fix it." I held up the chicken wire.

"You should make Pete fix it," Luke said, drawing his eyebrows together. "It's his fence, right?"

"Pete's not exactly speaking to me," I explained.

"He blames her for the fire," Sophie added.

"Well, that's plain silly," Luke said. "I heard through the grapevine it was an electrical fire."

"Either way, the siding is going to need to be replaced and painted to match—which means more work for you," I said with a smile.

"Speaking of work, I'd better get to it." Luke lifted his bucket to emphasize his words.

"See you," I said and turned toward the McMurphy. "I bet Sherman was looking for his dad last night." I opened the back door of the McMurphy and let Mal go. She gathered up her leash and raced off to find Frances.

"I bet that's it," Sophie said. "The kid is a bit of a shy one, typical teenager, though, slouching about. Luke did some work out at the airport. Sherman came to see him every day."

"Aw. Luke must be a good dad for his teenage son to want to hang around with him."

"He's a nice guy. His wife is a real sweetheart. In the summers, she works part-time for the Grand in the event planning area so I see her a lot."

"Who are we talking about?" Frances asked as she stood up from taking off Mal's leash and harness.

"Luke Archibald," I said. "He's painting trim on the lower floor of the Oakton. Pete put in a business center for his guests."

Frances frowned. "What business person wants to stay at a B & B?"

"That's what I was thinking." I put down my bag and chicken wire. "It's not like they have to print off plane tickets when they leave."

"I think offering Wi-Fi is too much," Frances said as she went back to her perch behind the reservations desk. "People come to Mackinac to get away from all that Internet stuff. They want to unplug and experience another, more genteel way of living."

"And here I thought they came for the fudge," I said with a laugh.

Sandy was working in the fudge shop. The candy counter shelves were full and she was working on chocolate centerpieces for a wedding.

"It does smell good in here," Sophie said.

"Frances, have you met Sophie? Sophie, this is Frances. She is my hotel manager."

"You're the pilot, right?" Frances held out her hand.

"Yes," Sophie shook Frances's hand. "We've met before a couple times."

"I thought so. Pretty gutsy being a female pilot." Frances looked over the top of her red reading glasses at Sophie. "Good for you."

"Thanks. I don't see it as gutsy."

"She was born into it," I said. "Like me and the McMurphy."

"'Some people are born into greatness,'" Frances quoted with a smile.

"'Some people have it thrust upon them.'" I finished the quote and picked up the bag with the cat food. "I bought stuff to fix the fence. Can you have Mr. Devaney do it? We're going upstairs for beignets and coffee. Do you want me to bring you anything?"

"I'll let Douglas know," Frances said. "You realize that he will tell you that it's Pete Thompson's fence."

"I know," I laughed. "Tell him I want to do it anyway."

"Fine." Frances waved us off. "I don't need anything. You two go visit. Take that little rascal with you."

Mal wagged her stub tail and raced up the stairs in front of us.

"Mal loves to show off the apartment," I said as we climbed.

"How's the puppy feel about the cat?" Sophie asked.

"I'm sure the cat will grow on Mal or at the very least Mal will grow on the cat."

Sophie laughed. "Somehow, I imagine it isn't Mal you have to worry about."

Mal stopped a few steps ahead of us and wagged her tail at us as if to say hurry up. I think Sophie was right. Mal got along with all creatures. I just hoped the cat felt the same way.

Chapter 11

"So I have some interesting information," Liz MacElroy said as she leaned over the candy counter. It was after five PM and the big crowds had begun to thin out. I was cleaning up the kitchen and setting up for the morning.

Liz had her dark hair pulled back in a thick braid. She wore a pale blue tank top under an open khaki camp shirt, a pair of jeans, and thick hiking boots.

"Spill," I demanded, my eyes lighting up. "Is it about the explosion?"

"Better, it's about Rodney Rivers. My research uncovered a couple threatening notes in his e-mail."

I paused in the middle of wiping down the cooling table. I wasn't going to tell her that Shane had told Jenn about the threats on Rodney's phone. I'd learned to keep my mouth shut about investigations when talking with Liz. "How?"

She grinned and her blue eyes sparkled. "I know someone who can hack through anything."

"Is that legal?"

"It is if he works for the police."

"Oh." I nodded. "An inside job."

"Yes. A girl has her friends."

"And knows how to bribe people," I said with a laugh.

"That, too," Liz agreed. "Anyway, Rodney owed some not very nice people money and he was getting threatening e-mails and text messages."

"You don't think his death was a mob hit or something, do you?"

"Here on Mackinac?" Liz shook her head. "No, no mob hits, but my source says that the threats led them to send Rivers Productions accounting to forensics for an audit."

"They do forensic audits?" I asked and made a face. "Why?"

"To see if anything fishy was going on in the business."

"Oh." I pursed my lips. "Does that mean that Rodney's partner Henry might be in danger?"

"That or if he's hiding anything, it could be a motive for murder."

"Let's hope not. I still need someone to light the fireworks for the shows and Henry can't do that if he is in jail."

"Or dead." Liz frowned. "When did you last see the guy?"

I froze. "Oh, no no no." I turned to her. "I need him. He can't be dead."

"Maybe he's not dead. When did you last see him?"

I tossed my cleaning cloth into the sink and pulled off the pink and white striped apron I wore. "It was yesterday. He was here to let me know about the insurance. He's supposed to be staying at the Hamilton. I left him a message but he never called."

"Let's go over there and see if we can find him," Liz said.

"I agree." I hung the apron on the hook in the metal corner that held the glass walls in place. "Frances, I'm going out with Liz for a while. Can you keep an eye on the fudge?"

"Sure," she said, not looking up from her computer. Sometimes when things were slow, Frances played games like Candy Crush or Farmland. I suspect that's what had her engrossed at the moment. "Take Mal with you, would you? She needs a walk."

As if on cue, the puppy came racing over. She stopped and slid across the floor until she hit my legs with a *humph.*

"You little nut," I said and picked her up.

She kissed my cheek, her stumpy tail wagging fiercely. I grabbed her pink halter with the white hearts on it and her matching pink leash. She stepped into the halter and I snapped it closed then hooked the leash and grabbed some poo bags from the box near the coatrack where we kept Mal's things. "Okay. Let's go."

Liz had her hands in her pockets and watched us, bemused. "You sure do love your pup."

"Yeah, she keeps me out of trouble," I said and then thought about it. "Mostly," I qualified.

Liz laughed.

We walked down Main and turned down a side street to hit Market and the streets beyond. The Hamilton was one of many lovely summer cottages that had been built in Victorian times, complete with turrets and gingerbread cutouts.

We walked past two ladies sitting in the white rocking chairs on the porch and gabbing about their day. Liz pulled the heavy lead glass door open and held it for Mal and me. We walked through into the cool, main foyer. It smelled of beeswax and candles. A giant chandelier hung in the center of the ceiling with stairs going up the left side of the hall.

"Hello," Mrs. H called as she came in from the backdoor like she had done the day before. "Oh, hello, Allie, Hi Liz. Who's this?" She bent down to give Mal a pat on the head and some scratches behind the ears.

"This is my puppy, Mal," I said.

Mrs. Hamilton wore neatly pressed jeans and a thick, blue T-shirt with a boat neck and three quarter length sleeves. She had white athletic shoes on her feet and her gray hair was pulled back into a neat, low ponytail. "Hi Mal. Are you the intrepid doggy who has a knack for finding dead people?"

"The very one," I said with chagrin.

Mal held out her paw for Mrs. Hamilton to shake.

"My, you are smart," Mrs. H said and shook Mal's paw and then straightened. "What can I do for you girls?"

"We are looking for Henry Schulte," Liz said. "We have reason to believe he might be in some kind of trouble."

"Oh, dear," Mrs. H said. "That's not good. We don't like trouble at the Hamilton."

"Have you seen him today?" I asked. "He never got back to me after I left the note yesterday."

"I haven't seen him today." She drew her eyebrows together. "I don't remember seeing him yesterday, either. I usually make up the rooms but he had his No Thanks sign on his door handle."

"Did you give him my message?"

"I placed it under his door. Do you think he's all right?"

"We have reason to believe his partner was getting death threats before he was killed," Liz said.

"And you think someone might try to kill Henry as well?" Mrs. Hamilton's voice rose an octave. "Oh, no, not in my hotel. I won't have that in the Hamilton. Let me go get my husband. We can go to Mr. Schulte's room and ensure he is safely alive."

"Okay," Liz said. "We'll wait here."

Mrs. Hamilton scurried through the kitchen door into the back of the hotel. I noticed that across from the stairs was a formal front parlor with a fireplace and two pastel striped settees with a cherry wood coffee table between them and a couple winged back chairs in a floral pattern. On the mantel of the fireplace was a wooden cuckoo clock.

The second doorway off the main foyer contained a breakfast room with four round tables covered by long tablecloths with pastel skirts and white tops. Around them was a wide assortment of dining chairs. In the space of a bumped out window box was an antique buffet. I could imagine that breakfast was served from the buffet.

A door on the back wall led to the kitchen, I assumed. It was the door Mrs. Hamilton had come out of each time I had visited. To the right of that door was another door which was closed. Under the stairs on the right was a third doorway. I glanced in to see a finely appointed library with cherry wood bookshelves that went from floor to ceiling. Two long windows let in the light. The bookshelves had a single ladder on rollers that helped reach the top shelf.

Inside were cozy chairs, each with a small table that held a reading lamp. Between the windows was a long antique desk and matching chair. On the desk was a computer system complete with printer.

"Huh. It looks like the Hamilton has a business center, too," I said.

"We just put that computer in the library," Mrs. Hamilton said behind me.

I turned to find her behind me with a tall, thin, bald man who I assumed was Mr. Hamilton.

"We argued for months about putting one in or not," the man said. "But eventually we decided it was time to bring a little bit of the twenty-first century into the business."

"Alex wanted three computers," Mrs. H said. "But I put my foot down at one. When people come to Mackinac, they come to get away, not to sit at a computer and answer e-mails."

"That said, there is an entire business center in the new Grander Hotel. Have you seen it?" Mr. Hamilton asked.

"No." I shook my head.

"I have," Liz said. "It's got six computers, three printers, one of which is full color. They also offer a lending service."

"Lending service?" I asked, my eyebrows drawn in confusion.

"They lend out tablets and laptops for people who want to use one in their room."

"Is it popular?" I asked and raised an eyebrow.

"The Grander claims it is." Mr. Hamilton shrugged.

I noticed that his brown eyes darkened. "It's pretty darn hard to compete in this tight market when they have all the newest gadgets."

"I agree with Mrs. H," Liz said. "People come here for the old-fashioned peace and quiet. If I had my way, they would ban the Internet from the island." She crossed her arms.

"I bet that would sell more papers," I said with a smile.

"There is something to be said about unplugging," Mrs. Hamilton said.

"I don't think people know how any more," Mr. Hamilton said. "I'm Alex by the way." He held out his big square hand.

"Allie McMurphy." I shook his hand. "This is my doggie Mal."

Mal sat and lifted her left paw for a shake.

Mr. H laughed and squatted down and shook Mal's paw. "Please to meet you both." He stood, his long legs encased in jeans. He wore work boots on his feet and a green shirt with *Hamilton B & B* embroidered across the top of the pocket on the left side. "My wife told me you had some concerns about the safety of one of our guests."

"Yes," Liz said. "We have reason to believe that Henry Schulte may be in trouble. My investigation into the murder of his partner Rodney Rivers has shown that Mr. Rivers received death threats before he died. It seems that the company was dealing with some pretty shady characters."

"And you are worried that those characters may have harmed Mr. Schulte," Mr. Hamilton surmised.

"I hope not," I said. "I left Mr. Schulte a message yesterday to contact me and never heard from him. Your wife tells us she hasn't seen him in almost two days."

"It is important that we know he's okay," Liz said.

"Did you contact Rex Manning?" Mr. H asked.

"We weren't sure we had to go that far," I said. "Right now, we simply came to see if you had seen him lately. I would rather believe he is alive and ignoring my message than to find out he was hurt like Rodney."

"Well, all we can do is knock on the door and see if he answers," Mr. Hamilton said. "Until he misses his check-out date, we really can't go into his room. It's not like the cop shows where they just give them the key to go inside."

"Okay. Please knock and see if he's in," I said.

"Fine," Mr. Hamilton said. "If you ladies don't mind, I'd prefer you didn't go up. The man's room number is private unless he tells you."

"Fine," Liz said. "If he answers the door, let him know two good-looking women want to speak to him."

Mr. Hamilton smiled. "If that doesn't peak his curiosity something is really going on here."

We waited with Mrs. H while he went upstairs and did his thing. I tried to be patient and not speculate if Henry was dead or not. Mal spent the time begging Mrs. H for pets and the older woman was happy to oblige.

"You are the sweetest puppy," she cooed. "What a cute dolly."

"She has a whole repertoire of tricks," I said. "I'll have to bring some treats with me next time so that she can show them off."

"I've heard this little one has quite the reputation

of sniffing out danger," Mrs. H said with a smile. "Don't you, Mal? Yes, you do."

Mr. Hamilton came down the stairs with a look of concern on his face. "He's not answering the door. I slid a note under it. It's the best I can do."

"When is he supposed to check out?" Liz asked.

"He paid up for the full week," Mrs. Hamilton said. "He still has the privacy note hanging from the doorknob. There's nothing we can do until Saturday."

"If he's dead, the body is going to start to stink," Liz pointed out.

"We'll be sure to keep an eye on any foul odors coming from the room." Mr. H crossed his arms. "I'm still not sure that is reason enough to enter the room. With the privacy sign on the door, we can't even go in and make up the room. Look, girls. It's only been a day or so. Let's give it a little more time. Okay?"

"Okay." I sighed and looked at Liz. "Let's go see Rex. He needs to know that his witness may not be safe."

"I agree," Liz said. "Thanks for checking, Mr. Hamilton."

"You're welcome, girls," Mr. H said, his big Adam's apple bobbing in his skinny throat. "Keep us posted if you hear anything."

"I'll give you a call if I see the man," Mrs. H added. "That way you won't worry. You'll know he's rude and not dead."

We both laughed. It was the first time either of us wished someone was just rude.

Pumpkin Pie Fudge

½ cup cream cheese, softened
1 3.4 ounce package of vanilla instant pudding and pie filling
1 teaspoon vanilla
¼ cup canned pumpkin
1 teaspoon vanilla
1 teaspoon cinnamon
1 teaspoon pumpkin pie spice
6 cups powdered sugar, sifted
Optional—2 cups chopped walnuts

Butter 8x8x2-inch cake pan.

Mix cream cheese, unprepared instant pudding, pumpkin, vanilla, cinnamon, and pumpkin pie spice. Add powdered sugar 1 cup at a time until you reach the desired thickness. Add chopped walnuts and mix well.

Scoop into prepared pan. Pat until smooth. Score into 1-inch pieces with butter knife.

Refrigerate for 2-3 hours until set.

Break into 1-inch pieces along score and serve in individual paper candy cups or on a platter. Store leftovers in covered container in the refrigerator.

Enjoy!

Chapter 12

"How's the fireworks show planning going?" Mrs. Amerson stopped us on Market Street as we walked toward the administration building where the police offices were. The older woman was five foot nine inches tall and wore jeans, tan athletic shoes, and a white T-shirt with flowers embroidered around the scooped neckline. Her gray hair was cut short and her face clean of makeup. Her appearance was as no nonsense as her attitude.

"Hello, Mrs. Amerson," I said as Mal sat down in front of the older woman and lifted her paw to shake.

Mrs. Amerson ignored the puppy. It was something she had to do on purpose because Mal was difficult to ignore.

"Did you talk to Rivers Productions and get the shows straightened out? We don't have many days left and people expect the usual three shows."

"I've got fireworks," I said. "I'm still hunting down a technician to run the show."

"We've been trying to get ahold of Henry Schulte," Liz said. "You haven't seen him, have you?"

"Who is Henry Schulte?" Mrs. Amerson narrowed her eyes.

"He's Rodney Rivers' business partner. He's on Mackinac Island and contractually obligated to run the show," I said. "That is, if I could find fireworks and I did."

"Well, then he'd better do the shows," Mrs. Amerson said. "Did you call him?"

"I've left several messages."

Liz backed me up. "We just went over to the Hamilton where he's staying, but he's ignoring us."

"Do I need to get the lawyers involved?" Mrs. Amerson asked. "Because I can."

By this time Mal was pirouetting in front of her to catch her attention.

"Thanks, but I think we should try to track him down first. If he says no when we speak face-to-face then I'll call the lawyers." I tried to hide my sigh.

"See that you do." Her expression was pinched as if she smelled something bad. "The show must go on. If I have to, I'll find someone to light the fireworks myself."

"I'm sure you won't have to," Liz said. "Schulte is contracted to do it. He'll do it."

"He'd better." Mrs. Amerson glared at me. "For your sake, young lady, he'd better." She walked off toward her shop on Market.

"Did she just threaten me?" I asked Liz.

"I believe she did." Liz took out her notepad and made a note.

Mal tugged on the leash, her busy little nose pressed to the ground.

"We're going," I said with laughter in my tone. Mal liked to go to the administration building. Officer Brown and Rex were her buddies and had started to keep doggie treats behind the counter.

"Your puppy knows the way to the police station," Liz noted. "Is somebody special there?"

I felt the heat of a blush rush up my cheeks. "No."

"Uh-huh."

"Seriously. I'm dating Trent. We are going sailing next week. That is, if I can find Henry Schulte and get him to do the fireworks show."

"And yet, Mal certainly knows the way to the administration building," Liz said again and raised one beautifully arched eyebrow as Mal trotted along at a good pace, dragging us behind her.

"Officer Brown keeps treats behind the desk," I explained as nonchalantly as I could.

"I'm going to pretend that is true." Liz grinned at me.

"It is true."

"And I've seen the way you look at Rex."

"Everyone knows I'm dating Trent, even Rex," I said. "Now stop it."

"Why?" She laughed, the sound echoing along the street. "You are so much fun to tease. You should see your face."

I pressed my hot cheeks with my palms. "I'm not the kind of girl who gets this kind of interest. Seriously."

"That's why it's so much fun," she said.

"Who are you dating?" I asked trying to turn the subject around on her.

"I've lived my whole life on Mackinac. That means,

at one time or another, I've dated about every single guy who is eligible."

"Even Trent?" I teased.

"Yes, even Trent," she replied.

"Really?" I drew my eyebrows together. Clearly she was prettier than me. Plus, she was a true native and thus, higher up on the social chain. "What happened?"

"It was sixth grade and when he tried to tongue kiss me, I punched him," she said with a shrug. "He's sort of kept his distance ever since."

I laughed. "Well, I know he's a smart man."

We arrived at the admin building. I opened the door and Mal went straight to the police offices. Liz sent me a look.

"It's the treats," I said again and felt as if I protested just a bit too much. I bit my lip.

"How's my favorite puppy?" Officer Charles Brown said as he got up and came around to greet Mal. She sat and lifted her paw for a shake.

He shook her paw and patted her on the head. "Come on. You know where the treats are."

I let go of her leash so she could follow him and sent an *I-told-you-so* look to Liz. She grinned and shrugged.

"What brings you lovely ladies here?" he asked after he put Mal through her tricks and gave her a treat.

"Has Henry Schulte been in the station?" I asked. "I've been trying to get ahold of him."

"He was in yesterday. Rex asked him to stay on the island for forty-eight hours in case there were more questions."

"Is he a suspect?" Liz asked.

"If you are referring to the Rodney Rivers murder case, there are no suspects yet. That's the official statement." Charles gave a short nod, his brown gaze sincere.

"There is reason to believe that Henry may be in danger," I said.

"Really?" Charles tilted his head. "Why?"

"We know that Rodney Rivers was being threatened," Liz said. "He had e-mails and phone messages that said he wasn't paying his bills and some pretty shady characters were threatening him."

"Where did you get that information?" Charles put his hands on his hips.

"I can't reveal my sources, but if Rodney was being threatened and is now dead, his partner Henry could be in grave danger."

"As far as I can tell, you were the last ones to see him," I said. "Mrs. Hamilton at the Hamilton B & B said no one has seen him there in a couple of days."

Charles drew his eyebrows into a scowl. "He could have left the island, but that would be against the request of the investigating officer."

"If he did leave the island, he had to take a ferry or an airplane," I thought aloud.

"Unless he had a boat," Liz pointed out.

"I'll need to inform Rex." Charles went around the desk and picked up the phone.

I pulled Liz aside. "If he was here yesterday, then he could be just hiding out in his room."

"Or he could be dead in his room," she insisted. "I need to find out if he left on the ferries."

"I'll get Jenn to ask around and see if anyone has seen him. I really need him to be alive. I need to have someone do the fireworks shows."

"I'd be calling the town lawyer if I were you," Liz said. "If Henry Schulte isn't dead, he's either going to help you or he's going to wish he were dead."

"Come on, Mal." I made a kissy noise and my puppy ran to me from behind the desk. I grabbed her leash. "Please have Rex call me," I said to Charles. "I need to see Henry as soon as possible."

"From the sound of things, you aren't the only one." Liz nudged her head in the direction of Officer Brown.

He was on the phone with Charlene the island dispatcher. "That's right. Apparently Henry Schulte has not been seen since he left the police station early yesterday." He waved good-bye to us as we headed out the door. "Rex asked him to stay on the island. If he skipped town, we need to know about it as soon as possible."

Chapter 13

"Hey beautiful." Trent came into the McMurphy at ten the next morning and smiled at me as I worked behind the counter of the fudge shop. He wore a light-pink dress shirt with the collar open and the sleeves rolled up to three-quarter length. He had on dark-wash blue jeans and cowboy boots. His skin was tan and his dark hair perfect.

"Hi." I couldn't help the smile that crossed my face at the sight of him. "What brings you in?"

"The fudge." He wiggled his eyebrows. "I hear you have a lemon meringue."

"Oh. Yes, I do." I tried not to let my disappointment show.

He laughed and it echoed around the room, drawing Mal over with a run and a slide. "A kiss for the beautiful woman first." He leaned over the counter and gave me a sweet kiss that left me wanting more. We were early in our dating and things were at that stage where I wanted, but was afraid to really let him know how much I wanted to be with him. It didn't do to give up my power too early.

Good relationships took time and space. I pulled him back for one more quick kiss over the counter and then let him go and took a step back. "Mal wants attention," I teased.

My puppy was bouncing on her back legs, begging with her black button eyes.

Trent leaned down and scratched behind her ears. "How's my second favorite girl?"

"She is excited for the Fourth of July celebrations," I said.

He glanced up at me. "Does she do okay with fireworks?"

"I imagine so. She seems to be fine with the cannon." As if on cue, the cannon boomed in the background. The fort reenactors fired it on the hour during the season. "How much of the lemon meringue fudge do you want?"

"I'll take a quarter pound, but that's not really why I came."

I grabbed a tissue paper and pulled the tray of lemon meringue fudge from the glass container and expertly estimated a quarter pound. I set it on the scale and was dead on. "So the fudge was a ruse to see me."

The guests leaving for the day had begun to come down with their suitcases in tow.

"I have good news for you," he said.

I wrapped up his fudge, put it in a pink and white striped bag with the McMurphy logo on it, and folded the top. "I like good news." I smiled at him and handed him his bag.

"I have the name of a guy who is free to do your fireworks show."

"Oh!" I got so excited by the news that I came around the counter and gave him a big hug.

Not to be out done, Mal leapt up and pawed at my pants leg.

"Thank-you! We are only days away and I can't find Henry Schulte. I didn't know what I was going to do."

Trent held me close and I reveled in the feel of him from knees to shoulders. He was tall and broad and solid. I knew that he ran daily and, even though he was the owner of the stables, he was not above mucking them out when he had to. Plus, I had spotted him handling one of the big carriage horses. The man had muscle to spare and I wanted it to all be mine.

"Wow, I need to make you happy more often." Without letting go of me, he freed one arm and pulled a business card out of his shirt pocket. "Here's the guy's card. He said for you to call him to work out the final details."

I took the card and gave Trent a kiss on the cheek. "You are the best boyfriend ever." My eyes grew big as I realized what I'd called him. I glanced at him sheepishly. After all, it had only been three dates.

His face lit up. "I like it that you call me your boyfriend. What are you doing on the Fourth?"

"Well, I guess I'll be busy seeing that the firework shows go off without a hitch."

"Right." He chuckled. "Will you have time to go for a picnic? I know this nice little place where we can see the show without the crowds."

"I'd like that."

"Great. I'll come by at two o'clock if that's okay?"

"Do you want me to pack my picnic basket?"

"No, I've got it." He lifted his bag of fudge. "How much do I owe you?"

"That one's on the house."

He sent me a confused look.

"In exchange for the help with the fireworks." I tapped the card.

"Wow, a beautiful woman in my arms and free fudge. I need to do good deeds more often."

"That said, I've got to get back to work. I've got another fudge demonstration in forty minutes."

"How're sales?" he asked and let me go.

"Pretty good. That reality show I taped last month is showing and people are starting to come in and mention they saw me on television."

"A celebrity in the making," he teased. "What can't you do?"

"Get rid of my Fudgie status on the island." I pulled down the ingredients for the red, white, and blue fudge recipe I was working on. The contest winner was red velvet for the red, and I was making cream cheese for the white. The blue was blueberry. Blueberries were in season and grow in Michigan so I thought it was a good choice even if it was a bit expected.

"I'll call you later," he promised and patted Mal on the head. "I bet you need a treat, don't you?" He took her over to the reception desk and dug out a doggie treat from the jar on the desk.

I heard Frances tell him to make Mal do her tricks as I poured fresh blueberries into a bowl and mashed them. I'd tried using a juicer and only use the blueberry juice in the fudge, but I found that having a few actual berry pieces enhanced the flavor.

"Hey." Trent stuck his head into the fudge shop area. "What ever happened to the cat?"

"It's been hanging out on my fire escape. No one has come to claim it."

"You fed it, didn't you?" His eyes twinkled.

"Yes," I said defiantly. "I know that means it has now adopted me, but I couldn't see the poor baby starve."

Trent laughed. "I can take it back to the stables with me. We like having a barn cat or two around to keep the rodents down."

I made a face. "It's too pretty to be a barn cat."

"It's better than being an alley cat," he pointed out.

I took a deep breath and let it out slow. "I suppose you are right. I want to catch it first and take it to the vet in St. Ignace. That way, I'll know it has all its shots and is spayed or neutered."

"I'll catch it for you the next time I come by," he offered.

"You are a true gentleman." I smiled.

"I try," he replied, his eyes twinkling. "I do try."

"Okay. I've got some news," Jenn said later that afternoon when I went upstairs to change.

"Good news or bad news?" I asked as I tossed my chef coat and black slacks into the dirty clothes pile and put on a summer dress. I was going to call the number Trent had given me and then go to see Mrs. Amerson and Mrs. Jones to report that the firework shows were good to go.

"Well, that depends," Jenn said as she leaned against the door jamb and watched me rummage through my closet. "Why are you changing? Do you have a hot date?"

"I'm meeting with Mrs. Amerson and Mrs. Jones. That is, if the phone call I need to make goes well."

"You got Henry Schulte to agree to do the fireworks shows?"

"No." I pulled out a short cream-colored dress with sprigs of pink flowers on it. It was a fit and flare style with short sleeves and was at once comfortable and lady-like. "Trent got me the name of another guy. Henry Schulte seems to be missing. Either he skipped the island or is in the same state of hurt as Rodney. Remember, you told us that Rodney was having money troubles and had several threats. Well, Liz said the same thing. She thought maybe Henry was in the same kind of trouble as Rodney and might even be dead."

"Well, that's where things get interesting," Jenn said. "Did she tell you that Henry Schulte will get a ten million dollar life insurance payment because Rodney died?"

"What? How?"

"They had a life insurance plan on Rodney to cover the company because he was the technician. If anything happened to him, the company would go belly up."

"So Henry had motive," I said as I tossed the dress over my head and zipped up the side. "I bet he skipped the island.

"You know what? I'm going to call this guy to do the show and then I'm calling the lawyer. If Henry has the ten million dollars, he can pay this guy's fee to do the shows. We have a contract that covers more than the loss of the fireworks."

"The fireworks are here, by the way," Jenn said as I brushed out my hair and applied lip gloss. "They are in two trailers with strong locks and are sitting in a safe place in St. Ignace."

"Good. Let's not take the chance of them exploding on the island again."

"I agree. When you contact your new guy, tell him that they will have to be set off via barges like what they have done in the past. It's the safest way."

"I intend to. How did you find out about the insurance money anyway? That's not something your boyfriend would know. Isn't he all about the crime scene?"

"I found out from Missy Kastler," Jenn said.

"Who?" I was confused. It was the first time I had heard that name. It was just like Jenn to be more with the in crowd than me.

"Missy Kastler. She called me to plan her wedding reception. She wants it on the grounds of the yacht club. Anyway, Missy heard from her fiancé's uncle who is in the insurance business that Rodney Rivers had a ten million dollar pay out. The yacht club was all a buzz about the fact that if they catch the killer and that person is a relative or, in this case, a business partner, the insurance company doesn't have to pay."

"Let me guess. They are waiting to pay Henry until the investigation is done."

"Yes." Jenn wagged her eyebrows. "That could take years."

"So there really isn't a motive for Henry to kill his partner."

"Or he was silly enough to think that he would get paid regardless of how Rodney died, unless it was suicide."

"Have they ruled out suicide?" I asked.

"Pretty much. Shane tells me that there was a bullet in the ashes, but no gun at the scene."

"If Rodney had killed himself, they would presume

the gun would be found near the body," I surmised. "Unless it somehow went missing from the ruins of the warehouse." I chewed my bottom lip. "Wait. When I saw Rodney, he was covered in a string of screaming chickens. Who tangles themselves in a string of screaming chickens, lights the fuses, and then kills themselves? It doesn't make any sense."

"No, it doesn't. This is the first I've heard of the screaming chickens."

"It was weird. They just started to go off, but no one was in the room with him so it had to be a slow burning fuse. Do we know when Henry Schulte arrived on the island? I mean, if he was there . . ."

"Then he could have lit the fuse and caused the explosion to cover up the suicide," Jenn finished.

"Exactly. So many people were helping put out the embers it's impossible to tell if Henry was there or not."

"I know, right? You would think a stranger would stand out in a crowd, but we all were worried about the explosion and the surrounding forests and the loss of the fireworks."

"How can we find out when Henry got on the island?" I asked as I headed toward the apartment door. I was going to call Trent's guy from the McMurphy's office phone.

"We can ask the ferry owners to check their records of tickets purchased," Jenn suggested.

"That shouldn't be a problem. They are already checking to see if he purchased a ticket to get off the island. I'll call Rex and ask him to check. While I'm at it, I'll call Sophie and see if Henry took the airport shuttle any time."

"I don't know," Jenn said as we entered the office.

"Flying in and out on the Grand's jet is expensive, especially if you aren't staying at the Grand Hotel. Henry didn't dress like a rich man. Besides, if he were rich, there would be no need for threats over unpaid bills."

"I agree he didn't look that well-off," I said, remembering his worn athletic shoes. "But, if he thought he was coming into ten million dollars, he might take the plane."

"But the only way he would know that he was coming into that kind of money would be if Rodney didn't commit suicide."

"Darn it." I sat down in front of my desk. Jenn sat down at her desk across from mine in the center of the overcrowded room full of bookcases and file cabinets. "We've come full circle in our reasoning and we still don't know if Henry Schulte is alive or even still on the island."

"What a mess," Jenn agreed. "Call your guy and get the fireworks shows back up and running. I sent you a list of the fireworks we were able to purchase. You can e-mail that to him and he can come up with a nice show. I'll contact Rex and ask him if he's seen Henry Schulte. I'll tell him we have to know because we have a contract with the man."

"Great!" I dialed the number on Trent's card.

"This is Ashton Cooper," a male voice answered.

"Hello, Mr. Cooper. This is Allie McMurphy. Trent Jessop gave me your name and number. I'm looking for a pyro technician for three fireworks shows on Mackinac Island. He said you were available."

"Yes, that's right. I understand your contracted guy did not follow through."

"Yes, you could say that. There was a tragic mishap and the business partner refuses to get back to me."

"A tragic mishap?" The man sounded concerned.

"Yes. We lost all of our original fireworks and our pyro tech in a warehouse explosion. We were able to get new fireworks for the shows—I have the list I can send you—but the business partner refuses to get back to me."

"The guy was killed?" Ashton Cooper really didn't sound happy. "Trent didn't mention that part."

"Oh, don't worry. It wasn't an accident. We're pretty sure the fireworks were set off after Rodney died."

Jenn was shaking her head and signaling me to stop talking.

"Excuse me?" he asked.

I put my hand over the receiver. "What?" I asked Jenn.

"Don't tell him that. He'll never work for you if he thinks he could get killed."

"But it wasn't because of the fireworks shows or our contract," I stage whispered.

Jenn rolled her eyes. "He doesn't need to know that."

"Hello?" Mr. Cooper said.

"Yes, hi. Sorry." I turned my back on Jenn. "I'll e-mail you the list of fireworks we were able to get and you can let me know if you can plan three shows at least thirty minutes in length. We're planning on firing them from barges in the Straits of Mackinac."

"Okay, look. I'm starting to get a bad feeling about this job."

"No, no. No bad feelings," I said. "It's pretty cut and dried. We have the fireworks and we have the barge. What we need is you. What is your going rate? I can increase it by twenty percent."

"I'm not sure. . . . I mean, if this thing is jinxed in some way—" He paused.

"There's no jinxing, no bad juju. Everything is fine. After all, if it were jinxed, we would not have been able to replace the fireworks so quickly. Therefore, it was certainly meant to be."

"I'll have to think about it."

"What's to think about?" I tried not to let him hear the panic in my voice. "It's a simple job. It's only days away and you are free. We are paying. It's great."

"But the original pyro tech died, right?"

"That merely means our shows were freed up for you to step in and do them," I pointed out. "It's really good luck for you."

"Bad luck for the dead guy, though," he mused.

"I've got your e-mail. I'll send the list of fireworks we have purchased and the dates and times along with a copy of the contract. I'll give you two-thirds down once the contract is signed and the last third an hour after the last show. You have nothing to lose and everything to gain."

"Unless I die."

"You won't. Even better, if you do a great job, I will be sure to sign you for next year's shows, as well." I fidgeted with my pen, doodling scared faces on the pad of paper near my computer along with the words *please, please, please.*

"Fine," he said. "I'll look over everything and get back to you."

"Don't take long. We have only a few days until the shows and I must have someone signed by tonight. If you don't do it, I'll find someone else."

"I'll take that into consideration." He hung up.

I hit the END button on my phone, tossed it on my desk, and pouted. "What is it with men and thinking I have bad juju?"

"Well, it would help if you didn't tell them the last guy died," Jenn teased.

"I almost offered to let him borrow Mr. MacElroy's rabbit's foot, but I don't think the old man trusts me enough to give it up."

"He's just teasing you," Jenn said with a twinkle in her eyes.

"We have to solve Rodney's murder." I straightened in the chair. "It's the only way to prove that it's not me and it's not the show that is cursed."

"You'd better get on it, then. You only have a few more hours to sign someone."

I stuck out my tongue at her. "Call Rex," I ordered and got on my computer to send out the promised e-mail. "After I send this out, I'm going to go see Mrs. Amerson and company."

"Ooh, what are you going to tell them?"

"That I have hired a new man . . . because I have. Then I'm going to scour the island until I find Henry Schulte. I have a feeling he is the key to this entire mystery."

"Good luck with that," Jenn said sincerely. "Sandy and I will look after the fudge shop."

"Thanks." I hit SEND on the e-mail. I gathered up my purse and phone and kissed Jenn on the cheek. "Wish me luck."

"Good luck. You're going to need it."

Chapter 14

Mrs. Amerson and Mrs. Jones were pleased as punch when I told them that I had a new pyro tech. At first, they were skeptical, but I explained that Trent found the guy and after that, they were all smiles.

Thank goodness. Once I left the tea house and the two society women, I headed toward Market Street. I highly doubted Henry was anywhere near the tourist-filled Main Street. Someone would have seen him and phoned me.

I pulled out my cell phone and glanced at the front. No phone calls. I frowned and put it back in my purse. The Hamilton was the only place I could think of to begin my search. I mean, the man couldn't simply disappear between the police station and the B & B on Market. Could he?

Silly as it sounds, I began to glance under the bushes as I walked down the sidewalk. It was too bad I didn't have Mal with me. If Henry was dead somewhere in the open, she would have found him. Not that I wanted Henry dead. In fact, it would be best for me if Henry weren't dead—if, in fact, it was Henry who did his partner in. Then I could tell Mr. Cooper that it wasn't bad luck at all, but a bad business relationship—something that didn't have anything to do with me or Mackinac Island.

"Hi Allie."

I stopped and turned at the sound of someone calling my name. It was Sophie, looking gorgeous as usual in her pilot's uniform.

"Hi, Sophie. How are you?"

"I'm good. I heard you were looking for Henry Schulte."

"Yes. Have you seen him?"

"I didn't fly him off the island if that is what you want to know. Not this time."

"Not this time?" I drew my eyebrows together. "Have you flown him off the island before?"

"Yes, that's what I came to tell you. Henry Schulte is sort of a regular at the Grand."

"Sort of?" I put my hands on my hips. The skirt of my dress blew around my knees.

"Yes, he comes in and stays a few days once a year. He hates water so he pays the extra money to fly."

"Why does he come to an island if he hates water?" I had to ask.

"I have no idea," Sophie said with a shrug. "He isn't particularly rich. The staff at the Grand said he always got a cheap package deal and rarely tipped."

"Maybe he likes the fact that we don't have any cars on the island," I wondered out loud. "Or maybe he has family here?"

"Not that I know of," Sophie said. "But then I'm not exactly a native myself.

"It's something to look into. If he has family, he could be visiting them right now and that's why no one has seen him."

"You mean his family might be hiding him?"

"Yes." I chewed on my bottom lip. "That's assuming he has a reason to hide."

"Liz told me about the death threats," Sophie said. "Those would make me hide."

"But not if the threats weren't against him personally . . . unless he was the reason those guys were making threats in the first place."

"What do you mean?" Sophie asked.

"I got the feeling Henry was sort of a silent partner. The entire business was built on Rodney's reputation as a great showman. But Rodney didn't have time to work on the business end. Henry was the one who did the billing and kept the books."

"You think that he might have been the one not paying those guys?"

"It makes the most sense," I said. "If the money mess was his fault, I don't blame him for hiding. I'd be hiding out, too. We need to figure out who he knows on the island."

"Yes, and since word has gotten out about the ten million dollar insurance payment, the bill collectors have to be coming out of the woodwork."

I nodded. "Frances knows everyone on the island. If Henry Schulte has a connection to Mackinac, she should be able to find it."

We walked through the alley that ran behind the McMurphy. The cat was back, sitting halfway up the staircase sunning itself.

"Hello kitty," I said in greeting.

The cat did not seem interested in me or my greeting.

"Is this your cat? She's beautiful."

I turned to Sophie. "How do you know it's a girl?"

She shrugged. "Just guessing. She is gorgeous and acts aloof. That's pretty typical for a girl cat in my experience."

"You have cats?"

Sophie smiled and reached down and scratched the kitty behind her ears. She purred loud enough that we could hear it. "I've had a cat my whole life. They are such cutie-pies."

"This cat has been here for nearly a week. I left some food on a plate near the landing."

Sophie laughed. "Oh, then she's your cat now. Are you going to keep her as an indoor cat or an outdoor cat?"

"First off, I've still got posters up to see if she belongs to someone. She is so pretty and just showed up at the McMurphy. Someone has to be missing her." I flicked my wrist as if introducing the cat. "Secondly, I'm going to have Trent catch her and we are going to take her to the vet to be checked out. Then I guess it is up to her if she is an indoor cat or an outdoor cat." I frowned. "Except if she is indoor, I'll have to get a door to close off the fudge shop. The food inspector has trouble with Mal and she's trained not to go in the shop. From what little I know of cats, you can't train them not to do something."

Sophie giggled. "There's no training cats. That's one thing I learned early on with my first cat, Matilda. The best you can do is come to an agreement with them."

"An agreement?"

"Yes," Sophie said as we climbed to the landing at the top of the steps. "You agree to feed the cat and see to its health and it will agree to do whatever it wants."

"Oh. Sort of like my hair. I've agreed to not make it be something it's not—like straight—and it agrees not to have too many bad hair days."

Sophie glanced at my wind tossed waves. "I don't think I've ever seen you with a bad hair day."

"Clearly, you haven't spent enough time with me," I replied and opened the door to my apartment. "Don't let the cat in. She can find a hiding place faster than I can say 'there's a cat in the house.'"

"Right," Sophie said, and we both carefully skirted the doorway and closed the door safely behind us.

We cut through the apartment to the hallway. I stuck my head into the office where Jenn was seated. "Jenn, you know Sophie, right?"

"Yes, of course," Jenn said with a smile and stood up to shake Sophie's hand.

"Sophie didn't take Henry Schulte off the island, but she does taxi him in a couple times a year."

"I thought you only brought in the Grand's patrons."

"Henry stays at the Grand Hotel when he comes for a few days," Sophie said. "He hates the water and stays at a place that is willing to fly him in . . . at a price."

"It's a steep price," Jenn said carefully. "No offense meant." She waved her hands in front of her.

"Oh, none taken," Sophie said. "It's expensive to fly anywhere. Fares have to pay my salary, pay for fuel, maintenance, and housing of the vehicle, plus hanger fees and airport use fees."

"Wow," Jenn said. "That's a lot."

"It's stuff people don't think about."

"We think Henry might have family on the island and if he does—"

"Frances will know," Jenn finished my sentence.

"Yes." I smiled.

"How'd the meeting go with the Star Spangled Fourth committee?" Jenn asked.

"Not bad," I hedged.

"You didn't tell them he hasn't signed yet," Jenn accused.

"Who hasn't signed what?" Sophie's dark eyes held suspicion.

"It's nothing important." I turned Sophie away from the office door and I sent Jenn a look.

She shrugged. It seemed I wasn't the only one making a few social blunders today.

"Trent got me the name of a new pyro tech and I called him this afternoon and sent him a contract to sign along with a fee schedule."

"And you told Mrs. Amerson that it was good to go even though he hasn't signed a contract yet," Sophie surmised.

"He'll sign," I said. "I'm certain."

"Certain enough to lie to the leaders of Mackinac Island society . . . who are counting on you, by the way."

"I know." I walked with Sophie down the stairs where we were greeted by a sleepy pup who rose slowly, did her downward dog stretch followed by an upward dog. Thoroughly stretched, she came over for her head pats.

Sophie obliged her with a few pats on the head followed by a good behind the ear scratch.

"I think Mal likes you," I said with a laugh.

"She is a cute puppy," Sophie said.

"Hello, girls," Frances said from her perch behind the receptionist desk. She studied her computer screen through purple granny reading glasses she bought at the dollar store. She had so many different readers in a variety of colors and designs that it seemed she wore a different pair every day. "Sophie, what brings you to the McMurphy?"

I jumped in before Sophie could answer. "We were wondering if you know if Henry Schulte has family on Mackinac. No one's seen him since he left the McMurphy."

"Oh, dear. That's not a good sign," Frances said.

"Exactly," Sophie said. "We don't want to find him like Allie found Rodney."

"Why would you think he has family here?" Frances tilted her head and studied us over the top of her reading glasses.

"I've flown him in once or twice a year ever since I started working for the Grand. I figured he was a regular."

"Hmm." Frances pursed her lips. "Schulte, Schulte, Schulte . . . no, there is no Schulte on the island." She tapped her computer to life. "Let me check the phone directory."

I looked at Sophie and she looked at me and we shrugged. I hadn't used a phone directory ever. All my friends had cell phones. In fact, landlines were so scarce, we just assumed we could text everyone.

"I'm right. There is no Schulte in the phone directory."

"But it could be his mother's family," I pointed out.

"Or an aunt," Sophie said. "How could we find out that information?"

I grabbed my phone and Googled Henry Schulte. He had a LinkedIn profile for Rivers Productions but no Facebook page and no Twitter. Henry was older so I kind of doubted he had an Instagram page. "Nothing on Google." I frowned.

"Someone should know," Frances said. "I'll check with my friends and see if we can't track down your fellow. I'll let them know he's missing. People are helpful if they know someone could be in danger."

"Thanks, Frances," I said.

"How'd the meeting with Mrs. Amerson and Mrs. Jones go?" she asked.

"Not bad."

She gave me a look that said I was a bad liar.

I shrugged. "We'll talk later."

"I'm sure we will." She went back to her computer.

By this time, Mal was charming Sophie with her twirling. Mal had become quite clever about charming people for treats. She stood on her back legs and twirled while everyone around said "Awww."

Sophie reached inside the treat jar and pulled out a tiny biscuit. "How can you resist this?" she asked me as Mal sat and lifted her paw for a shake.

"She is irresistible," I said with a laugh as Sophie gave her the treat.

Mal took it gently and ran off to her bed to savor it.

With a smile, Sandy came out of the fudge shop

area. The girl was so pretty with her copper skin and long black hair. As always, she had her hair pulled back into a no nonsense braid that draped down her back. She wore a McMurphy polo shirt, black slacks, athletic shoes, and a pink and white McMurphy apron. "Hi Allie. Everything's prepped and ready for the morning. If you don't mind, I'm going to take off a bit early today. My grandmother's birthday is tomorrow and we're planning a celebration."

"Is that what the chocolate dragonfly sculpture is for?" I asked.

She had been working all week on an elaborate dragonfly. The body was six inches long and the delicate wingspan was a marvel of chocolate engineering.

"Yes." Pride shone in her eyes. "My grandmother's spirit guide is the dragonfly."

"You should see the centerpiece," I said to Sophie. "Sandy really is a master."

"I would love to see it." Sophie smiled and held out her hand. "Hi, I'm Sophie Collins."

"Oh, I'm sorry. You two haven't met? I should have introduced you. I have the worst manners," I said as they shook hands.

"Sandy Everheart. You're the lady pilot for the Grand."

"That's me," Sophie said. "And you are a chocolatier?"

"Yes," I answered, not giving Sandy the opportunity. "She studied in New York, but she came back to Mackinac to be with her family and I was so lucky to hire her."

"She gives me space to work my sculptures on the side," Sandy said with a serious nod.

"So you're from the island," Sophie said. "Do you happen to know Henry Schulte?"

"Henry Schulte?" Sandy repeated.

"He's Rodney Rivers' partner and he's missing," I explained. "Sophie says he flies into Mackinac at least once a year. We think he might have family here."

"Evie Garnier has an uncle named Henry. Perhaps he is the same one. She says he has a silly fear of water and will only come to see his family if they will fly him out."

"Well, that makes more sense," Sophie said. "I never thought he dressed or acted like someone who could afford the plane ticket here."

"The family pays, even though they can't afford it. Family is family." Sandy smiled.

"Of course it is," I agreed. "And we are keeping you from yours. I'll see you tomorrow—unless you want the day off for your grandmother."

Sandy's dark eyes lit up. "Is that all right?"

"Of course. Family is family."

Sandy smiled again. "Then I will see you the next day."

"Perfect. Please tell your grandmother happy birthday for me," I said as Sandy grabbed up her backpack from the cubby behind the reception desk.

"I will. Thank-you."

"Nice to meet you," Sophie added.

"So," I said as Sandy left out the back. "We have a lead."

"I heard." Frances's eyes were twinkling. "And I have an address."

"Great!" I practically clapped my hands. "Do you have time to go with me?" I asked Sophie.

"Sure. I can take a few minutes." She patted Mal on the head as we realized my puppy had stashed her treat in the cushion on her bed and come back for more attention. "Can we bring Mal?"

As if on cue, Mal looked at me and then ran to get her leash.

I laughed. "Okay. If Henry is truly missing, perhaps she can help us track him down."

"Let's hope he is alive," Sophie said as I bent to put on Mal's halter and leash. "I'm not as excited to find a dead body as you are."

"Not me. Mal. She's the one who seems to enjoy it most."

"Be safe, girls," Frances said. "If there is a killer out there, he may not like it that you are investigating."

"We'll do our best." I let Mal draw me out the back door.

Cherry Cream Pie Fudge

2½ cups white chocolate chips, melted
1 3 ounce package of cherry flavored gelatin dissolved in ¼ cup hot water to reduce graininess
1 16 ounce can cream cheese frosting
1 cup dried cherries, chopped into tiny pieces
1 cup dark chocolate chips
1 tablespoon butter plus 1 teaspoon butter for pan prep

Butter 8x8x2-inch pan.

Carefully melt white chocolate chips and dissolved gelatin in the top of a double boiler. Hint: White chocolate burns faster than regular chocolate. Melt slowly and stir constantly.

In a medium bowl, mix can of frosting, melted chocolate-gelatin mixture, and chopped cherries. Stir until combined.

Pat into pan. Score into 1-inch pieces with butter knife.

Refrigerate for 3 hours.

Remove and cut into 1-inch pieces following the score marks. Serve in individual paper cups or on platter. Cover leftovers in air tight container and store in refrigerator.

Bonus: I melted 1 cup of dark chocolate chips with 1 tablespoon of butter in the microwave and poured a thin ganache on top. Yum!

Chapter 15

"What are you doing here?" The female officer scowled at me and ignored Sophie.

We had arrived at Henry's aunt's house and were met by Officer Lasko.

She was petite and looked gorgeous in her police blues. Her blond hair was neatly tucked up off her collar. She was all business and yet still looked like an actress who played a police officer on television. I have no idea how she managed it. Or why she so blatantly didn't like me.

"We are looking for Henry Schulte," I said. "We were told he may be at his aunt's house. This is her house, right?" I tried to look around Officer Lasko, but she stepped into my view.

"Step back," she said, her tone official. "This is a police investigation." She held out her hands to push us off the sidewalk and into the street.

Mal tugged on her leash and wrapped herself around Officer Lasko, stopping the woman in her tracks.

"Sorry. She prefers standing on the grass rather

than standing in the street." I carefully unwound Mal's leash and then picked her up and took a step back from the frowning female officer.

Henry's aunt lived in a small worker's cottage near the airport. The place was neatly painted a pale green with cream shutters. A short sidewalk flowed into a small front porch which framed the 1920s bungalow. In comparison to the painted ladies called "Summer Cottages" this was a modest home most likely holding only two bedrooms and one bath.

"What is going on?" Sophie glanced around.

There were no ambulances or fire trucks. That was a good thing as far as I was concerned. It meant that no one was hurt or worse . . . dead.

"We're here to talk to Henry about the contract his partner Rodney Rivers signed with the fireworks committee," I offered. "We're not impeding an investigation and we are definitely not investigating anything. Are we Sophie?"

"No," Sophie said, backing me up. "We are trying to find Henry to get him to fulfill his contract."

"Henry Schulte does not live here," Officer Lasko said. "I have been told he is staying at the Hamilton." She pointed away from the house.

"His aunt lives here," Sophie said. "We want to talk to her about Henry's whereabouts."

"He's not answering my calls or responding to my messages," I said. "We are concerned about his well-being."

"I'm certain he is fine," Officer Lasko said. "Leave him another message."

The cream-colored front door opened and Henry Schulte came out, his hands clearly cuffed behind him. Rex had his hand around Henry's elbow. Henry looked disheveled. His shirt was wrinkled as if he had slept in it a few days. His jeans were wrinkled and his shoes were untied. His blue-tipped, spiked hair stood up in places it hadn't the last time I'd seen him. It appeared that Rex had disturbed Henry's nap.

Mal's stubby tail wagged hard against me as she wiggled to get down and greet Rex.

"Is Rex arresting Henry?" I asked, holding tight to Mal. The last thing I needed was to give Officer Lasko an excuse to accuse Mal of obstructing justice.

"As I said," Officer Lasko repeated, "this is an official police investigation. Please back off. And keep that dog out of the way."

Sophie pulled out her phone and snapped a few quick photos of Rex hauling Henry out of the little bungalow. "What is he being arrested for?"

"An official statement will be given at seven PM." Officer Lasko kept her body between us and Rex.

"It's not like you are going to be able to keep this secret," I said. "We're blocks from the police station and Rex is going to walk Henry through town. People talk."

"And take pictures." Sophie shot a few more pics and then quickly texted them. "I'm sending these to Liz. She'll be at the police station before Rex."

"Rex," I called. "Why are you arresting Henry?"

"There will be an official announcement," he said as he pulled a reluctant Henry past us. "But I recommend you find yourself another pyro tech for the fireworks show."

"That's all I needed to know," I said.

Sophie looked at me.

I looked at her. "I'll bet a year's worth of fudge that Rex is arresting Henry for Rodney's murder."

"I won't take that bet. I told Rex I flew Henry in the day before the explosion. As far as I know, he was on Mackinac when it happened."

"Great," I said with a breath of relief. "Now I can tell my new contact that the murderer has been caught and the show is no longer jinxed."

"We can't make any such statements at this time. Everyone is innocent until proven guilty." Officer Lasko's gaze was serious.

I frowned. "Wait. I thought you would be happy to catch a murderer."

"I'm happy when justice is done. I'm not so reckless as to make statements like you just did. I believe in the law."

"Fine." I worked to keep from rolling my eyes then stopped and looked at her. "No, you're right."

"Of course I am." She stood up straighter.

"Listen, somehow we got off on the wrong foot. Why don't you come over to the McMurphy sometime? We can have coffee and get to know each other better."

She drew her eyebrows together. "Why would I want to do that?"

Really?

She turned on her heel and followed Rex, ensuring that anyone on the street did not get too close or take pictures.

"Wow," Sophie said as we watched them go. "She does not like you."

"One of my claims to fame."

"What did you do?"

I shook my head. "Heck if I know."

"Well, listen. Now that we've solved the murder, I've got to get back to work. There's a couple from Chicago who are coming out for the week." Sophie patted me on the shoulder. "I don't want to be late picking them up. They're big tippers."

"Sure. Thanks for your help. Come by anytime. There's always coffee."

"Will do." Sophie headed in the opposite direction.

"Come on, Mal. Let's go home, get some dinner, and call a man about signing a contract."

We were a few blocks from the McMurphy when Mal started to tug on her leash. She usually walked very well, keeping beside me unless there was something not quite right.

I had learned to pay attention to her antics. "What is it, Mal?"

She wanted to go left—not right toward the McMurphy.

I let her tug me off toward a group of small cottages rented by summer hotel staff and shop workers. The area was a bustling mini city where minimum-wage workers stayed for the summer. Often in the early morning, maids and porters and reception-desk workers could be seen walking from this area toward the hotels that employed them.

The little bungalows were clean and neat and simple. Some of them dated back to before the McMurphy—over 100 years. The waitstaff was often given weeklong ferry passes and free room and board in the smaller cottages—usually at two people per bedroom.

I had always stayed at the McMurphy growing up and so I rarely had a chance to venture into the staff housing area. Mal had decided that it was a good time to do that.

Then I smelled it—the scent of smoke on the damp evening air. "Oh, no. Not another fire." I let Mal pull me between two buildings.

We came around the back corner of a tiny white cottage to find a small shed on fire. Mal sat a few yards away and looked at me. I pulled out my cell phone and dialed Charlene.

"9-1-1. Please state your emergency," she said.

"Hi Charlene. There is a shed on fire at 900 East Marrow Street."

"Is this Allie McMurphy?" Charlene asked.

"Yes, this is Allie. I was out walking my dog when she smelled something. We approached and there is a small shed on fire. It looks like one of those wooden sheds that holds lawnmowers and racks and such."

"Oh, dear. Step back. Where there are lawnmowers there is usually—"

A loud explosion knocked me back against the bungalow. Debris smacked against me. Mal leapt into my lap and I turned my body so that my back was to the fire and Mal was between me and the house.

A second explosion rattled my teeth and smacked me with pieces of wood and glass. The heat of it warmed my back. I struggled to catch my breath and braced myself for more.

Everything moved in slow motion as I breathed in and out. I could feel Mal shiver in my arms and my ears rang from the blast. I couldn't hear anything. I was too scared to see if anything was left of the shed.

Suddenly, I felt a hand on my shoulder and looked up into George Marron's dark black gaze. I could see that he was saying something, but I had no idea what. I shook my head. "I can't hear you." My voice sounded muffled as if I had cotton in my ears or a bad head cold.

He nodded his understanding and then gently took ahold of my elbow and helped me up. He motioned that we were going to move between the two bungalows and away from the fire. I followed on shaky legs with Mal safely tucked in my arms. She seemed more excited than scared as she licked my face.

The ambulance was parked in front of the bungalow and the fire truck was parked behind it. The firemen in full gear hauled hoses around the homes and commanded the scene. Mal took it all in without a bark.

George guided me to sit on the back of the ambulance then gently took Mal from me. She licked his face and I smiled. I knew if he wasn't careful she'd French kiss him. He was a handsome man any girl would be lucky to snuggle up next to just like Mal was doing. I suppose it was one of the privileges of being a fluffy white doggie.

The air smelled of soot and petroleum. George handed Mal off to Officer Brown who'd arrived at the scene via his bike. They talked, but I couldn't make out what they were saying. I blinked and George turned back to me. He carefully listened to my lungs and then put an oxygen mask over my nose and mouth.

I think I was still a bit dazed. The oxygen had a tinny scent to it and I tried to breathe deeply. Everything seemed to move in slow motion. George checked my pulse and shone a light into my eyes. He then put up his finger and expressed that I should follow it. I did and passed the test just fine.

He nodded and then gently moved my arm looking for broken bones. I winced when he touched me. I glanced over to see that I had a gash in my left forearm.

George's expression was solemn as he checked all my limbs. I learned that my left shoulder hurt. My right thumb was swollen and my ears still rang from the explosion. He went to work splinting my thumb and triaging the shrapnel wounds and bits of glass from my arms and back.

The gash was deep enough that he motioned I would have to have stitches and he wanted me to get on the stretcher.

"I'm fine," I said into the mask and shook my head. I didn't want to get on the stretcher. I didn't want to go to the clinic.

He shook his head in disagreement and insisted I get up on the stretcher.

Rex appeared on the other side of the ambulance just as my ears popped. "Concussion?" I heard him ask George.

"Her eyes look fine," George said. "I'm pretty sure

her thumb might be broken and she needs stitches and glass removed from her back."

I lifted the oxygen mask. "That is exactly why I should not lie down on the stretcher."

"Put that back on," George commanded, gently pushing my hand up so that I had to cover my mouth and nose with the mask. "Your hearing has returned?"

I nodded as he turned my head and looked into my ears.

His breath was warm and minty on my face. "Your ear drums are irritated. You need to keep the oxygen mask on. An explosion and the resulting heat can collapse or scorch your lungs. You're at risk for pneumonia."

"I feel fine," I said into the mask. It came out muffled and Rex frowned at me.

"You need to go to the clinic."

I lifted the mask. "What about Mal?"

George pushed the mask back to my face.

"Charles called Frances," Rex said. "She is on her way. As far as we can tell, the dog is completely unhurt."

I sent him a look that meant that I didn't believe him.

He blew out a long breath. "Frances will see that Mal goes to the vet and gets a thorough checkup. You need to go to the clinic where they can do some X-rays and get you stitched up."

"Fine." I attempted to cross my arms, but the pout didn't work. It hurt to move and I winced.

Rex lifted his eyebrows and nodded at me. "Get on the stretcher."

I lifted the mask. "I'll go, but I'll sit."

George pushed the mask back. "Fine," he agreed and helped me up and into the back of the ambulance.

"I'll be over there in a bit," Rex said, "to ask questions."

I suddenly felt exhausted. "Okay." I was regretting not getting on the stretcher.

George put a blanket gently around my shoulders as Rex closed the ambulance doors on us and pounded on the back. The vehicle took off in a slow roll away from the smoke-filled scene.

George sat beside me and I leaned against him. The trip to the clinic took only a few minutes. The ambulance ran silent through the back roads of the island, honking at the bicyclists and buggies to watch out.

I must have nodded off. The next thing I knew, I was in the clinic on a bed. I was lying on my stomach, my back free of clothing as someone worked on removing glass and wood.

The oxygen mask was still on my nose and mouth. I winced as the person tugged on my back.

She finally moved so I could see her face. "Hello, I'm Doctor Seager. I put an IV in your hand, but we aren't going to give you pain meds until we know for sure you don't have a concussion. We've taken some X-rays of your head, your lungs, and your thumb. Those results will be in soon. Meanwhile, you lie there and relax. We're nearly done cleaning up your back and shoulder.

I raised my thumb as a way of indicating that I understood.

I faded in and out while they worked on me.

Finally they gave me pain meds and the next time I woke up the entire night had passed. I was in a curtained area still on my stomach. The mask was gone and I had oxygen hooked to my nostrils. "Ugh," was all I said.

"Hey Allie." Jenn came around into my line of sight. "Don't move yet, okay?"

"Sure. What's going on?"

"You've been out for a while." Trent came into view and I was embarrassed. I mean, I must look a fright, what with lying on my stomach and drooling.

"Hi." I tried a smile. "How long have you been here?"

"I've been here for a few hours." He brushed the hair away from my face. "How do you feel?"

"Silly," I said, wishing he weren't so good-looking. "How's Mal?"

"Mal's fine." Frances's voice floated from over my shoulder. "We ran her over to St. Ignace and the vet checked her out. I understand you covered her with your body. She didn't have a scratch on her."

I swallowed and my throat was like sandpaper. My lips were dry so I licked them. "How are her lungs?"

"Fine," Frances said. "I called your parents."

I tried not to roll my eyes at that news. "I'm fine. Did you tell them I was fine?"

"She did," Trent said and took hold of my hand. His big warm palm engulfed my hand and he stroked me with the pad of his thumb. "They are on their way up."

"Oh." I planted my face in the pillow. "They don't have to come."

"They love you and want to see for themselves that you are all right," Frances said.

"Well, well. Our girl is awake," Dr. Seager said as she came into view. "Let's give me some time with her, okay folks?"

Trent squeezed my hand and planted a kiss on my cheek. "I'll be back."

The doctor busied herself checking my IV and waited for the room to clear out. "How do you feel?"

"Fine. Can I sit up?"

"Sure, I suggest you turn on your side and move carefully from there. You've got the IV to think about and the oxygen hose."

I slowly rolled onto my right side and felt the stinging tug of the IV in the back of my left hand. I managed to sit up and let my feet dangle a bit off the edge of the bed. I was not in a room, but still in the curtained area of the clinic. Most likely there weren't patient rooms. The clinic was mostly for emergencies and such. Anything to do with actual hospitals was done off the island.

I wore a cream-colored hospital gown with small, blue, flowers sprinkled on it. As best I could tell, I still had panties on but otherwise was naked under the cotton gown. My wavy hair bunched around my shoulders.

"Now how do you feel?" the doctor asked. She checked my eyes with her small light. "Follow my fingers."

I did what she told me.

"Any light-headedness?"

"No."

"Good. Your X-rays came back. You have a slight concussion and broke your right thumb in three places."

I glanced at my thumb and frowned.

"There's nothing more we can do than splint it. But it means you can't use it for six weeks."

"Wait. No! How will I make fudge?"

"I understand you have people who can help you with that. You've got twenty-five stitches in your right forearm, a couple nasty contusions on your shoulder, and we took out about twenty pieces of glass and wood from shallow cuts in your back. You will want to sleep on your stomach for a while until those heal. Other than that, you're good. You were lucky. Your lungs are clear."

"I smell singed," I commented, surprised that I could smell anything with the oxygen being pumped through my nostrils.

"It's your hair. It got a little hot at the initial blast." The doctor turned to a person behind her. "This is Nurse Goldberg."

"Hi." The young woman with black hair and cream-colored skin stepped out of the corner.

"Hello," I said.

"She'll get you some water and lunch," the doctor said. "Once you eat, I'll check your vitals one more time and you'll be free to go home."

"Thanks," I said.

She smiled. "You have a room full of visitors. I promised Rex Manning he could see you first. Are you up to questions?"

"Yes." I took the glass of water the nurse handed me. "You wouldn't have any mouthwash, would you? I feel like I've got cotton in my mouth and don't want to talk to people if I have bad breath."

Dr. Seager laughed a bell-like sound. Her even teeth gleamed in the hospital light and her hazel eyes twinkled. "I suppose I'd feel the same way when faced with Trent Jessop and Rex Manning."

"A brush for my hair would be nice, too." As I sipped water, I couldn't help but smile at my own vanity.

"Nurse Goldberg will help you get cleaned up before we let them back in. How's that sound?"

"Sound's perfect. "Thank-you!"

Thirty minutes later, I was feeling better already. I had been allowed to visit the restroom, wash my face and hands, brush my hair and teeth, and felt more human. The oxygen was put away as my lungs were good, but I had a lovely, bright black bruise on my left cheekbone that highlighted the paleness of my skin.

"Well, this is the best I can do," I said as I came out of the restroom pushing my IV pole.

"You look good," Nurse Goldberg said. She was five foot two and wore a turquoise smock top, white slacks, and white shoes. Her oval face was well proportioned and her eyes were big and brown.

"So do you. How long do I need the IV?"

"Doctor says she wants you to continue until it's done. Then we'll take it out."

I glanced to see that there was a third of the fluid left in the bag.

"It will be done by the time you finish your meal," she said as she helped me back into the bed.

I leaned back and winced. I'd already forgotten that my back was tender. I scooted up to sit straight.

"I've got a nice ice pack that will help with that," she said and left to get it.

I tucked the blankets in around my bare legs.

The nurse came back in with a thin pad the size of a pillow. "This is kept in the freezer. We'll put it behind you for ten minutes and try to ease some of the swelling." She covered it with a piece of thin cotton and tucked the cold pad behind me. "How's that?"

I leaned back gently. "It feels good. Thanks!"

"I'll let Officer Manning in and go get you some lunch." She ducked behind the curtain and a few minutes later Rex stepped in.

He wore his finely pressed uniform, his hat tucked under his arm. His shoes shined. "How are you?"

"Starving," I said and sent him a wry smile. "Seems I missed dinner and most of the night yesterday and breakfast this morning."

"Doc says you had a mild concussion."

"I guess explosions can do that to you."

He nodded and pulled out his notebook. "You called in the fire."

"Yes. Mal and I were walking back from Henry Schulte's aunt's house. By the way, I missed your press statement, didn't I?"

"Let's talk about one thing at a time," Rex said his expression solemn. "You were walking Mal . . ."

"Right." I closed my eyes to help remember what happened. "I was walking Mal when she started tugging on her leash. I've learned to simply go whenever she wants to go off the path."

"You followed your pup."

"Yes." I opened my eyes to see him writing notes.

"She must have smelled the fire first. I was halfway between the two bungalows when I smelled it. At first, I thought maybe someone was having a cookout, but when I rounded the corner, I saw that the shed was on fire. So I called Charlene."

"You called Charlene right away."

"Yes." I no longer took his statements personally. I figured he was simply stating the facts as I gave them to him. "Once I explained what was on fire, Charlene suggested I step back, but it was too late. I'd realized what she meant at the moment the shed exploded. I had enough time to grab Mal, turn my back, and duck. The next thing I was aware of was George Marron touching me. I have no idea how he got there so fast."

"George was in the area because Henry Schulte's aunt Dorothy was having chest pains," Rex said.

"Oh, no. Is she all right?"

"Yes, it was the shock from my finding Henry in her basement."

"Henry was hiding in his aunt's basement and she didn't know it?"

"One thing at a time," Rex said, steering me back to the shed. "Did you see anyone before you saw the fire?"

"No." I drew my eyebrows together. "No, the street was empty. I didn't think it was unusual. That area usually has the summer temp staff and most work that late in the afternoon."

"Did you see anyone in the backyard? Anyone near the shed?"

"No. Did the firemen find anyone in the shed?"

I had a sudden horrifying thought that someone could have died in the explosion.

"No," Rex said. "It looks like an accelerant was used on the side of the shed."

"Similar to the pool house?" I asked.

"It could be. It's still—"

"Under investigation," I finished.

"Right."

"I didn't see anyone." I frowned. "I wasn't even aware of any curtains moving or anyone inside the houses. That's why I called Charlene right away. I figured no one was home to report the fire."

"Okay." Rex put his notepad away. "You'll let me know if you remember anything else. Right?"

"I always do. Now, about Henry Schulte . . ."

Rex's eyes crinkled at the corners as he smiled. "You can read about it in the paper."

"Mean." I pouted. "You are so mean."

He laughed with his head thrown back. His dark eyes twinkled and his muscled shoulders shook. "Glad to see you are going to be just fine."

Nurse Goldberg came in carrying a plastic tray of food. It looked like an old school tray. She put it on the bedside table and adjusted it so that it was in front of me. "There you go."

I took note of the coffee, cup of broth, and Jell-O. "Oh. Clear liquid diet?"

"Only lunch," she said with a smile. "It's been awhile since you have eaten. There will be plenty of time for steak later."

"Enjoy," Rex said with a grin.

"You only say that because you don't have to eat it," I said.

He chuckled and left me to Nurse Goldberg.

I looked at her. "Seriously? No burger and French fries?"

She looked at me with a smile. "I'm certain your family will get you some when you go home. For now, let's make sure you can eat this and keep it down. Okay?"

"Okay." I took the plastic wrap off the top of the cup of broth and spooned some out. My thoughts went back to the scene of the fire. Someone had to start that fire. Who?

A sense of dread crept down my spine. Had the arsonist still been there when I arrived? Don't they like to watch things burn? If so, they know I called in yet another of their fires.

The worst part was, they knew who I was, but I had no clue who they were.

Chapter 16

"Well, you are a sight!" my mom declared when she entered the apartment and saw me on the couch.

"Hi Mom," I said as she embraced me in a tight, painful full-body hug which was hard to do since I was sitting down. Mostly my entire torso was squeezed into Mom's Chanel sweater set and Calvin Klein jeans.

"Now, let me see the damage." She pushed me away. Her strong hands grabbed my chin and turned my head this way and that.

"Ow!" I said through fish lips.

"Look at that bruise!" She grabbed my splinted hand. "And your thumb! How are you going to make fudge with a splint on?"

"I'm going to make the fudge, Mrs. McMurphy," Sandy said from her perch on the footstool next to the chair where Jenn sat.

Frances had opened the apartment door to let my parents in. My father followed my mother, huffing and puffing with his arms full of suitcases.

"Hi Dad," I said from my seated position. "You can put the suitcases in the master bedroom."

"Nonsense," Mom said. "We'll take a room. Frances, there is a room free for us, isn't there?"

"Yes," Frances said with a slight smile. "I ensured the blue room was free before I called you."

"The blue room on the second floor?" Dad asked.

"Yes, two-twelve. I have the key waiting downstairs."

"Wish someone would have told me before I lugged the bags up here."

"The elevator works," Mr. Devaney said from his perch on the bar stool on the living room side of the breakfast bar. He sat with his arms crossed. His dark blue cardigan matched the blue in his blue and red and orange plaid cotton shirt. He wore deep navy corduroy pants and dark brown deck shoes.

Frances took the bags from my dad and placed them near the door. "I'll have one of the interns deliver these to your room."

"You have interns?" Dad's eyebrows rose.

"Yes, two," I said as he came toward me and kissed me on the cheek. "I budgeted for them. Papa approved it last fall."

"Huh." Dad patted me absently on the head. "How are you, kiddo?"

"I'm a little worse for wear," I said and hugged him. "Good to see you, Daddy."

He hugged me back. "Good to be here." He wore a light blue chambray shirt, the neck open and the sleeves rolled to three-quarter length, and dark-wash jeans with brown deck shoes.

Dad was still handsome in his late fifties. His dark brown hair had gray along the sides and was thinner on top than I remembered. His hazel eyes sparkled with pride as he looked around. "You've made this your own. He turned back to look at me. "Looks like you've filled it with friends."

"Oh, Daddy, let me introduce you." I sat up straighter. "You remember Frances." I pointed to her first, then to Mr. Devaney at the bar. "Mr. Devaney is my new handyman."

Dad went over to him. "Nice to meet you." The two men shook hands.

"You remember Jenn from school, don't you?" I asked.

Dad turned to Jenn and smiled. "Of course. How are you?"

"I'm well, Mr. McMurphy," Jenn said as she stood to give Dad a hug. "How have you been?"

"Better, now that I'm here to see my kid for myself."

"This is Sandy Everheart," I said as she rose to her full height of five foot four. Her long black hair hung in a single braid down her back. She and Jenn both wore the standard McMurphy uniform of pink polo shirt with the McMurphy logo above the left breast pocket and black slacks with serviceable shoes. "She is a chocolatier who studied in New York City. She's been a great asset this year."

"Nice to meet you," Dad said and shook Sandy's hand. "I hear very good things about you." He looked over her head at me. "You need to include her in next year's budget."

"I have." I felt the heat of a blush rush up my battered cheeks. "Plus I've offered her the use of the kitchen for her own chocolatier business."

"Smart choice." Dad winked at Sandy.

"Finally, Daddy, this is Trent Jessop," I said as Trent rose from the chair on the opposite side of me.

"Yes, I remember." Dad stuck out his hand. "How are you doing, son?"

"I'm well, sir."

It was so weird to see the two men in my life in the same room face-to-face. It was even weirder to hear Dad call a buff guy like Trent *son.*

"How are your mom and dad?" Dad asked. "I believe I saw them last year at the yacht club."

"Yes, you did," Trent said. "My parents are well. I'll let them know you asked about them."

"Mom," I said. "You remember Trent."

"I do," Mom said and gave Trent a smothering hug. "How are you, dear?"

"I'm good, Mrs. McMurphy." He patted her awkwardly on the back. "Good to see you."

Mom let him go. "Well. Good to see that everyone is here and taking good care of my baby."

As Trent sat on the arm of the couch, Mal popped up and pawed at her for attention.

Mom bent and picked up the pup. "Hello little one." She gave Mal a squeeze and a scratch behind the ears.

"Is this the girl who keeps getting you in trouble?" Dad asked as he gave Mal a pat on the head.

"She usually keeps me *out* of trouble," I protested. "This time, she was showing me that something bad was going on. She likes to keep me posted on what is going on around me."

"Did you find that fire?" Mom cooed and hugged Mal. "You are such a good puppy. Don't listen to that mean man." She gave Dad a look and then took Mal to the kitchen to get a treat from the ever-present treat jar that sat on the counter.

Dad shook his head and sat down in the chair that Trent had vacated. "This is not the first fire you found, is it?"

"No," I said. "We found the pool house on fire just a couple days ago."

Dad shook his head. "Strange to have an arsonist on the island. It's so small. It's almost like he or she wants to get caught."

"Or they can't help themselves, but they've gone too far." Trent reached for my hand. "One man was found dead in the warehouse fire and now they've hurt someone else. The entire island is on alert." He kissed the back of my hand. "We'll get this guy."

"You think it's a man?" Mom asked as she came out of the kitchen and put a contented Mal down.

Mal came over and leapt up into my lap. I winced at the contact.

Trent picked her out of my lap and held her in his. The dog was perfectly content. "Arsonists are more likely to be male."

"Are you an expert?" Dad asked.

"No, I Googled the profile."

"Oh," Dad said with a nod. "I see. So we are on alert for a male fire starter. Is there anything else these fires have in common?"

"Officer Manning is looking into that," Frances said. "We haven't spotted any pattern, except for the fact that the fires have moved on from small fires in the park areas to the housing area of the island."

"And the arsonist most likely knows who I am," I said. Everyone in the room looked at me. "Well, they say that arsonists stay to watch the fire. I've been in two locations. The arsonist has to know who I am."

"That means they know Mal is finding the fires and keeping the burns short," Jenn said thoughtfully.

I frowned. "You don't think they will come after my puppy, do you?"

"Arsonists are generally more interested in the fire than anything." Trent patted Mal. "I think she's safe."

"I worry." I chewed on my bottom lip.

"You've been through a trauma," Mom said as she sat beside me. "You should see someone."

I drew my eyebrows together. "I saw my doctor. I promise, I'll go back in ten days when my stitches need to come out."

Mom patted my hand. "No, dear. You need to see a counselor. You've been through some shocks in the last few months."

"What? No. I'm fine." I felt a blush rush up my cheeks. "Really, Mom, let's not talk about my mental health in front of my boyfriend and my entire hotel staff."

She reached for her purse, pulling it toward her from where she'd left it on the end table. "I know the perfect person to call." She pulled out her wallet and dug out a card. "Dr. Mackay is great with trauma. My friend Anna's daughter went to see her after a severe car accident."

I waved off the card. "I'm fine."

"See her," Mom said forcefully, putting the card in my hand. "I can have her call you if you prefer."

"I'd prefer not to have anyone call me," I said and took the card. Sometimes protesting only made a bigger deal out of something. Sometimes it was simply easier to agree to whatever Mom proposed at the time and then simply let it go.

"How's the fireworks show coming along?" Dad asked. "I understand that you lost your pyro technician in an explosion."

"Oh! The pyro technician," I exclaimed at the reminder. "I was in the middle of negotiations with the new guy. I need to check my e-mails."

"I've taken care of it," Trent said, patting Mal absently.

"You took care of it?" I parroted, confused.

"After they told us last night that they were keeping you overnight for a mild concussion, I talked to Jenn."

My gaze went from Trent to Jenn.

She smiled at me. "I knew you would worry."

"She asked me to take over the negotiations," Trent said. "So I called the guy. He said yes the moment I explained that Rex had arrested a suspect in Rodney Rivers' murder."

"That was what I was going to do." I slumped my shoulders and relaxed against the pillow. It still stung to lean back, but not as bad since I'd taken a pain pill. "Please tell me you didn't tell him about the latest fire and explosion. He was convinced I have bad luck and he might use it as an excuse to back out."

"I didn't tell him," Trent said. "I explained that he didn't even have to set foot on the island to do the show. Then I added a twenty percent bonus and he agreed to do it."

"Did you tell the fireworks committee?" I asked. "Because Mrs. Amerson wasn't certain I would get it done."

"I told them." He picked up my hand again and kissed it. "Don't worry. The committee has nothing to complain about." He glanced up at my parents. "You should stay through the weekend and enjoy the shows. Allie is certain to be a huge success."

"Thanks to Jenn and Trent." I squeezed his hand.

"We plan on it," Dad said. "Since we're here, we thought we'd stay the rest of the week and watch the shows and the other celebrations."

"There is going to be a big picnic in the park," Jenn said. "I plan on having baskets catered and inviting our guests to picnic on the lawn or one of the great vantage sites for the fireworks."

"That's a great idea. Picnics in the parks and fireworks can be so romantic." Mom smiled at my father. "Isn't that right, dear?"

"I remember a few good ones," Dad said with a wink.

"Allie and I have a picnic date set," Trent said. "Would you like to come with us?"

"That might be fun," Dad said.

My eyes grew large as I looked from Dad to Mom. I'm certain that I sent Mom a look of *please-don't-come-on-my-date-with-me.*

"Thanks for the offer," Mom said smoothly, but we have plans for the Fourth."

"We do?" Dad drew his eyebrows together.

"Yes." Mom raised her right eyebrow. "We do."

"Okay."

Frances stood and Mr. Devaney stood with her. "Well, it's been quite the day. We should be getting home."

"We'll see you in the morning," Mr. Devaney said

to me. He turned to my parents and shook their hands. "Nice to meet you both. You have a hard-working daughter. You should be proud."

I was surprised. Mr. Devaney was usually gruff and never gave out praise. It was nice to hear him say that.

"We are proud," my dad said. "Thanks for your help with the McMurphy. She's getting up there in years so I know the daily list of things that need worked on."

"Gives me a reason to get up in the morning," Mr. Devaney replied and then walked Frances out the door.

Sandy stood next. "I've got to make it an early night. I'm making fudge at five AM tomorrow."

"I have a list of five recipes for tomorrow," I said as she shook my parents' hands.

"I look forward to it." Sandy turned to Mom and Dad, "Nice to meet you both."

"Well," Mom said as we watched Sandy leave, "she is a very nice girl." To Dad, she said, "And, dear, you should see what kind of miracles she works in chocolate."

"You've told me." Dad stood. "We'll leave you young ones to your night. I'm exhausted."

"I'll ring Mike to come get your suitcases," I said and reached for my cell phone.

"Don't bother." Dad picked up the four suitcases, two stacked in each hand. "If you can get the door, honey, I'll take care of these myself."

"Got it." Mom kissed my cheek then went to the door and held it open for Dad. "Sweet dreams, Allie."

"Good night, Mom."

The door closed behind them and I heard them talking in the hall, their voices muffled. But I think Dad was telling Mom that I looked good . . . considering.

I closed my eyes and rested my head against the back of the couch. Jenn got up and went to the kitchen. Trent sat down beside me and I tilted my head against his broad shoulder. Mal climbed up on the couch beside me.

"Long day," Trent said.

"I should not be this tired," I said. "I've done nothing but rest for almost all day."

"Your mom's right," Jenn said, coming back into the living room with a glass of ice tea in both hands. She handed me one and handed Trent the other. "You should see someone about the trauma."

"I think trying to impress Mrs. Amerson gave me more trauma than finding Rodney dead."

"Trauma is not something to ignore." Trent rubbed my forearm, careful to stay away from the bandaged part.

"Is this a conspiracy?" I asked and raised my head to look my boyfriend in the eye.

He kissed me. It was a nice, slow, gentle kiss. "People care about you," he said against my lips.

I sighed and leaned into him. I could hear his steady heartbeat under my ear. "It's embarrassing to have everyone in the room hear my mom tell me I need to see a shrink."

Jenn came around with her own glass of ice tea and settled sideways into the chair. "It's not just Rodney. You've been through several traumas, including two explosions. It might not hurt for you to talk to someone about them before things get bad."

"You really mean it." I frowned at her.

"We both do." Trent kissed the top of my head.

I tried to sit up, but his arm kept me gently against him. "I'm not crazy."

"That's why you should see someone," he insisted. "Only a crazy person could go through what you have gone through since your grandfather died and not need to talk to a professional about it."

I wanted so badly to stick out my tongue at them both and flounce off in a huff, but I was tired and as much as I hated to hear it, I had begun to realize they might be right.

Time to change the subject. "Rex wouldn't tell me what happened with Henry Schulte," I said, my thoughts tumbling to the first explosion. "Do we know why he killed Rodney?"

"The official statement was simply that they had arrested Henry for the crime and that the evidence against him would be presented in court." Jenn made a face. "Not very satisfying."

"No," I agreed and wrinkled my brow. "I'd love to hear Liz's take on it. Did Henry use Rodney's threatening e-mails as a decoy to murder him? If so, why murder him here on Mackinac? Why not kill him someplace less dramatic. I mean, if I wanted it to seem like a professional murder, I wouldn't have killed him in a warehouse on a small island, lit the fuse on a string of screaming chickens, and then blown up the fireworks inside."

"I see what you mean," Jenn said, her expression puzzled.

"Also, when he left me the last message, Rodney said that someone was messing with the fireworks and I swear he saw someone in the warehouse."

"He could have seen Henry," Trent suggested.

I shook my head. "I don't think so. I think he said something like 'Hey, you. What are you doing here?' Which means—"

"He didn't recognize whoever was in the warehouse with him," Jenn finished my thought.

"The two things may not be connected," Trent said. "Anyone could have been in the warehouse before Henry killed Rodney."

"So why kill him here?" I asked again. "I mean, why not kill him someplace closer to home?"

"Or why not wait and make it seem like an accident?" Jenn said. "If it was that premeditated, I think Henry could have thought out the murder better. I mean, what better way than to have the fireworks backfire and explode in Rodney's face when he was doing a show? That makes more sense than using the death threats as a motive to throw the cops off his trail."

"Maybe that's what Henry was doing in the warehouse when Rodney saw him," Trent suggested. "Maybe Rodney caught Henry sabotaging the fireworks. Then Henry wouldn't have had a choice. He would have had to kill Rodney then and there."

"Again, it goes back to Rodney not seeming to recognize the person he caught messing with the fireworks. Do we know what Rex thinks the motive is?" I asked.

"Liz said something about issues with the accounts," Jenn said. "That plus a ten million dollar life insurance policy are pretty good motives to me."

I bit my bottom lip. "Yes, I suppose I can see that.

Thankfully, I never saw Henry at the warehouse. I shouldn't be called upon to testify, anyway."

"Speaking of witnessing crimes, did you see anyone at the scene of the fire?" Trent asked.

"No." I shook my head. "Rex asked me the same thing, but I didn't. It was eerily quiet. That's why I called 9-1-1 right away. I knew no one was home to call in the fire."

"So why start a fire and leave it?" Jenn tapped her lips then shrugged and got up. "We're just talking in circles and it's late. I think I'll head to bed." She poured the remains of her drink in the sink, rinsed her glass, and wiped her hands. "Don't stay up too late, kids." She winked at us. "Sweet dreams."

"Good night, Jenn." Trent's voice rumbled through his chest and comforted me.

Mal slept beside me and for a moment, I drank in the warmth of being surrounded by love. "Thanks for being so nice to my parents. I know they can be a little strange sometimes."

Trent chuckled. "They're good people. I'm glad they came up."

"But you didn't have to invite them on our date." I pouted.

His chuckled deepened. "I was being polite." He tilted my chin up so he could look me in the eye. "I like your folks, but I enjoy being with you. I figured it was better to invite them on our date than to miss out altogether because you wanted to spend time with them while they are here."

"Oh."

He kissed me then and the evening was perfect.

Chapter 17

Two days later, I felt better and excited for the holiday. July third dawned bright and beautiful. The whole island was gearing up for the celebrations to come. Mom and Dad came in from a morning walk with pink cheeks and sparkling eyes.

"Did you have fun?" I asked.

"Oh, my," Mom said. "I forget how much fun the Fourth is here on Mackinac."

"We have one of the only two remaining all original Revolutionary War forts in America," I said with pride. "They have so much going on. There's a thirty-one gun salute and tomorrow there's a picnic at the lawn at the foot of the fort catered by the Grand Hotel. Everyone will be there."

"If I remember right, doesn't the fire department put on a shindig?" Dad asked and pushed the hair out of his eyes.

"Yes, Mr. McMurphy," Jenn said from her station at the reception desk. She was covering for Frances while the older woman ran some errands. "They host the Fun and Games at Windermere Point."

"Right," Dad said with a fond smile. "They have the Greasy Pole Climb and old-fashioned sack races."

"The Ladies Auxiliary hosts a lemonade stand," Sandy said as she leaned on the back of the candy counter. We had finished our first demonstration of the day. She had done the work, while I walked around telling the crowd the story of fudge making. It actually worked out well. I was able to cut off some small bites with my good hand and a stainless steel scraper. I passed them around to the delighted crowd and then took orders filling pink paper boxes with pounds of fudge. As much as I missed doing the work myself, I knew the McMurphy fudge was in good hands with Sandy.

The crowds had dissipated after Mom and Dad came inside.

"Do they still have a three-legged race?" Mom asked. "Honey, remember the time you and Allie tried the three-legged race?"

"I think Dad cheated." I smiled at the happy memory.

"It wasn't cheating," he protested.

"You picked me up and ran with me under your arm," I pointed out.

"Papa jumped the gun and had a three-stride lead," Dad said. "As I saw it, the old man should not get to win. Besides, your leg moved with mine."

"If I remember right, you and Papa both tripped and Pat Keller and his son Marvin won that year," Mom said, her eyes sparkling.

"Papa tripped us," my father grumbled. He went to the coffee bar and poured two fat cups of coffee.

From the way he fixed them, I knew he filled one for Mom and one for himself.

It made me smile to see the simple act of getting coffee for my mom. It meant that things were okay between them. My heart blossomed. After Mom's last visit, I wasn't sure how things were going, but watching Dad take her an unasked for cup of coffee with two creams and no sugar let me know that things were okay.

"That sounds like something Liam would do," Frances said as she came in through the back hallway. She let go of Mal's leash. My puppy gathered it up and raced toward me to say hi.

I bent down and patted Mal on the head. Then I gently took off her halter and leash. "There you go, little girl." Thankfully, the clip leash was easy to work with my left hand.

I stood. "I was reminding Mom and Dad of all the things going on around the island this week," I said to Frances.

She wore a long, comfy brown skirt with a red, white, and blue, long-sleeved blouse that was untucked, but pulled together with a brown belt that had a gold, star shaped buckle. "Always lot's going on."

She waved Jenn away from her perch behind the receptionist desk. "The three nights of fireworks, which Allie put together, starts tonight. I recommend you take chairs and set them up in the schoolyard early. I was just by that way and people were already staking claim to the best spots."

"But the fireworks are twelve hours away," Mom said, checking her watch.

"There are some folding chairs in the basement,"

I said. "If you hurry there might still be a few good spots left."

Dad nodded. "I'll get on it." He went to the basement.

Mom looked from me to Frances. "Really? Twelve hours before?"

"It gets crowded," Frances said.

"Do you stay there all day?" Mom asked. "Because if that's what is happening, then I need to go up and make some picnic food for Allie's dad."

"You can leave the chairs and blanket there," Frances said. "People are good about respecting staked out spots."

"Until about seven PM. Then all bets are off." Sandy turned from the counter to the dishes in the sink behind it.

"Oh, good," Mom said. "Two hours outside is much better than twelve hours."

"When was the last time you and Dad were here for the Star Spangled Fourth celebrations?" I searched my memory and didn't recall them being there since I turned twelve.

"It's been forever," Mom said. "Your father's office has a mandatory company picnic on the Fourth."

"How did you get out of it this year?" Jenn asked as she grabbed her own coffee mug and draped her lanky body across one of the overstuffed chairs. Her dark hair floated over her shoulders in a soft cloud. She wore a pale blue sundress with cream-colored flowers sprinkled on it. It was pretty and went well with the thick blue and white stripes of the chair.

"Allie being hurt was our excuse," Mom said, her gaze going to my bandaged arm and my splinted thumb. "How are you feeling?"

"I'm fine."

"Really?" Mom narrowed her eyes. "You look a little pale."

"Sandy did all the work," I said quickly.

Jenn ratted me out. "But you have been working since five o'clock this morning." She ignored my stink eye and sipped her coffee. "I'm just saying that it's been five hours. You should sit down and take a break."

"Allie, sit down before you fall down," Mom commanded and pointed to the pale pink chair that sat across from Jenn's blue and white one.

"I'm not going to fall down," I muttered. Sulking, I scooted over to sit in the chair.

Mom shook her head, her mouth flat and slightly down turned. "You almost died in an explosion three days ago. Don't push it, young lady."

"It's not like I'm going to cheat at a three-legged race," I muttered. Still, I had to admit to myself that it felt good to sit and take the pressure off my legs.

The McMurphy's front door opened with the accompanying jingle of the bells attached it. I glanced over to see Liz walk in. Her curly hair was put up in a messy bun. She wore tan peddle pusher shorts, a white tank top, and a green camp shirt with the tail hanging out over the top. "Hey kids, what's shaking?" she asked with a big smile.

"Someone's happy," I observed as she made her way to the coffee bar and poured herself a cup.

"New boyfriend? Jenn asked. "Spill."

"I take it you know her," my mom stage whispered to me. She was dressed in pressed blue jeans and a polo shirt in a lovely mint green. Her dark hair was perfect in its low bun at the nape of her neck.

"Mom, this is Liz MacElroy. Liz, this is my mother, Ann McMurphy." I waved my introductions.

"Hi." Liz came over with her coffee in her left hand and shook my mom's hand with her right.

"Liz works with her grandfather Angus at the *Town Crier,*" I added.

"Oh," Mom said. "I remember Angus as a nice fellow—a little nosey but nice."

"Mom!"

Liz laughed and sat on the arm of Jenn's chair. "It's okay. He is nosey. So am I, I suppose." She sipped her drink. "It's what makes us good journalists. If we weren't nosey, there'd never be investigative journalism."

"So, who's the guy?" Jenn asked, her blue eyes crinkling.

"No guy," Liz said. "But I may have solved the arson problem."

"Really?" I sat up straight. "Who? How? Did you tell Rex?"

Liz put her hand up in a *stop* motion. "I said, I *may have* solved them. Remember, Rex doesn't want theories. You can't prosecute theories."

"What is your theory?" I asked.

Dad came through the basement door. "Got four chairs, a tarp, and a blanket." He grinned. His arms were full of rolled up bundles. "Do you think we'll need more?"

"Do you think a tarp is necessary?" Mom moved toward him. "How can we see the fireworks if we have a tarp over us?"

"The tarp is for the picnic," Dad said, his face darkening a bit. We can tear it down after the sun sets."

"Sounds perfect." I stood. I was set to defuse the brewing argument, but it wasn't necessary.

"Oh, of course. What a great idea." Mom kissed Dad on the cheek, restoring his smile. "Pat, this is Liz MacElroy. She is a reporter at the *Town Crier.*"

"Oh, hi," Dad said. "I would shake your hand, but mine are full." He raised his to show off the bundles he juggled.

"Liz has a theory on the arsons." Mom put her hands around Dad's bicep.

"Great." Dad moved forward. "Are they arresting the jerk who hurt my little girl?"

"Not yet," Liz said with a twinkle in her eye. "I have a theory. What I need to do now is see if I can shake the arsonist into admitting their guilt."

"How are you going to do that?" I asked.

"I'm not sure," Liz said. "Like I said, I have a theory. I thought I'd ask you all what your opinions are about it."

"Let me put this stuff down, Dad said.

Mom stopped him. "No, we don't want to lose a spot at the fireworks display."

"She's right," Frances said from her perch behind the receptionist desk. "Spots were going fast."

"Not fair." Dad blew a puff of bangs from in front of his face.

"It's all right, Mr. McMurphy," Liz said. "We can fill you in on the plan when you get back."

"Fine." His shoulders sagged a bit in disappointment. "I'll be back in a few."

We watched him walk out, hands full and shoulders square with purpose.

"Theory?" I asked Liz, bringing everyone's attention back to the story at hand.

"Do you have a white board?" Liz asked.

"Oh, are we going to do a murder board?" Jenn asked, sitting up. "I love how they do that on crime shows. Except ours will be an arson board, I guess."

I frowned. "No . . . Wait." I went out to the sidewalk and grabbed the SPECIALS board and its easel. I tucked the board under my left arm and Jenn held the door as I brought them inside. "We can use this." I set it up in the lobby near the chairs and settees beside the basement door and erased the words *Today's Specials—Red, White, and Blue Fudge and Apple Pie Fudge.*

"Oh, apple pie fudge," Liz said. "Really? Grandpa would love that."

"I'll box you up a pound," Sandy said.

"Allie has a whole series of pie fudges," Frances said as she came around the receptionist desk to join us in front of the arson board. "I was skeptical at first, but the lemon meringue won me over."

"Okay." I handed the erasable markers to Liz. "Spill your thoughts."

"Okay, this is the island." She quickly sketched the familiar outline of Mackinac. The island was thought to be the back of a great turtle. Liz had done a good job with it. "Now"—she put down the black marker and grabbed red—"these *X*es are where the fires have been since February."

"There were fires in the winter? Jenn asked. "Isn't it kind of cold and snowy for that?"

"Yes," Liz said. "That's why no one realized it was arson at first. The snow kept the damage to a minimum and it was thought that someone was out snowmobiling and stopped to eat lunch and built a fire to keep warm."

"That could have been the case at first," Frances pointed out.

"Sure." Liz nodded her agreement as she made X marks on the board. "It may have started that way. The fires may have started even earlier but they might never have come under the notice of the fire department." She pointed to a mark in the east portion of the state park near Eagle Point Cave. "This is the first that we can reasonably call part of the arsonist's series. It was a large bonfire. The starter had piled huge branches and twigs and pine needles. The wood was wet and the smoke was thick and black. People called it in because it looked so out of place."

"Is there anything around where this fire was started? Like a shed or something that gave the person a reason to be in the area in the first place? Did the arsonist talk to anyone?" I asked.

"No, by the time the guys got the truck out there, it was out of hand and whoever started it was gone. The only clue was the snowmobile tracks that led back to town so it was dismissed as a tourist who didn't know what they were doing."

"Because everyone knows that wet wood does not make for a warm fire," I said.

"And it looked like it got out of hand because they kept adding more wet fuel in an attempt get it to burn warm," Liz said.

"Since there were snowmobile tracks there must have been snow on the ground, right?" I asked.

"Yes," Liz confirmed. "I checked the weather report

for that day. There were ten inches of snow. Whoever started the fire really had to work to collect combustibles. That means they were at it for some time."

"Do we know anything about the tracks?" I asked. "Do we know how many snowmobiles were in the area? What sizes? It could be a good clue to the identity of the arsonist."

"That's what I thought, but the report only mentions the fire, which was substantial by the time the firemen got there. Even with the snow and damp the fire crew had quite a time to get in there and douse it."

"Did you interview the guys? Did anyone remember the fire?"

"I did," Liz said with a nod. "Frank Blessing said there were plenty of boot tracks. He figured it was two guys, but one snowmobile."

"Two of them." Jenn pursed her mouth. "Do arsonists work in pairs?" She grabbed her phone. "Let me do a Web search on that."

"Actually, I already did," Liz said. "The profile for arson is rarely more than one person. It was why the thought of arson never crossed anyone's minds. They figured whoever started that fire were kids or ignorant tourists."

"When was the next fire?" I asked.

Sandy walked out of the fudge shop with Liz's box of apple pie fudge. She put it on the end table next to the settee and sat down on the arm of the couch. "Was it the early March fire?"

We all looked at her.

She shrugged. "I was in New York, but that fire was close to my grandmother's home. My family was worried." Sandy crossed her arms.

"Yes," Liz said, drawing our attention back to the board. "The second fire was here along the edge of Great Turtle Park. This one was much closer to homes. It, too, was assumed to be a hiker or picnicker who'd started a fire for warmth or to cook hotdogs and such. The thing is that the fire was started on the ground, not in an empty grill. What caught the fire chief's eye was the fact that the fire was set next to some brush stacked against a shed."

I tilted my head. "The arsonist wanted to see if they could get the fire to leap?"

"There was accelerant found on the ground between the original fire and the brush," Liz said.

"You said the first fire was in February and this one in March. Why do you think they are connected?" Frances asked.

"The two fires had the same shape. The first fire was set high, causing fear that the nearby trees would catch fire. This one"—Liz tapped the second *X* on the board—"was similar, but not as ambitious. This one was set to leap to the shed."

"Do fires have signatures like bombs?" I asked.

"Yes," Liz said with a smile. "But you have to look for them. This second fire was when the fire department started to catalog the fire signature. It was only because of the strangeness of the first fire that Frank remembered some of the details. After the second fire, he made notes for comparison. He told me that he had hoped his suspicions would come to nothing."

"Sadly, they did not," Frances said. "The next fire was two weeks after, wasn't it?"

"Yes, the second week of April. Allie, were you on the island by then?" Liz asked.

"I was. Papa died about that time. I don't remember any fire." I frowned and shook my head.

"You had other things on your mind," Mom said and patted my shoulder. "I remember a small article in the paper when we came up for Liam's funeral. It started in a trash barrel, didn't it?"

"Yes, the third fire was started in Harrisonville," Liz pointed at her map. "It was set in a barrel meant to look like someone was burning trash."

Frances turned to my mom. "You know that it's not unusual for the locals to burn trash in burn barrels."

"Yes, I remember," Mom said.

"How did they connect a burn barrel fire to the other fires?" I asked.

"The barrel had a hole punched in the bottom and traces of accelerant that led to kerosene soaked rags held to the ground with a rock."

"I don't get it," I said. "What is the arsonist doing?"

"It looks like they want to see how the fire moves under certain conditions," Liz said. "It's almost as if they are studying the fire."

"I read where some people see fire as an animal," Jenn said.

"An animal?" Mom asked, drawing her eyebrows together.

"Yes, it is born"—Jenn raised her index finger—"breathes, consumes, reproduces, and dies." She counted off the facts on her fingers. "Do you know of any other definition of life?"

"Strange," Mom muttered.

"Our arsonist is trying to manipulate fire," I said. "Why?"

"We don't know yet," Liz said. "The next fire was two weeks after that. It was a very slow burn of old bicycle tires near North Bicycle Trail and a boarded up cabin."

"I remember that," Frances said. "Didn't the report say that trash had been built up next to the house?"

"That's what it looked like," Liz said. "It takes a lot to start rubber on fire, but once it starts it's hard to stop. Frank thinks that the arsonist piled pitch filled pieces of bark and other tinder on the wet pile of trash. Then they started the fire, slowly feeding it until it burned through the pile to the bicycle tires below."

"That was a heck of a fire," Mr. Devaney said as he came in from the back hall. "What a mess. Luckily, a spring storm helped cool that down enough for it to burn itself out."

"After that fire," Liz said, "the public became watchful and the fires stopped."

"They stopped?" I narrowed my eyes. "That would be why I hadn't heard anything about them before I found the pool house on fire."

"Why would an arsonist accelerate for a short time, stop for eight weeks, and then start back up?" Jenn asked. "Don't they tend to continue to accelerate?"

"Maybe they were off the island," Sandy said as she studied Liz's map. "Maybe they were accelerating their fire starts elsewhere."

"Yes!" Liz said, her eyes sparkling. "That is exactly what I thought. So I did some digging. I wanted to see if I could figure out who was on the island during the first part of the fires—"

"And who was not on the island when the fires stopped," I said.

"Then who was back on the island when they started back up," Jenn continued. "So, who is it?"

"Ten people fit that profile," Liz said.

"Ten? Let's see the list." I said.

Liz went back to the board. Mr. and Mrs. Castor," she said as she wrote. "They own a place near the airport. They also run the Boar's Head Inn and Pub during the tourist season."

I frowned. "Why were they off the island for the first four weeks of the season?"

"Their daughter lives in South Carolina and she was having their first grandbaby. It was a girl born June fifteenth," Liz said as Frances opened her mouth to ask. "They just got back on Mackinac the day before the pool house fire."

"They are friends with Pete Thompson," Mr. Devaney said. "There was no reason for them to set the pool house on fire."

"Next we have Oliver Crumbley."

"Wait. His Mom runs the Old Tyme Photo Shop next door," I said. "It can't be Oliver. He porters for me sometimes."

"He was off the island visiting his father in June," Frances said. "He did get back the week of the pool house fire. He also lives close enough to have started the fire without being seen. Combine that with his mom Cyndy having trouble with Pete Thompson the week before."

"I don't buy it." I shook my head. "He's too nice a kid for that."

"At this point, no one is too nice. We have to look at all the suspects or the real arsonist will continue and more people will get hurt." Liz looked pointedly at my splinted thumb.

I winced. Mal jumped into my lap and I held her tight. Whoever was behind the fires was a neighbor. No one could be ruled out no matter how much I wanted them to be.

Key Lime Pie Fudge

½ cup cream cheese, softened
¼ cup milk (almond milk is a good nondairy substitute)
1 3.4 ounce package of vanilla instant pudding and pie filling
1 teaspoon vanilla
3 tablespoons lime juice
6 cups powdered sugar, sifted

Butter 8x8x2 inch cake pan.

Mix cream cheese, milk, unprepared instant pudding, vanilla and lime juice. Add powdered sugar 1 cup at a time until you reach the desired thickness.

Scoop into prepared pan. Pat until smooth. Score into 1-inch pieces with butter knife.

Refrigerate for 2-3 hours until set.

Break into 1-inch pieces along score. Serve in individual paper candy cups or on a platter. Store leftovers in covered container in the refrigerator.

Enjoy!

Chapter 18

"Who else is on the list?" Mr. Devaney asked. "You said ten suspects."

"Right, I'll finish the list before we go into each case," Liz said. "There is Henry Schulte."

"Wasn't he in jail for the shed fire?" Jenn said.

"Let her get out the entire list," Mr. Devaney said as he studied the fires on the map.

"Bruce and Penny Miller and their sons Ethan and Michael," Liz went on.

"But Bruce is the acting fire chief," Frances pointed out.

Liz did not stop writing. "Daryl and Terry Cunningham and their daughter Amanda."

"That's eleven," Mr. Devaney said. "You said ten suspects."

"Plus Luke and Sherman Archibald." Liz finished writing.

"That is thirteen suspects," Sandy pointed out.

"I wrote down everyone who was off island during the appropriate time period. That said, I ruled out Daryl, Terry and Amanda," Liz said drawing a line through their names. "They felt like outliers. Most arsonists are male and most between the ages of twelve and nineteen or twenty-six and thirty."

"That's right," Jenn said, reading her phone. "This article says that arsonists are difficult to profile because a majority of arsons go undetected or unsolved." She glanced up at us. "Wow, it seems arson is a crime you are more likely to get away with." She glanced back at her phone. "Most arsonists are white males between the ages Liz described. The ones that are caught seem to be of lower intelligence." Jenn raised her index finger as if to make a point. "That said, it says here that it could simply be that the less intelligent arsonists are the ones who get caught so you can't count out intelligence."

"That makes sense," Mom said with a lift of her eyebrows.

"The prevailing emotion behind arson is anger," Jenn read, "unless there is insurance fraud."

"That's not the case here," I pointed out. "None of the fires have done that kind of damage."

"Unless you count the fireworks," Liz said. "That could be insurance fraud."

I nodded. "That's why Henry is on your list."

"Plus he fits the time frame. After I spoke to Sophie about the dates that she flew him onto the island, they match up with all the fires, including the warehouse fire that killed Rodney Rivers."

"Or they were set to look like arson so that Henry could kill Rodney and blame it on an arsonist," I said.

"How did Henry start the last shed fire?" Jenn asked. "You saw Rex dragging him to the police station in cuffs and then fifteen minutes later, you were calling in the shed fire. There is no way that could have been started by Henry."

"Unless he has a partner," I mused.

Everyone was thoughtful for a moment.

"I suppose anyone could have a partner," Jenn said. "In which case, we might have more suspects."

"Darn." Liz's shoulders slumped and she sat down against the back of the settee that faced away from the board. "I didn't think about a partner. That would screw up this entire list."

The front door opened with a jingle. Dad came in looking windblown and bright-eyed. "What did I miss?"

"They just blew away my line of thinking." Liz sighed.

"Great." Dad came around to give Mom a kiss on the cheek. "That means I can help come up with a new theory."

"It seems that statistically most arsonists don't get caught," I said. "Of those that get caught, the universal emotion behind the act is anger."

"Okay." Dad nodded. "I can understand that."

"They are also more likely to be white males in their teens or late twenties and lower in intelligence," I added. "At least the ones who get caught."

"And this is our list?" He pointed at the names on the board.

"These are the people who were on the island during the fires and off the island during the times when no fires occurred," Liz said. "I thought I had figured out who our main suspects were, but it was pointed out that the person who was causing the arsons might have used a partner and therefore the real person didn't have to be on Mackinac."

"Oh." Dad studied the map. "So you think there's an argument for using a young man's lack of intelligence and anger to light fires to hide a premeditated crime."

"Such as the warehouse explosion," I said. "And Rodney Rivers' death."

"Well, that definitely puts a twist on your list of suspects." Dad shoved his hands in the pockets of his jeans. "It could be anyone."

"But it wasn't just anyone," I said. "Let's rule out the partner idea for a moment. Remember, things are not usually as complicated as they seem. Do we know if there is any way that Henry could have started the shed fire before Rex arrested him? I mean, didn't you say the tire trash fire was experimenting with slow burns?"

"Yes," Liz said as she studied the map. She turned to me. "Did you see a pile of trash or a tire or anything when you called in the shed fire?"

I shook my head. "No, I saw smoke, but the fire was started inside the shed. The smoke I saw was thick and black and came through the gaps around the window."

"We need to find out what started the shed fire," Mom said.

"The official report was that the fire was set with an accelerant. The gas cans inside the shed along with a couple lawnmowers caused the explosion."

"So it could have been a slow burn," I said. "The smoke was quite thick and black. Not like paper fire or even wood."

"I'll double-check with my sources inside the fire department and see if the fire was a slow burn. If it was, we can't rule out Henry. In fact, he may have set the fire knowing Rex was close to arresting him. That way, he would seem innocent in the whole thing."

"Do you think Henry Schulte is that smart? I asked. "He didn't exactly come across as a criminal mastermind. The man has blue-tipped, spiked hair for goodness sakes."

"Desperate men can do desperate things," Dad observed.

"He would have to be pretty darn desperate," I said.

"He may have gotten the same death threats that Rodney did. Or worse," Liz said. "Rodney could have discovered that Henry did something that caused the death threats. Perhaps Henry was cooking the books and not paying the bills, for example. In that case, Rodney may have threatened to go to the police."

"There has to be a good amount of evidence that Henry killed Rodney or Rex would not have arrested him," I said. "Do we have any details?"

"No." Liz shook her head. "Rex is playing it close to the vest. What I do know is that Henry hired a lawyer who got him out on a hundred thousand dollar bail."

"Only a hundred thousand dollars?" I said. "For murder?"

"There is no evidence of flight risk as Henry didn't leave the island."

"When does the trial start?" Dad asked.

"They go to the grand jury in two weeks," Liz said. "Meanwhile, Henry is staying with his aunt on the island."

"One hundred thousand is pretty cheap when you have a ten million dollar payday coming," I said.

"That's the thing," Liz said. "The insurance company won't pay as long as Henry is under suspicion for Rodney's murder. They're waiting to see what the outcome is in the murder trial."

"Well, that's enough to make a mad man even angrier," Dad said.

"So Henry is still our main suspect." Mom studied the board. "Let's look at them all individually. "Frances, you know Mr. and Mrs. Castor. Can you find out if they know anything about the fires?"

"Sure. I'll check in with them and see what they have to say. At the bare minimum, they might have seen or heard something on their trips back and forth to the island."

"I'll check with Cyndy about her son Oliver," I said. "I haven't really gotten to know her yet."

"I can talk to Bruce and Penny," Liz said. "With Bruce being the fire chief, it's not very likely they are involved, but I want to rule them out, anyway."

"If the arsonist is Bruce's son, he has grown up around fires and knows about how they are set and grow and such," Dad said. "He might just be an angry kid in trouble."

"True," Liz said.

"I can talk to Luke and Sherman," Jenn said. "I got to know them pretty well when we were putting out the ashes from the fireworks explosion."

"Great. Let's reconvene tomorrow morning before the picnic," Liz said. "How does that sound?"

"Sounds great." Dad glanced at his watch. "It's nearly noon. What say we go get some lunch?" He held out his hand to Mom.

She smiled, stood, and took his hand, then looked at me. "Come with us. We know you're going to spend tomorrow with Trent. We didn't come all this way to not have a good visit."

"But the McMurphy," I protested.

"Is in good hands with Frances and Sandy and Jenn," Mom said.

I glanced at my friends who all nodded in turn. I sighed. I did trust them. I simply felt guilty not doing my share of the work.

"Go enjoy lunch with your parents," Frances said. "The work will be here when you get back."

"Fine. Thanks."

"Let's go out the back way," Dad suggested and put his free arm around my shoulders careful not to bump my stitches. "Main Street is already filled with tourists."

"Are you going to sit with us for the fireworks?" Mom asked as I bent to put Mal's leash and halter on her.

"Sure," I said. "Since I put so much work into the shows, I really want to make sure they go off well and that people are happy."

"Are you still worried about the Star Spangled Fourth committee?" Dad asked.

"It's Mrs. Amerson," I said and straightened. "Wouldn't you be worried?"

Dad laughed. "Yes," he agreed. "Yes, I most certainly would be worried. That woman is a barracuda."

Chapter 19

After lunch, I left my parents at the bike rentals. Mom had decided it would be fun to bike the road that went around the island. It was an easy eight mile track that showcased the shoreline.

Before I went back to work, I figured it was a good time to pop in to my neighbor's shop and ask about Oliver. He was fifteen and I kind of hoped he'd be looking for part-time work next summer. At sixteen, he could do more than porter. I would like to see if he might work the front desk to relieve Frances a few hours a week.

The Old Tyme Photo Shop had red, white, and blue bunting draped across the front. In the windows was an ever changing kaleidoscope of tin-type pictures of smiling Fudgies in period dress from the revolutionary war to the World War II era. The glass doors were held open with a brick and the sound of laughter and music greeted me.

The set up was simple. A front counter with a cash register and blown up poster-size pictures was positioned to the right of the door. To the left was a seating area currently occupied by a family of six. Mom and Dad wore 1900s costumes—full suit for dad and mutton sleeve blue jacket, white shirt, and floor length skirt for Mom. A set of twins, blond boys who looked to be about eight years old, wore short pants and sailor tops. A girl of about thirteen had draped herself in the chair in the most bored manner while she flipped through her cell phone. She wore a calf length white dress with a drop waist set off with a pale blue sash. Her blond hair was pulled back into a braid that ran down her back. The little girl who looked to be three years old was in a cute pink and white striped dress with pantaloons. The family was adorable.

Beyond the waiting area was a small hallway. I made my way down it to see two rooms to the right. One held a variety of backdrops and photography equipment. The one behind held racks and racks of costumes. To the right were restrooms marked BOYS and GIRLS.

"Hello?" I called.

"I'll be right out." Cyndy Crumbley popped her head out of a tiny office in the back of the building. "Oh, hi, Allie. How are you?"

Cyndy was a gorgeous blonde. At age thirty-eight she still could pass for a woman in her twenties. She had big blue eyes that she'd lined with blue eyeliner and black mascara. She wore her hair in a messy bun on top of her head. Cyndy was five foot four and wore a white peasant blouse with violets embroidered across the top and a long loose skirt in purple. Her perfectly manicured toes peeked out of open-toed wedges.

"I'm good. You look busy." I pointed toward the waiting family.

"Being busy is good." In her hand was an envelope clearly filled with proof pictures. "How's business?"

"It's going well. Except for the thumb, I'm enjoying every minute of it." I held up my splint.

"Oh, that's right. I heard you were in an accident." She winced at my thumb. "How are you making fudge?"

"Sandy has to do it for a few weeks. I supervise, but it's not the same."

"I bet."

"Listen, I stopped by to see how Oliver is doing."

She paused and looked at me earnestly. "Why? Did you hear something?"

"I didn't see him around for a while. I hear he recently came back from some sort of trip?"

She scowled. "His father is angry because Oliver hasn't been taking any of his calls. The divorce didn't go that well and Oliver is a teen and mad at his dad. I tried to explain that, but there's no talking to the man."

"I'm sorry to hear that. Is that why Oliver was gone for a while?"

"Yes. The courts made me send him to his father's for a month as soon as school let out." She shook her head. "Oliver was with him four days before my ex sent him off to summer camp."

"What?" I blinked. "He made you send Oliver to stay with him and then he sent Oliver off? Was it a day camp?"

"No, it was an overnight camp," she said and I noted that her hands curled into fists. "Oliver called me after the first night and asked if he had to stay if he didn't want to be there so I sent him a plane ticket to come home. As far as I know, his father still thinks Oliver is at camp."

"That's so weird."

Cyndy shrugged. "My ex was trying to get back at me by taking Oliver and the courts didn't see it that way."

"Poor Oliver. I bet he's pretty angry right now."

"Wouldn't you be?" Cyndy asked.

"Yes, I would. One quick question. I know Oliver was back the night the pool house was set on fire."

"Are you implying he did that?" Her blue eyes flashed. "Because he would never."

"Oh, no." I raised my hands. "I'm not implying anything. I was wondering if he might have seen something that night."

"Oh. Sorry." Cyndy's shoulders dropped. She ran her free hand over her face. "I'm a little defensive when it comes to my boy. He's a teenager and that means he's no angel, but he's a good kid. He wouldn't do anything malicious."

"I know"—I put my hand on her arm—"but he may have a better idea of who would do such a thing. I mean, he hangs out with the other island teens, right? Maybe they know something."

She looked at me thoughtfully. "I'll ask him."

"Thanks. Let him know that I'm really hoping to bring him on part-time at the McMurphy next summer when he's sixteen. That is, if he's interested. I'll need someone to give Frances a break at the receptionist desk."

Cyndy smiled. "I'll let him know."

"Thanks," I said again. "I'll let you get to that nice looking family in the waiting area."

"The Gunthersons. They are so cute, aren't they? They come every year for their family portrait. Then put it on their Christmas card."

"I love repeat customers. You get to know them and they become part of your friends and family."

"I agree." She patted me on the shoulder. "Thanks for thinking about Oliver. I'll ask him if he saw or heard anything."

"One last thing. Did you see the calico cat that's been hanging around the back alley? If so, do you happen to know who it belongs to?"

"Oh, yes, I've seen it. I thought it was yours. I saw the food and water dishes on your fire escape."

"It's been hanging out and I couldn't let it starve. I'm going to catch it and take it to the vet and ensure that it's healthy."

"And you're keeping it, aren't you?" She winked at me. "It's a pretty cat. Let me know what you name her. Okay?"

"Are you sure you don't want her? Maybe Oliver?"

She stopped and thought about it. "You know, maybe having a pet would be good for Oliver. But I can't afford the vet and spay bills." She bit her bottom lip. "Sorry."

"I'll pay the bills and if Oliver wants the cat, that would be great. I already have Mal and I am pretty certain the health inspector would frown about my having another pet in the fudge shop."

"Sounds perfect," Cyndy said her eyes lighting up. "Thanks!"

I left out the front as she placed the envelope on the reception desk and then called the Gunthersons back to the studio for their photos.

With Cyndy's door always open, I wondered why

the cat hadn't gone inside the photo shop instead of the McMurphy in the first place. If Oliver took the cat, I would still get to see her. Cyndy and Oliver lived in the apartment above the photo shop—which meant the cat would be hanging out on their fire escape instead of mine.

"What did you find out?" Frances asked as I entered the McMurphy.

"Oliver left the island because his dad protested the custody situation and forced Cyndy to give Oliver up for the month after school let out. But after a week, Oliver was put into summer camp. He called Cyndy in tears and she brought him home. She's expecting her ex to get wise and come storming back for Oliver any day."

"I wouldn't hold my breath. That one was always all about himself."

"Did you talk to Mr. and Mrs. Castor?"

Mal jumped up to greet me with a wagging stub tail and a little pirouette. I bent down and patted her on the head and scratched behind her ears.

"I called Jessica. They went on a once-in-a-lifetime cruise to the Greek isles for their thirty-fifth wedding anniversary."

"Wow. How fun. Kind of funny, though, that they left our island for a series of Greek islands."

"Once you're an island person, you are always an island person," Frances said.

"Do they know anything about the fires?" I went to the counter and got Mal a treat from the treat jar. I made her sit and twirl and shake her paw before I gave her the treat. It was always good to keep her well-practiced with her tricks. Not that she would ever forget. Sometimes she pulled out her tricks just to entertain the guests and try to get them to give her a treat.

"They told me to ask Luke Archibald," Frances said.

"Why?"

"It seems that Luke was doing some exterior painting work for them near the site of the first fire at around the same time."

"Really?" I glanced at the map Liz had drawn. "What is out by Eagle Point Cave?"

"The Castors have a guest house out that way. It's really a one bedroom cabin that belonged to Jessica's brother. When he died, it went to her. They wanted to fix it up and sell it to finance their cruise so they called Luke to come out and spruce things up a bit."

"Interesting." I picked up a blue marker and put a star by the sight of the first fire. "We know he was doing work at the Oakton when this fire occurred, as well." I put a star by the pool house. "Then there is the fire in Luke's trash barrel. Do you think he was working near any of the other sites?"

"I think he was working in Harrisonville around the time of the Great Turtle Park fire, but I can't be positive. Let me call around and see what I can find out."

"Sure." I studied the map. If Luke was at four of the sites, we had a pattern. Enough of a pattern, anyway, to get Rex involved. I put the cap on the marker and put it away.

I had just been talking to Luke and he seemed like such a nice guy, always helpful. It didn't make sense. There hadn't been any anger in his eyes. Why would he set the fires? For insurance? No, the Castors would hold the insurance on their cottage and I know for sure Luke wouldn't see a cent of insurance from burning the pool house. So where was the motive?

We were going to have to dig a little deeper.

Chapter 20

We closed the fudge shop at six PM so that everyone could go out to see the fireworks. It was tradition to close it early. Papa Liam had loved fireworks and always insisted that we shut down for all three fireworks shows. It made good business sense. The streets emptied as people grabbed picnic baskets and headed out to their staked out tents and chairs and blankets on the shore or the schoolyard.

Mom had packed a huge picnic basket full of her homemade fried chicken, coleslaw, potato salad, vegetable platter and dip, biscuits, and fig cake for desert. Dad carried a cooler full of glass bottles with ice tea and sodas. I carried a Frisbee, a portable bocce ball set, and horseshoes. Mal carried her leash and followed beside me.

It felt like a mass exodus as everyone left for the part of the island with the best views of the fireworks. The fire department had parked a horse-drawn replica fire truck in the schoolyard where the fire chief had a gaggle of children enthralled as they tried on fire hats and climbed up on the vehicle, imagining chasing through the streets ready to start a bucket brigade to save the fort or any of the houses on the strip. His face was animated and his Irish storytelling was in full gear.

"Bruce makes a great storyteller," I said to Mom.

"His dad was great at it as well."

"That whole family could tell a fat tale and make you believe every word of it no matter how ridiculous it was," Dad said.

Our mood was light as children squealed and ran around in front of us with red, white, and blue streamers and poppers. Once twilight set, they would have sparklers and screaming chickens and replica tankers who would move a few inches and then send out a pop of smoke and noise from their long noses. Mal was a little skittish around the kids as they tended to not look where they were going and run over little dogs carrying their own leash.

Dad had staked out a very good spot and we set down our things. I tied Mal's leash to one of the poles of the overhead tarp and she was content to rest on the blanket Dad had put down to mark our spot.

Mom went to work setting out the food on the top of the basket, piling plates and cups and utensils on the blanket.

"Hey, can we join you?" Trent came up from behind with his sister Paige and her boyfriend in tow. Mal jumped up and Trent gave her hello pats.

"Sure," Dad said, puffing up his chest. "I take it I got a better spot than you. Next time you need to get here earlier."

Trent agreed, but I noticed that Paige nudged her boyfriend when he opened his mouth to correct my dad. I followed her boyfriend's gaze toward a site closer to the lakeshore where their parents sat in elegant chairs under a mosquito screened tarp. They had a buffet table filled with plates of food, a couple tall bar tables covered in linens and their place settings were white china and crystal wine glasses. A man in a chef coat worked at a stainless steel grill. In comparison, our little fete seemed lacking.

Trent came over and put his arm around my waist and gave me a quick kiss. "Thanks for letting us crash your party."

"There's plenty of food. Who's this?" Mom asked of Paige and her boyfriend.

"Mom this is Paige Jessop, Trent's sister," I said. "And her boyfriend . . ."

"Reggie." Paige rescued me and patted the man's chest covered in a pale blue polo . "Reginald Owens the third."

Reggie had that New England old money look. He had light brown hair cut close and preppy. His jaw was square and his eyes brown. His teeth were braces straight and glowingly white. At six foot two, wearing a polo shirt with a sweater tied around his shoulders and plaid Bermuda shorts, he looked like a Ken doll.

"Paige, this is my mother Ann McMurphy and my dad, Patrick McMurphy."

"The last time I saw you, you were ten years old and all about horses," Dad said and shook Paige's hand and then her boyfriend. "Reginald Owens, are you local?" Dad drew his brows together. "I don't remember the name."

"Reggie is from Long Island," Paige said. "We met

at my sorority's national meeting in New York this spring."

"My mother, grandmother, and sister were all members of the sorority," Reggie said with a grin. "They dragged me along for a family weekend."

"Looks like you're happy you went." Mom opened the cooler. "Drinks, anyone? We have wine and beer and ice tea and soda."

She poured wine and beer into clear plastic glasses. Knowing that there was crystal glassware at the Jessop tent did not mean our plastic was any worse. Seriously, who uses actual glassware at a picnic? Besides, Trent and the others had come over voluntarily.

"I've got extra chairs," Jenn said as she and Shane approached with their hands full of folding chairs. Mal rushed over to greet her the moment she was close enough for the leash to reach. "Hi Mal. Are you being a good doggie?" She patted Mal on the head.

Trent and Reggie were quick to take the chairs from Jenn and set them up for everyone.

"Don't sit before you have your food," Mom warned. "We're eating buffet style."

Before we had a chance to think, Mom had corralled us into some semblance of a buffet line with paper plates and plastic silverware in hand as we dished up the picnic food. Soon Sandy and her grandmother and the rest of her family walked by, but they, too, had seats on the lakeshore so they didn't stay.

It was one of those nearly perfect days with the soft breeze off the lake keeping us cool and the bugs to a minimum.

Paige and Reggie left after we finished eating and went to be with the Jessops. The sunset was a gorgeous red and orange and green then blue. I sat cross-legged on the blanket with Mal in my lap. Trent lounged on his side behind me, his hand around my waist. Mom and Dad sat in their chairs and held hands.

Jenn sat in Shane's lap and the local summer band began to play the "Star Spangled Banner." We all oohed when the first firework screamed into the air and then exploded with a bang as the last strains of music floated through the air.

Fireflies came out winking in and out with their green lighted tails. Mal left my lap and tried to catch one or two before the next firework went screaming up. It split into three and gave us red, white, and blue giant flowers. She decided it was safest to be in my lap. I bundled her up in a blanket and held her close as the fireworks grew closer together and filled the sky with sparkles and rockets and large blooms that fell safely to the lake underneath.

Halfway through the show, I caught Jenn's gaze and smiled and gave her a thumbs up. After all, she had found us the fireworks to replace the ones that were vandalized. She smiled and gave me two thumbs up back.

I didn't know what I was going to do next year when she moved back to Chicago for a high-paying job. I watched how Shane looked at her with so much caring in his gaze and my heart squeezed. Maybe I wouldn't be the only one to miss her at the end of the season. Maybe, just maybe, she would have a reason to come back next year.

The finale was a spectacular five solid minutes of

every kind of firework along with a dizzying array of colors and booming sounds. Mal whimpered in my arms and I knew that tomorrow I would tuck her safely into her crate in the McMurphy for the fireworks. She didn't understand the booms and bangs and the human excitement. I gave her a comforting squeeze and the sky, once full of light, shimmered back to a soft black. Stars popped out giving us the real show of the night.

People were tired as they packed up. Moms and dads carried sleeping children. Preteens ran through the darkness playing games of flashlight tag. The air was filled with the scent of sulfur and I tried not to think about the explosion that killed Rodney. Still, the smell brought it all back so clearly.

"You okay?" Trent asked. We stood and he held me in his arms.

"Yes." I laid my head on his broad warm chest. "The smell brought back the day Rodney died."

"Mal seems a little unnerved as well." Trent hugged us both close.

"I don't think she liked the fireworks as much as we did," I said.

"Good job on the fireworks, young lady." Mrs. Amerson and her husband Richard strode by. He carried a chair in both hands and a large umbrella under his arm. He wore a windbreaker jacket, a dark T-shirt, and light-colored Dockers slacks. It was difficult to distinguish colors in the darkness left after the fireworks, but his bright white hair shone in the night.

"Thank-you. It was a team effort." I pointed toward Jenn with my head and then glanced at Trent to let Mrs. Amerson know that while I would have taken all the responsibility if things had gone badly, I wouldn't take all the credit for the success.

"It shows." She gave a nod and walked off. She wore a light-colored sweater over a V-neck T-shirt, and long slacks. Her hair was pulled up into a severe bun. In her hands, she carried a single blanket that might have been a quilt. It was difficult to tell.

"Can we keep our stuff up for tomorrow's show?" Mom asked.

"No," I said. "The Star Spangled Fourth committee ensures that all blankets and tarps and markers are taken down. No one is allowed to stake out a spot for the Fourth until twelve-o-one AM. That way, every day, everyone has equal chance of staking out a nice spot."

"I think this spot works well," Dad said as he pulled the tarp down. "Does everyone else agree?"

"We do," Trent said and stepped over to help Dad remove the tarp from the poles and the poles from the ground.

"I'll try to get out here first thing in the morning and put it back up," Dad said as he put the rolled-up tarp into its carrying case.

"I'm working third shift or I'd offer to stake it out for you, Mr. McMurphy," Shane said.

"Not a problem. I'll set my alarm and get out here by six AM."

"Maybe you should set it for five AM," Mom said. "My guess is that there will be more people out for the fireworks tomorrow."

"Hi Allie," Cyndy Crumbly walked by with Oliver beside her. They were headed back toward town, both carried coolers with blankets rolled up on top. "Great show."

"Thanks," I said. "Hi Oliver."

He lowered his head and muttered something in return. I assumed it was a nice greeting.

"We'll talk later," I said to Cyndy, who nodded and bumped into her son.

"Come on, Oliver. Let's get home."

"Is that the Oliver whose name is on the arson board?" Dad asked me as he picked up the cooler.

"The very same." Holding Mal in her blanket, I picked up the remaining chair with my good hand. Trent helped by carrying the drink cooler I had brought out. "I don't think he's the fire starter. At least I don't want to think so."

"He certainly has reasons to be angry." Frances and Mr. Devaney had come up the trail behind us.

"Where were you two?" Dad asked. "I had a great spot."

"Douglas has a private place where he goes every year," Frances explained quickly. Her tone sounded excited and embarrassed at the same time.

If it weren't so dark out, I'd swear she was blushing.

"Is it big enough for all of us?" Dad asked. "We could be together tomorrow."

"It's quite small," Frances said, her tone growing warmer.

"I keep it small so that my students can't stumble in and ruin my enjoyment," Mr. Devaney said. "It's perfect for two."

"I like where we were today, Dad," I said in an attempt to rescue Frances from further embarrassment. It was clear they had enjoyed their secret space and alone time.

"I have to agree with Allie, Mr. McMurphy," Trent said. "This really was a great spot."

I wanted to kiss Trent for saying that. Frances's shoulders relaxed a bit.

"Okay," Dad said with pride in his voice. "I'll come out early tomorrow and secure us the same spot. Frances, you and Doug are welcome to join us."

"We'll consider it," Mr. Devaney said. "Good night."

"We need to get to bed," Mom said, linking her arms through Dad's. "Especially if you are getting up early to stake our claim. Good night, kids. Don't stay up too late."

Good night, Mrs. McMurphy," Trent said. We let them stroll ahead of us.

"I wonder when Frances and Mr. Devaney are going to come clean about their relationship. It's not like they're hiding anything from anyone . . . except maybe my dad."

Trent chuckled. He had his arm around me and I could feel the rumble of it that ran through his body. "Let them have their secret for a while. Maybe things are just too new for them to share."

"They've been dating longer than we have," I pointed out as Mal wiggled in my arms.

"Yes, well, I made my intentions clear and public from the start." He squeezed me. "Come on. Let's take this stuff back to the McMurphy while we still have some time to make out on your couch." He waggled his eyebrows and I felt the heat of a blush rush up my cheeks.

"Oh." All my thoughts melted into a pile of mush.

He leaned over and kissed me for good measure. It was a sweet and lingering kiss that promised more.

I noticed that the park had emptied and the air was quiet. The stars twinkled overhead and the scent of dew was on the air.

Mal squirmed in my arms and I realized I was holding her tight. When I loosened my grip, she leapt out of my arms, gathered up her leash, and raced off.

"Wait, Mal!" I called. She was not headed toward the McMurphy. Silly puppy. She knew the way home.

"I'll get her," Trent said and handed me the cooler. He took off after her in the night.

While I didn't have to worry about her getting hit by a car, I still didn't like the idea of her running off. Anything could happen. She could be run over by a carriage or fall into a pit or something.

Okay the pit thought was a bit dramatic, but that didn't stop the worry. I hurried after Trent as fast as I could encumbered by the cooler, chair, and blanket. It was hard to rush and juggle things with a splint on my thumb. "Mal, come back here!"

"Allie," Trent called from the shadows ahead of me. "Stop!"

The tone of his voice made me freeze in place. "Trent?"

"Don't come any closer. I mean it."

"Trent, I can't see you. What is going on?"

Mal barked.

"Do you have Mal?"

"Allie, listen to me carefully," Trent said. "Do not come any closer. Do you have your cell phone?"

"Yes," I said. "Don't you? What's going on?"

"I have Mal," he said, his words careful. "We are tangled in what might be a trip wire for what looks like a bomb."

"Oh, my, gosh, Trent." I took two steps toward them before I realized what I was doing.

"Allie," he said sternly. "Stop. Call 9-1-1. I can't see where you are and I can't see what other trip wires are around. I've got Mal. Call 9-1-1. Trust me, I don't want to be the last firework of the night."

Chocolate Chip Pecan Pie Fudge

4 cups pecans, chopped
2 cups mini dark chocolate chips
1½ cups packed dark brown sugar
1½ cups granulated sugar
1 cup half and half
3 tablespoon dark corn syrup
1 stick butter plus 1½ teaspoon butter for pan prep
2 teaspoon vanilla extract
½ teaspoon maple extract

Preheat oven to 350 degrees. Place the chopped pecans on a baking sheet and toast them in the oven for about 8 minutes, stirring halfway through. Remove from the oven and allow the pecans to cool.

Prepare a 9x9-inch pan by lining it with aluminum foil. Butter the foil with 1½ teaspoon butter. Place 2 cups of dark chocolate mini chips in the bottom of the pan.

In a large heavy-bottomed saucepan, combine the brown and granulated sugars, the half and half, and the corn syrup over medium heat. Stir until the sugars dissolve. Insert a candy thermometer, making sure it does not touch the bottom or sides of the pan, and bring to a boil, stirring occasionally. Allow the mixture to boil, until it reaches 238 degrees on the candy thermometer. This takes approximately 10 minutes. (I set the timer to help understand how long it takes for the temperature to reach this point.)

Once at 238 degrees, remove from heat. Take out the thermometer and stir in the butter, maple and vanilla extracts, and chopped pecans.

Stir the fudge vigorously with a heavy wooden spoon. (I break more spoons making fudge. It will get thick.) Stir constantly for 10-15 minutes until the fudge loses its shine and holds its shape.

Pour fudge into the prepared pan and smooth it into an even layer.

Refrigerate the fudge for at least 1 hour to set it.

Once set, remove the fudge from the pan using the foil as handles. Cut the fudge into small 1-inch pieces to serve.

Store fudge in an airtight container at room temperature for up to one week.

Chapter 21

I swallowed my panic, put down everything I was holding, and hit 9-1-1 on my phone. It was very late. I wasn't sure who would be on dispatch.

"9-1-1. Please state your emergency," said a male voice.

"Hi, this is Allie McMurphy," I said, trying to remain calm. "I'm with Trent Jessop. He is tangled in what he thinks is a trip wire for a bomb."

"Do not move!" commanded the male voice.

"We're not. I'm going to put you on speaker. I think Trent can hear you."

"This is Officer Pulaski. Where exactly are you?"

"We're behind the school. We packed up our things after the fireworks and were moving through the lawn toward the McMurphy. My puppy Mal got loose and Trent went after her and got tangled."

"Jessop, can you hear me?" Pulaski's voice boomed out of my phone.

"Yes." Trent's voice was strangely calm.

"I've got Officer Brown and Office Lasko on their

way there. Can you tell me exactly why you think there might be a bomb?"

"Yes, sir. I saw the dog go under some bushes, so I crouched down to get her. When I did, my knee hit a wire."

"Do you have a flashlight?"

"I have an app on my phone." Trent said. "I tucked the dog under my arm and hit my flashlight app. There is a bundle of something about a foot in front of me with wires running out of it. One of them is stretched across my knee."

"Okay," the dispatcher said. "I've got the bomb squad scrambling. It will take some time for them to helicopter over. Can you sustain your position?"

"I kind of have to," Trent said.

"Good man," Officer Pulaski said. "Allie, are there any other people nearby you?"

"No," I said, looking around. "It's just Trent and Mal and me." I touched my own flashlight app on my phone and swung it around. The ground near my feet was clear. Luckily, when I put the cooler and chair down there hadn't been any wires nearby. "It looks like we are behind the Hummingbird Cottage's backyard. There's about a hundred feet between us and the back fence and nothing much closer."

"Okay. Take it easy. Allie, can you see any wires where you are?"

I looked around my feet. "I don't see anything near me." I squatted and flashed the phone's light. "I can see where Trent went in. It's damp enough that his footprints show. Okay, I think there is a wire about eighteen inches in front of me."

"Don't move," Officer Pulaski ordered.

"Allie, don't move," Trent said at the same time.

"I'm not. You don't move, either."

Officer Brown and Officer Lasko came up behind me, walking in careful motion of one step in front of the other. They had powerful flashlights that illuminated the lawn.

"The officers are here," I said to both Trent and Officer Pulaski.

"Okay," Trent said. "Come on, Mal. Don't wiggle."

I could hear my puppy whining. She must have seen the new people approaching and wanted to run off to greet them.

"Mal, stay!" I ordered. The whining stopped.

"She isn't going anywhere," Trent said. "I've got a strong hold on her."

"Allie McMurphy?" Officer Brown called my name.

I turned and had the flashlight shone in my eyes. I covered my eyes, blinking against the red dots left by the light. "Yes. There is a wire about eighteen inches in front of me. Trent is two yards in front and to the left of me. His knee is on a trip wire."

"Oh, man," Officer Lasko said, her voice sincerely concerned, her face deeply shadowed. "Who would do this? We're just a few feet from where everyone was set up. Children were playing nearby."

"Pull it together," Officer Brown said. "We've got a couple people in trouble here." He took a straight line path to me. "Are you okay?"

"I'm fine, but Trent is in deep trouble."

"There's a brick of something with duct tape wound round it and several wires coming out of it," Trent said. "I've never seen a bomb in real life, but this sort of looks like one."

"Okay." Officer Brown raised his right hand in a *stop* motion. "Okay. We're going to assume that it is. Lasko, have dispatch get the fire department out here to evacuate this block and the next."

"Roger." She held out her hand. "Allie, come with me."

"I'm not going anywhere," I said sternly. "Trent and Mal are in danger."

"You being in danger does not help us," Trent called.

"I'm not leaving you."

"Yes, you are," Trent said calmly. "Charles, make her go."

Officer Brown took my elbow and raised me to my feet. "You have to go Allie, so we can concentrate on getting your guy and your dog safely out of this situation."

"Trent—"

"Go, Allie."

I let Charles turn me, his bright flashlight ensuring that our steps were clear of any other wires. We took three steps before Mal started crying. I froze. "It's okay, Mal." I glanced behind me. "I'm not going to leave you."

"You have to get to a safe distance," Officer Brown said.

"Mal will fight Trent if I leave. She could slip out of his grip and trip a wire."

"I won't let her go," Trent said.

"You may not have a choice. She's persistent."

"Okay, okay. Talk to your dog. Let her know you are not going anywhere."

"Charles—" Trent said the name like a curse.

"No one's going to die today."

"It's okay, Mal," I said as calm as possible. "Stay. Stay." The whining stopped. "Good girl. It's okay. Mommy's right here."

"This isn't getting us anywhere," Officer Lasko said.

"We need to all remain calm. Lasko, evacuate the Hummingbird and the other cottages in the vicinity. The bomb squad will be helicoptering in. Pulaski has them landing in the schoolyard. We need to have the scene secure for their arrival."

"Yes, sir." She turned and walked carefully back to the sidewalk.

"Trent, are you doing okay?" Officer Brown ran his flashlight in front of him and took a few steps toward Trent.

"I'm okay."

"Good. You stay okay. Can you get any phone pictures of the bomb?"

"I don't have a free hand, but I can try."

"No." Officer Brown took careful steps toward Trent. "Don't try. Keep your hands on the dog and stay as still as possible."

After what felt like forever, the fire department arrived. They carefully set up hoses in preparation for fire. Rex showed up with four very large lights on five-foot-tall tripods.

I sat down on my spot and spoke softly to Trent and Mal while the lights were set up in a perimeter. "Hey Trent. Thanks for going after Mal. I may not have noticed the wire."

"She's a good dog," Trent said.

They turned on the lights one by one until the area was bright as daylight. I could hear a crowd of people in the distance.

"Keep those people back," Rex shouted and the firemen scrambled.

From where I sat, I could see Trent's back. He was down on his knees. Mal's tail wagged as she was tucked under his right arm. I couldn't see around him. I didn't want to see. I'd already lived through two explosions. I didn't want to experience a third.

"Allie," Liz called my name.

I turned my head to see her standing beside the fire truck. "Liz, back up!"

"What is going on? They're saying there might be a bomb?"

"Yes." I looked at her. "What if the arsonist is actually making bombs?"

Liz drew her darkly winged brows together. "Maybe . . ."

"It's got to be all connected. But why put a bomb in random bushes near an area where people are gathered to play and watch fireworks?"

"Terrorism?" Liz asked.

"No, terrorism doesn't make any sense. We're a little island. Not exactly a target like New York City or even Chicago."

"Maybe the bomber knew you were in the area and counted on Mal finding the bomb."

"Wait. Do you think this might be a way to get rid of me and Mal?"

"Maybe," Liz said.

"Then why not just put a bomb in the McMurphy?" I paused and stood. "Liz, call Jenn. We need to get everyone out of the McMurphy."

"I'm on it." Liz grabbed her phone and disappeared behind the fire truck.

"What are you thinking about, Allie?" Trent asked.

"There may be a bomb at the McMurphy. If this is an attempt to get rid of me, then it makes more sense to place a bomb there than here where I may or may not have tripped it."

"How could they put a bomb in the fudge shop?" Trent asked.

"We closed down for the fireworks. Everyone was here tonight. That means—"

"No one was at the McMurphy," Trent finished.

"Exactly." I wrapped my arms around my waist. "My parents are there. Jenn is there. I have a hotel full of guests." My voice broke and tears welled up in my eyes.

"Don't think about that," Trent said.

"Allie," Rex said as he came around from where he was talking to the firemen. "Liz told me what you think might be going on at the McMurphy. I've sent some firemen over there to walk through the building and make sure it's safe."

"Thanks," I said in a whisper. The spit in my mouth had dried up, leaving me with a dry mouth and scratchy throat. "Who would do this?"

"Someone with a lot of anger," Rex said. "Charles tells me that you are staying here to keep Mal from getting away from Trent and tripping wires."

"Yes." My stomach was in my throat. "Isn't that right, Mal?" Her stubby tail wagged brightly under Trent's arm. I turned to Rex. "We have to get them out of there."

"We're going to do just that," Rex said, his blue eyes serious. "The chopper is on its way."

Within moments, the loud sound of helicopter blades whipping through the air filled my ears. The copter landed in the schoolyard and four men dressed in full bomb gear got out.

The noise was loud and I glanced over to see Mal trembling and squirming. "It's okay, Mal. Stay. Stay with Trent. Please stay."

I have to say if I didn't know those were guys in the suit coming from that loud noisy bird, I'd freak out, too. It was all too much for my puppy. Mal burst out of Trent's arms and streaked straight for me. "No!"

The whole scene stopped. People literally held their breath. Mal could fly when scared and fly she did, barely touching the ground and leaping over two more trip lines straight into my lap.

In the next instant, everyone reacted. I cried and held my puppy. Trent turned to look at me with fear frozen to his face. His jaw was tight as if bracing himself for the coming explosion. When nothing happened, his expression turned to pure relief and I swear there were tears in his gorgeous eyes.

Officer Brown, who stood near Trent, had thrown his arm up to cover his face. He slowly put it down and turned to me with an incredulous look.

Rex rushed to me, grabbed me and Mal, and pulled us out of the pool of light and back an entire block behind the fire truck. He muttered something dark and dangerous under his breath.

Mal bathed my face with kisses, curious over the taste of the tears that ran freely down my face. My legs trembled, but I kept moving until Rex stopped and lowered us to the ground next to George Marron.

"Take care of her," Rex said and went back to the darkness and the pool of light.

All I could see from there was the large dome of

the light in the distance. George did a quick check of my heart and my eyes.

"I'm fine," I said through the tears.

"Sure." George put a blanket around my shoulders as I started to shake.

Jenn appeared next to me. "Honey, give me Mal. Okay?"

I let her take Mal's leash and pull my wayward puppy out of my arms. "Jenn, are you okay? Are my parents okay? Is the McMurphy okay?"

"I'm fine." Jenn patted Mal on the head. "Shane and I were in the lobby when the police came in. Your parents are good. They are with the rest of the guests in their robes a block from the McMurphy. When I heard about the bomb I came straight away. What happened?"

"Mal got away from us and when Trent went after her, he came face-to-face with a bomb. Jenn, there were trip wires everywhere."

"It's going to be okay." She put her hand on my shoulder. "The police and fire departments are doing all they can."

"Trent is still in harm's way," I said.

"Allie, thank goodness you are all right," Paige Jessop said as she came toward us. Reggie walked by her side. "Where's Trent?"

I swallowed hard. "He's near the bomb."

"What?" She started out in the direction of the light. Reggie grabbed her arm. In the next moment, there was a very large boom. Everyone instinctively ducked.

I screamed a little. Mal jumped into my lap. I leapt to my feet. "Trent!" I was off and running before I could think. In fact, the whole crowd ran with me. We came into site of the pool of light. Rex and Officer Brown were walking toward the fire truck with Trent safely between them.

"Oh, thank goodness!" I threw myself on Trent and hugged him and kissed his face, tears streaming down my own. "I heard the explosion."

"They brought in a robot. It took the tension on my wire and I got the heck out of there just in time as the motion caused the bomb to go off." Trent held me close and I could feel him tremble and his heart race.

"This really is a crime scene now," Rex said. "You people all need to get back. Lasko!"

She stepped up and pushed the crowd back as Rex and Officer Brown walked back toward the lights and the firemen who were hosing everything down.

"You need to be checked out," Paige said as she grabbed Trent's free arm and wiggled her way in to get a hug. "Come on."

We walked back to the ambulance. George's helper cleared the crowd of curious bystanders. The light from the back of the ambulance showed how pale Trent's skin was. His lips were blue. He had a few cuts and scratches from the explosion but was pronounced healthy except for the shock.

I couldn't keep my hands off him. What I really wanted to do was crawl up in his lap and feel his arms around me. It was as if he read my mind. He pulled me into his lap and George draped a blanket around both of us as we clung to each other.

"Rex wants you two here for questioning before he lets you go," Officer Lasko said.

"What about the McMurphy?" I asked her.

"The bomb squad is going through the building. They found a suspicious package near the front door."

I closed my eyes against the thought as anger rushed through me. My entire world was threatened tonight. It made little things like not pleasing the Star Spangled Fourth's committee seem inconsequential.

Frances came out of the crowd. She wore a trench coat over her night clothes. "I was getting ready for bed when I heard the commotion. What happened?"

"There was a bomb," Jenn said. "Mal found it."

"A bomb?" Frances had a flash of anger in her eyes. "This has gone too far."

"They found a package in the McMurphy as well," I said. "This fight has gotten very personal."

Trent gathered me closer to him. "There is no way the bomb under the bushes was directed at anyone in particular. It was simply in a random place as if the builder was hoping to catch someone but didn't care if it was a rabbit or a passerby."

"I suppose the bomber could have been a kid," I said, tears rushing back down my cheeks stinging my chapped skin. "A kid experimenting, maybe?"

"What kid thinks like that?" Jenn asked.

"This bomb might have been a distraction from the McMurphy." Liz was all business as she approached. "They found two bombs at the McMurphy, one inside near the fudge shop entrance and the second on the fire escape outside your door."

"Oh, no. The cat!" I nearly jumped up, but Trent tugged me back down.

"The cat's fine. I've got her. It was going to be a surprise for you. I lured her into my arms and got her to St. Ignace to the vet today. They're going to spay her and give her shots and such. I was going to bring her home to you the day after the Fourth."

"That would be tomorrow," Jenn said, looking at her watch.

Mr. Devaney arrived, tugging his jacket on over his under shirt. It was clear that he, too, had been getting ready for bed. "Is everyone all right?"

"We're good," Trent said.

"They found two possible bombs at the McMurphy," Frances told him.

Mr. Devaney scowled. "We left the arson board in the lobby. Whoever is doing this must have seen their name on the list and gotten scared."

A shiver ran down my back. I'd forgotten all about our arson board in the lobby. It meant that the arsonist, now bomber, had done more than left packages at my door. They had been in my home.

Chapter 22

For the second time this season, the McMurphy was a crime scene. Thankfully, all the guests felt safe enough to stay. No one wanted to check out immediately.

"After all," Mrs. Hamish said. "There was a bomb in the park. We don't know that there aren't bombs everywhere. Here, we know that the bombs are gone." She patted my hand and winked. "Safest place on Mackinac."

"We wouldn't want to be anywhere else," Mr. Jonas said. His wife Laura and their two kids, Joy and Stevie nodded in agreement.

"Everyone gets a free pound of fudge," I said. "It's the least I can do."

The lobby emptied as the guests went back to their rooms.

Rex studied the arson board thoughtfully.

Trent sat on the couch, facing the board with Mal in his lap. His broad capable hands stroked her fluffy fur. Somehow, she knew he needed comforting and made it her job to see that he got it.

Mom sat in the settee, her bathrobe clutched in her hands. Dad paced the length of the lobby in his striped pajamas and plaid bathrobe.

"This has gone beyond too far, don't you think, Manning?" Dad said, his voice stern. "I need to know that my family is safe here."

"Or what?" I asked from my place on the couch next to Trent. "You can't close the McMurphy. I own it."

"No, you run it," Dad said. "The family owns it and I am the head of this family. I won't let you stay here and get hurt."

"Calm down, dear," Mom said. "The family has been safe on this island for over one hundred years."

"This is different. This is our only daughter we're talking about. If we had a son—"

"Stop right there," Mom interrupted and stood. Her face was pinched in anger. "A woman can do the very same things as a man."

"This isn't about equal rights," Dad said, flinging his arms. "This is about some maniac out there trying to blow our kid up. If Allie were a man, you can darn well know that a bomber would think twice before pulling the stunt they pulled tonight."

"I won't let anything happen to her." Trent's voice was deep and sincere.

I squeezed his hand. Mal rested her head on his chest as if to say she would take care of him, too.

"When did you put this up in the lobby?" Rex asked, his attention still on the board.

"Yesterday," Mom answered.

"Liz came over," I explained. "She thought she

had an idea of who did it and was explaining her theory."

"Who was here when you discussed this?"

"Me, Mom, Liz," I said, counting on my fingers trying to remember where everyone sat. "Frances, Mr. D, Jenn . . ." Mal put her paw on my arm. "Mal," I said with a smile. "Oh, and Sandy."

"No one else?" Rex asked. "Not a guest or a fudge shop customer?"

"No," I said, thinking back. "It was one of those down times. We had finished the demonstration and the fudge shop was empty. The guests had checked out and it wasn't time for the check in yet."

"This is a listing of fires back to February?" Rex asked as he tilted his head to look at the map.

"Yes," Mom said. "Liz had a list of people who were on Mackinac Island when the first four fires happened, then were off the island during the down period, and then back on the island when the fires started up again."

"Henry Schulte is on this list," Rex said. "I had him in custody when the shed fire happened."

"There are two theories there," I said. "The first is that the shed fire was set to slow burn and could have been set prior to your arresting Henry."

"I'll check with the fire chief but I don't think that's likely." Rex shook his head and crossed his arms. "What's the second?"

"That Henry has a partner or accomplice," Mom said.

"In which case, the whole on-island, off-island theory is out the window," I added. "That's when we decided to ask the people on the list about where they went and why they came back."

"This is not your investigation," Rex said, his face stern. "You are not professionals and someone could get hurt."

"Someone almost got hurt, anyway," Dad pointed out.

"All we were doing was asking our friends and neighbors about their trips." Jenn came downstairs with an overnight bag. Shane followed her.

"Where are you off to?" Mom asked.

I sent her a look that it was none of her business, but she sent me a look saying it most certainly was her business.

"Shane's taking me off the island for tonight."

"The ferries aren't running this late," Mom said.

"I have an in with the helicopter pilot," Shane said with a grin. He pushed his dark framed glasses up his nose. He wore a T-shirt that had TESLA VS. EDISON emblazoned on it. The two inventors fought it out with electricity.

"We have to go if we're going to make our ride," Jenn said with a grin and a wave of her hand. "See you later. Happy Fourth of July!"

"Are you coming back for the parties tomorrow?" Mom called after her.

"*Today* is the Fourth, Mrs. McMurphy," Jenn smiled. "Allie gave me the day off. Good night!"

And out the door they went.

"I'm surprised you didn't hold her for questioning," Dad said to Rex.

"Shane told me that they were out walking when the bombs were found. They didn't see anything."

"Shane seems like a nice young man," Mom said. "Is Jenn serious about him?"

"Mom." I shook my head.

"Do you think the bomber saw this list and got nervous?" Trent asked Rex. "Or do you think he was simply mad because Allie and Mal have called in two of his fire sites?"

Rex paused for a moment and let out a long breath. "It could be either."

"If you had to hazard a guess, which would it be?" Dad asked.

"I'd guess the arsonist saw this board."

Dad slumped down on the arm of Mom's chair. "I was afraid of that."

"That means that whoever is doing this has been inside the McMurphy in the last twenty-four hours and not just to deliver packages," I said.

"The package at the front door was left by a porter," Rex said. "Frances identified the kid as Oliver Crumbly."

"Oh, no. Not Oliver," I put my hand on my mouth.

"Frances said Oliver told her the box was forgotten and left on the dock so the dock supervisor told him to deliver it. The box was marked COCOA so Frances told him to leave it at the opening to the fudge shop. That was where you usually leave your candy-making supplies."

"That's true," I said, "but my deliveries always come on Monday and Thursday. I'm surprised Frances didn't think something was off."

"He came as they were closing up for the fireworks," Rex said. "I'm sure she had other things on her mind."

"Oliver is on the list," Mom pointed out.

"I went to see Cyndy about him earlier today. She said he was having trouble with his dad." I looked at Trent. "I offered Oliver the cat. I thought perhaps it would give him a pet to confide in and help him with his anger."

"Anger issues are a hallmark of arsonists," Rex said. "So is being a teenage boy."

I shook my head. "I don't see Oliver doing that. I mean, if he blew up the McMurphy, then his own home would be damaged, as well. It's not his mom he's angry with."

"I'll have a talk with him," Rex said. "Maybe he knows more than we think."

"We can't discount him as the arsonist," Dad said. "He fits the pattern. Do you know why he was off the island when the fires stopped?"

"His dad went to court and got custody of Oliver for a month."

"But he wasn't gone a full month," Mom said.

"No, after a week, his father put him in summer camp. Oliver hated camp and called his mom. Cyndy sent him a plane ticket and brought him home."

"You could check with the camp," Dad said to Rex. "See if they had any unexplained fires."

"I'll ask Cyndy what camp he went to," Rex agreed and wrote in his notebook.

"You can cross the Castors off the list," I added. "Frances said they were concerned about the fire . . . no wait! She said the Castors told her that Luke Archibald was working on a summer rental they had near Eagle Point Cave when the first fire broke out."

"Wasn't he also working on the pool house when that fire broke out?" Mom asked.

"Yes." I looked at Rex. "We were going to see if he was doing any jobs near any of the other sites—besides the one in his trash barrel."

"He's working at the Hummingbird this week," Rex said. "I saw him out on the picnic table eating lunch. He said it was a good job. The owners are repainting the entire interior of the cottage. They're thinking about selling the property and wanted to spruce things up."

"There you go," Dad said. "Another suspect."

"I don't get it," Trent said with a shake of his head. "Luke's an okay guy. He's always smiling and joking around. I don't see him as the brooding angry type."

"And he certainly won't get any insurance money from the places that were set on fire," I added. "He doesn't fit the typical profile of an arsonist, either. Does he fit with a bomber?"

"I'll figure that out," Rex said. "What's going on with the rest of the people on this list?"

"We hadn't gotten that far," I said.

"I'm going to take this board in to the station and have it printed. It might just give us a clue as to who was angry enough to try to blow up the McMurphy."

"Okay," I agreed and stood. "Do you need help with that?"

"No." He snapped on gloves and lifted the board from its easel. "My advice to you all is to stop investigating. Leave it to the professionals. Okay?"

We all nodded. I wondered how many of us had our fingers crossed behind our backs.

"Get some rest. It's going to be a crazy day." Rex left.

I locked the doors behind him. My parents said good night and went to their room.

"Can you stay?" I asked Trent. He stood in the lobby with Mal in his arms. "I don't want to be alone tonight."

"Your couch is pretty comfortable," he agreed. "I know I'd feel better keeping an eye on you and Mal."

"Thanks," I said and we walked upstairs arm in arm. "I'm pretty tired of explosions."

"Yeah. Me, too."

Chapter 23

The Fourth of July dawned warm and bright on the island that time forgot. The apartment windows were all open to let in the cool lake breezes. The sounds of gulls and the crash of waves came in on the dew-scented air.

I got up at the sound of the back door of the McMurphy closing. A quick glance out the bedroom window showed me that it was my dad with picnic tarp, chairs, and blankets in hand. After last night's fiasco, he was still going to stake out a spot for tonight's fireworks. I watched as his jeans and T-shirt covered body disappeared down the alley.

I was restless and hurt in places I didn't know I had. It made me wonder how Trent was. I trotted into the kitchen with Mal at my heels. I wore silk boxers and a navy T-shirt. My hair was wild, but I didn't care. If Trent was serious about being my boyfriend, he'd have to see me with bed head sometime.

I poured kibble into Mal's bowl and started the

teakettle for my French press coffee. I ground the beans fresh for every pot. It wasn't because I was some kind of coffee purest. It was because I read somewhere that some coffees weren't all coffee. They had fillers in them. The only way to know you were drinking the real thing was to buy the beans and grind them yourself. So I did.

The sound of the grinder made Trent groan. I glanced over to see him sprawled out on my couch. His head was buried in the pillow I had given him. The sheet under him was rumpled and the blanket slipped down to expose his bare broad back. He had one bare foot on the floor and the other hung over the arm of the couch.

For a moment, my heart stopped. It was a sight I would hold in my mind for the rest of my life. Then Mal ruined it by jumping up on his back and licking his face.

"What the—" Trent opened his eyes and sat up. His hair stood up on one side. Mal jumped into his lap, put her front paws on his broad chest, and licked his whisker-covered cheeks. "Whoa, down girl." He pushed Mal to the side and glanced up to see me staring and then grinned. "Good morning."

"Hi," was all I could get out of my mouth. My brain had dropped below my waist and the spit dried up in my mouth.

He got up and stretched. He wore only dark blue boxer briefs.

I decided to concentrate on the coffee. Besides, the kettle was whistling. By the time I put the grinds in the press and added the hot water, Trent was sidling up to the breakfast bar wearing his jeans and a white T-shirt.

"You didn't have to get dressed on my account," I said as I stirred the coffee and then placed the top on it and the quilted cozyaround it to steep.

"My Mom taught me that it's polite to get dressed before any meal," he said, looking down at the wrinkled T-shirt stretched taut across his well-muscled chest. "I hope you don't mind a few wrinkles."

"Wrinkles look good on you." I went around to plant a kiss on his whiskered cheek.

"Wow, kisses from two lovely ladies first thing in the morning and French press coffee. I might have to sleep over more often."

"You'll scandalize the neighbors," I teased and moved to pull down two fat white mugs. I had to admit I was getting pretty good at using my left hand. The splint on my right thumb barely slowed me down . . . except when there was fudge to be made. Then I didn't even try. My ego wanted to keep going, but my teachers ingrained in me that when dealing with hot sugar, you didn't take any chances. If you got burned, you might be out of your career entirely. I wasn't going to take that kind of chance.

I put the mugs on the counter and let Trent pour the coffee. "Sorry to get you up early."

"It's the Fourth," Trent said with a shrug and added cream to both of our mugs. "I have to get to the stables early so I have time to take my girl out for a picnic and some fun and games at the fire department."

"Oh, no no no." I wound my fingers around the mug of coffee. "I'm not playing any games. No more three-legged races and definitely no greasy pole for this girl." I held up my splint. "I'm wounded. All I want is a nice shady blanket, a good picnic lunch with a nice bottle of wine, and my boyfriend to share it."

Mal whined and jumped up on me. I laughed. "Oh, and Mal, of course."

"Of course," Trent said. "Sounds like a plan. So, want to go for a bike ride and find a nice quiet picnic spot in the park?"

"Yes. I have to check on Sandy and make sure all our guests have fudge delivered to their rooms to make up for last night. What time do you want to meet?"

"Let's meet at one. That gives us a few hours before we have to join the families for the dinner picnics and fireworks."

I kissed him on the cheek. "Sounds perfect."

A couple hours later, I was downstairs in the fudge shop watching Sandy do a demonstration.

She was good. She had the crowd enthralled. She asked for my help and together we lifted the copper kettle and poured the liquid fudge onto the cold marble slab of the cooling table. "You'll notice the metal frame. Not every table has one, but we use this one so that we can pour the candy on the table and not worry that it will spill over at this critical point when the sugar mixture is super hot."

We set the empty kettle in the pot holder where it was left to cool before it was cleaned. "We use marble because the cold stone wicks away the heat slowly and evenly. We will let the candy cool on the table for ten to fifteen minutes. That's why you see me pouring the candy but the demonstration isn't scheduled until ten-fifteen." She pointed at the hands of the little paper clock on the candy counter that said NEXT DEMONSTRATION and the hands of the clock were set at 10:15. "While we wait, you can see that today's specials are as American as apple pie, and cherry pie, and coconut cream, and lemon meringue."

The crowd chuckled.

"We'll take orders while the candy cools," I said. Some of the people surged forward and I grabbed a prebuilt pink fudge box and paper square and filled the order of the couple in front of me.

Meanwhile, Sandy filled the order of a single mom with three little kids hanging off her. The kids were wide-eyed and rosy-cheeked. Mom didn't even look the tiniest bit frazzled. I admired women who could do that.

The time flew while we were busy serving up fudge. The timer buzzed and Sandy and I raised our hands like they do at the end of a televised competition.

"That's it for the moment folks as it's time to continue our demonstration. Sandy . . ." I motioned it was all hers and took a seat on a metal stool between the candy counter and the cooling table so that I could watch from the customer's point of view.

Sandy washed her hands and dried them on a paper towel. "As we said when we poured the hot candy, the marble table is a special cooling table. The marble wicks the heat away slowly and evenly. Then, to encourage the process, the marble is cooled from the bottom with water. The table is prepared with butter or coconut oil depending on the type of fudge. We pour the hot liquid candy on the table to begin the cooling process. Now you'll see as I remove the frame that the fudge has begun to thicken. It's much less likely to drip off." She pulled a long handled stir paddle off the wall. "These paddles have long wooden handles that do not transfer heat so that I can safely begin to stir the fudge as it cools."

She stuck the metal paddle end into the fudge and scraped it off the bottom and flipped it onto itself. "We stir the fudge from one end and then the other. As we do that, we add air to the liquid, making it nice and creamy."

She flipped one end and then walked around to flip the other. "We want to be careful not to let any of the fudgy goodness run off the table. This stage of hand whipping goes on for roughly eight to ten minutes. As you become more experienced with scraping and turning and folding fudge, you get a feel for the density of the chocolate." She silently turned the table a couple times. "Do you see how it's stacking up on itself and maintaining its height? When I first started, it would simply slip back down to the original height, but as I fold in air and the candy cools it starts to take shape.

"When it is able to stand three or four inches high, we know it's cool enough to start to shape the loaf. Before we do that, though we add the extras. This is pecan pie fudge, so we take the dark chocolate base and throw on chopped pecans." She put the long handled stirrer in the sink and reached for a measured white bucket of chopped pecans. Then she layered them on the top of the fudge. "Next we add a layer of salted caramel to help give it the taste of pecan pie." She poured a thin ribbon of caramel custard. "Now we take out a small spatula and start to fold the pecans and caramel into the shape of the classic fudge loaf you see in the counter in front of you."

She quickly scraped and flicked the fudge, expertly giving it the fudgy wave shape as she walked around the table. "Things go very fast at this stage. You see how quickly it's setting up?"

I looked at the crowd and smiled at the little kids who were standing still, in awe, and the little girl who was a tad too short who kept jumping up to see better. A blond-haired little boy sat on his dad's shoulders, watching through the window glass. This was the reason I loved the McMurphy. I lived for these moments when we passed on our heritage of candy making to the next generation of Fudgies. These demonstrations made impressions and lasting memories.

"Finally," Sandy went on, "we take a long buttered knife and cut approximately one-quarter pound sections and plate them on the trays and fill the candy counter." She cut the sections carefully and stood them in classic rows.

I got up and picked up a white platter and snipped off demonstration pieces and put them on the tray. Then I took the tray to the crowd to offer up free tastes. "The pecan pie fudge is part of this month's American pie fudges," I said as greedy hands, young and old, grabbed the just set, still warm fudge from the tasting plate.

My smile grew as I watched the expressions of the people sampling the fudge. The kids popped it in and chewed fast and nodded, more enthralled with the process than the candy. The adults, on the other hand, understood the dark chocolate pecan pie taste. Their expressions went from eager to eyes closed in pure enjoyment.

Yes, that was exactly why I loved being a fudge maker and continuing the McMurphy tradition.

The orders went fast and furious after that. People were grabbing fudge and hurrying off. The games at the fire department had begun. The streets were a crowded party of Fudgies and locals, laughing and shopping and enjoying the old-fashioned sights and sounds of a Fourth of July with no cars. Horse and buggies vied with bicycles for space on the roads. People walked five and six across as they moved like an endless wave from the ferry docs and on down Main Street.

"Great job," I said to Sandy when the crowd finally cleared. "I'm so happy to have you on my staff."

She nodded. "There is something about the crowds, isn't there? I think it's the kids."

"No, it's the grownups," I said. "The little kids may be seeing it for the first time, but it's the grownups who are remembering what it is like to be a kid again on the Fourth of July."

In the distance, firecrackers popped. Kids laughed and jumped up and down. The cannon boomed on the hour. As the door opened and closed, the sounds of the crowds carried on the wind along with the smell of the lake and sun-warmed vegetation.

"All right. Time for you to take off, Allie," Sandy said, her voice full of authority. "It's your Independence Day. Go have fun. I've got the fudge shop covered and my cousin April has the front desk."

"It's your Independence Day, too. Many indigenous people fought for the United States."

Sandy smiled. "We were already independent. We were fighting against our enemies."

"The ones who sided with the English?" I asked.

"The ones who were trying to kill us," Sandy said. "Now go. I know you have plans."

"Thank-you," I said. "The police are stationed at the front and the back of the McMurphy to ensure we don't have any bombs nearby."

"It'll be okay." She gently turned me toward the door. "I will handle the fudge shop until it closes at six. My cousin has the front desk until then. I'm sure it will be boring. Everyone will be at the picnic and fireworks."

I went upstairs to get ready for my picnic when there was a knock at the back door. Mal raced to the door barking. I peered out to see Trent standing there. "You're early," I said as I opened the door.

The man was drop dead gorgeous in his turquois polo shirt, khaki shorts, and deck shoes.

"I brought you a present," he said with a smile on his face. He brought a cat carrier out from behind his back.

Mal stood on her hind legs to smell the carrier. The cat inside was bored by her aerobatics.

"Is that the kitty?" I asked and peered inside to see the beautiful dark eyes of the calico cat.

"Yes." He set the carrier on the breakfast bar to be at eye level. "She is healthy and caught up on her shots."

"She is wearing a cone," I noted.

"She has been spayed and must be kept quiet for a few days."

"Oh, dear. Quiet does not really happen around

here." Mal was pawing at my leg to get a closer look. "Do I . . . can I take her out of the carrier?"

"Let's leave her in there while we go on our picnic."

I filled the water holder that hung on the outside of the carrier. The water holder's mouth was metal with a bead inside that when pushed aside the water would be accessible but not drip on the cat. "Does she need to eat?"

"I have some kibble," Trent said and pulled a small baggie out of his pocket. He poured the kibble into a tiny feeder.

"What am I going to do with her? I can't have a cat in the fudge shop." I waggled my fingers in the carrier and scratched the top of her head. "But she is so pretty."

"I thought you said you were going to see if Oliver would take her."

"As long as Oliver isn't our bomber," I said with a sigh.

Trent drew his eyebrows together. "You really think he might be?"

"No. I can't imagine that boy hurting anyone. I know he's a bit moody, but all teenagers are and he's dealing with his parents fighting and their divorce."

"Let's give the kitty some time to recoup and Rex time to find the bomber before we worry about what to do with her, okay?"

"Okay." I gave Trent a hug. "Thank-you for catching her and getting her to the vet and taking good care of her."

He hugged me back and gave me a nice kiss. "It

was my pleasure," he said a few inches from my lips. "I know that you were worried about her."

"I was. I hate to see a beautiful animal lost and homeless. Mal was worried, too. Weren't you Mal?"

She barked.

Trent shook his head with a smile. "Mal thinks she's going to get a treat. Isn't that right Mal?"

Mal barked.

We both laughed.

I got a small treat off the counter and made Mal do her tricks before I let her have the treat. Then I picked up the cat carrier. "I'll put her in a nice quiet spot." I moved her to the corner of the living room with a view outside. "Wait. What about a litter box?"

The door to the apartment opened and Jenn walked in. "Oh, is that our kitty?" She made a beeline to the carrier.

"Yes," I said. "Trent had her spayed and she needs to be quiet for a few days."

"Hi baby." Jenn opened the carrier and pulled the coned cat out and held her carefully. She looked accusingly at me. "You weren't going to leave her in that carrier were you?"

"I thought it would keep her safe and quiet."

"With no access to a litter box?" Jenn frowned at me.

I winced. "I'm a bad cat mother."

Mal was up on her hind legs sniffing at Jenn to let her see the cat. The cat on the other hand watched Mal with disdain. Her tail twitched ever so slightly. Then suddenly, she smacked Mal on the nose.

"Hey!" I said.

Mal dropped to all fours.

Jenn laughed and held the cat close and scratched her behind the ears. "I guess you told her who was boss. Do we have a name for the cat?"

"I thought I would leave that to Oliver."

"Oliver?" Jenn looked at me confused.

"I can't keep a cat." I stuck my hands in the pockets of my black cotton pedal pushers. My white sailor top with black trim floated around my shoulders. "It isn't safe with the hot sugar in the fudge shop. So I asked Cyndy if Oliver would like to have a pet."

"Oliver, the skulking boy next door?" Jenn asked. "That Oliver?"

"Yes. He's going through some tough times and he needs a pet. Cyndy said she thought he would like to have a cat."

Jenn petted the cat as it curled up contented in her lap. "Good luck with that. You can't just give a cat away. Cats choose you or they don't. I think this one has chosen you."

"Looks like she prefers you," Trent pointed out.

Jenn laughed. "I do love cats." She picked up the cat and squished it next to her face. "And you're such a pretty kitty, aren't you? Yes, you are."

Mal came over by me and whined. It was my turn to laugh. "Mal says you can't love on someone else without including her."

The cat looked pleased that it clearly had an advantage in the household.

Jenn and Trent laughed.

"New sister problems," Trent said.

"We can't get too attached," I said, my tone firm.

"It would be dangerous for a cat in the fudge shop. I won't see any animals hurt."

"You could just keep her in the apartment," Jenn suggested.

"How fair is that?" I argued. "We let Mal roam the place."

Mal did a little twirl to show that she knew I was talking about her.

"No, the best thing is to find her a new home."

"Let's hope Oliver thinks the same thing." Jenn rubbed the cat's head. "Let's hope."

Lemon Meringue Fudge

½ cup butter, melted; plus 1 teaspoon to prep pan (coconut oil is a good nondairy substitute)
¼ cup milk (almond milk is a good nondairy substitute)
1 3.4 ounce package of lemon instant pudding and pie filling
1 teaspoon vanilla
6 cups powdered sugar, sifted

Butter 8x8x2-inch cake pan.

Mix butter, milk, unprepared instant pudding, and vanilla. Add powdered sugar 1 cup at a time until you reach the desired thickness.

Scoop into prepared pan. Pat until smooth. Score into 1-inch pieces with butter knife.

Refrigerate for 2-3 hours until set.

Break into 1-inch pieces along score and serve in individual paper candy cups or on a platter. Store leftovers in covered container in the refrigerator.

Enjoy!

Chapter 24

Trent and I found a quiet shaded spot in Great Turtle Park. I rested on the blanket we brought and he rested his head on my stomach. Mal cuddled near us.

"You're not relaxing." Trent's deep voice rumbled through my body. "We had a nice meal, shared a bottle of good wine, and have the best lazy day company ever. You should be more relaxed."

I pillowed my head on my crossed arms. "I keep thinking about yesterday's bombs." I reached down and stroked his dark hair. "I almost lost you. If the bomber had been successful, I would have lost you and Mal and my parents and the McMurphy all in one day." My breath caught in my chest.

Trent rolled over to look me in the eye. "You didn't lose anyone. That's why we're here now . . . to celebrate life and to enjoy the holiday."

"But the bomber is still out there."

"Rex is on it." Trent took my hand in his. "It's a small island. He'll find the person who did this." He pulled me into his arms and kissed me. It was a sweet, soft, perfect moment.

Mal jumped up and barked, drawing our attention.

We both laughed at how bad her timing was.

"What is it, girl?" Trent asked.

Mal tugged on her leash, her tail bob wagging.

"Don't let her go," I said. "Maybe she saw a squirrel."

"Is it a squirrel, Mal?" Trent rested on his elbow, his hand on my stomach.

Mal stood and pirouetted.

I raised my head. "She usually only does that when she wants to impress someone she knows."

A sudden shriek and a pop sounded as a screaming chicken firework shot our way.

"What the heck!" Trent sat up fast as a second and a third and a fourth screaming chicken pierced the air.

I sat up and Mal jumped into my lap. The noisy fireworks scared her and made her shiver.

"Stop it. You're scaring the dog!" I shouted.

Trent got up. "Stay here." He rushed off.

I heard someone take off in the brush and Trent followed. The scent of fire caught my attention.

"Oh, no." I stood and held Mal to my heart. She barked and wagged her tail. Scanning the woods, I looked for the fire. I tried to tell myself it was simply a picnic bonfire, but the way my week had been going I knew better.

Screaming chickens were found on Rodney's body. It was all connected. "Trent?" I called.

I heard nothing. Mal shivered against me. I pulled out my cell phone and dialed 9-1-1.

"9-1-1. This is Charlene. Please state your emergency."

"Hi Charlene. This is Allie McMurphy."

"Please tell me you have not found another dead person." Charlene sounded pained.

"No, as far as I know there is no dead person."

"Oh, thank goodness." Charlene was verbally relived. "What is your emergency?"

"This is going to sound stupid. . . ."

"Honey, nothing you say anymore sounds stupid."

"Thanks, I think. We are picnicking in Great Turtle Park and were attacked."

"Oh, that's not good. What exactly is going on?"

"Someone threw lit fireworks at us." That sounded much more of an emergency than screaming chickens. "Trent ran after whoever did it and now I smell fire."

"Okay," Charlene said. "I'm sending out a patrolman. Do you see the fire? I don't want to call the fire department away from their fun day in the park if you smell fire and it turns out to be a campfire."

"I understand. No, I don't see fire."

"Then it sounds like a vandal. I'm sure Trent will catch the miscreant."

I swallowed as I glanced through the woods. "What if it's related to yesterday's bombing?" It was a question I had to ask.

"Let's think this through, dear," Charlene said. "Why would a bomber attack you with fireworks? Wouldn't they attack with a bomb?"

"I suppose." I glanced around. "I still smell fire and Trent is not back yet."

"I promise I've sent patrolmen out your way. Officer Brown should be there on his bike soon. Okay, honey?"

I began to feel foolish. Maybe I had misjudged. After all, screaming chickens were not bombs. "Okay. Thank-you."

"You're welcome."

I hung up the phone. "Trent?" I moved away from the blanket and picnic basket toward the woods where he had disappeared. "Trent?"

Mal barked, startling me. A loud crunching sound came from the bushes to my right. Trent strode out of the brush, dragging a tall skinny kid by his collar.

"Oh, my goodness." I put my hand on my heart. "You scared me. Who? Sherman?"

Sherman Archibald sulked as Trent dragged him to me.

"I caught him with his pockets full of screaming chickens," Trent said.

"Sherman, why?" I asked.

The kid shrugged. His oversized green T-shirt barely moved with the gesture.

I looked at Trent. "I thought I smelled fire."

It was then I noticed the smirk that flashed over Sherman's face. I looked at the kid instead of Trent. "Sherman, you started another fire, didn't you? Where is it?"

"You're so smart. You find it." He shoved his hands in the pockets of his skinny jeans. His hair fell into his eyes and I saw a glint of anger and defiance.

"Okay. I smell it, too." Trent handed me Sherman. "Watch the kid. I'll hunt it down."

"It can't be far." I put Mal down. "Take Mal. She might help you find it."

"Stupid dog." Sherman moved as if to kick her.

I yanked hard on his collar. "Knock it off!" I pushed him down. "Sit. Stay! Officer Brown is on his way."

"You can't prove anything," Sherman said.

"Oh, we know a lot more than you think."

Trent and Mal went racing off into the woods.

"I think you'll have a lot of explaining to do when Officer Brown gets here."

"Let my kid go!"

I turned to see Luke Archibald standing a few feet from me with what looked like a bomb in his hand. I blinked. That couldn't be a bomb. I mean, who holds a bomb in their hand? "Luke, are you okay? Is someone making you do this?"

"I said, let my kid go." Luke sounded calm. His eyes were a little glassy. He wore painters pants streaked with paint and a green T-shirt that matched Sherman's.

I raised my hands to show that I wasn't holding Sherman any more. "Luke, you need to put that thing down."

It was a glass bottle with what looked like nails and screws and shards of glass surrounded by a greenish powder. The top was wired with an ignition button, which Luke held his thumb over.

"Sherman, walk away," Luke said.

"Aw, Dad. I want to see you blow her up. I missed it when you blew the other guy up."

"Sherman, walk away," Luke said again, his voice stern and far off.

"Wait. You killed Rodney Rivers?" I asked. "Why, Luke? Did you know him?"

"He was going to call the cops on Sherman."

I glanced at the boy. "You were the one who sabotaged the warehouse."

"I wanted to see how it would blow," Sherman said with a fire in his eyes. "Those rich people treat us like dirt. I wanted to see what would happen if their world got messed with." He smiled and shrugged. "They get scared, just like us little people. They get scared like you are right now."

"I don't understand." I turned to Luke. "You knew Sherman was starting fires?"

"I suspected. I followed him the day of the warehouse explosion. That pyro guy was going to turn my kid in to the authorities."

"So you killed him?"

"We had a disagreement." Luke's thumb wavered over the button.

"Dad hit the guy so hard he went down, boom," Sherman said, using his hands to mimic the moment.

"You panicked and decided to blow up the warehouse to hide the body," I said.

"You can't prove any of that," Luke said. "Now, Sherman tell the nice lady good-bye and go home."

"Oh, man." Sherman stomped his foot. "I want to see her vaporize."

"Do as I tell you or I'll vaporize you," Luke said. His eyes narrowed.

"Fine." Sherman shoved his hands in his pockets again and walked toward the path.

"Keep going!" Luke said.

"I'm going," Sherman grumbled and disappeared.

"You can't just blow me up," I said, my hands in the air. "People will know. Trent knows about Sherman. I called Charlene. Officer Brown is on his way. Too many people know, Luke." I saw him thinking. "You didn't build that bomb, did you? Sherman built it and you thought you would commit suicide."

"He's not a bad kid," Luke said. "He's just a little screwed up."

"Committing suicide and taking me with you is not the answer."

"Please. Everyone will assume I did it all. Trust me, people are quick to judge. I saw how you were putting that on your arson board. I saw that you were lining up my paint jobs with the arsons. Officer Manning will think it was me and Sherman will be free."

"Sherman will never be free. He will go on making bombs. No matter how smart he is, he'll be caught, eventually. You know that, Luke. You know that he likes people to know what he can do. For all you know, he's watching in the wings right now."

"I told him to go home." Luke started to shake. Sweat beaded on his forehead.

"He's a teen. Do you really think he did what you said?"

"He did what I said." Luke was determined to be right.

"You really want the last time your kid sees you is when you press that button? Really?" My heart was racing. All the spit in my mouth dried up. I kept talking, hoping beyond hope that Officer Brown would show up.

"Sherman, you better not be out there," Luke hollered. "Answer me straight up, boy, if you are."

Silence.

"I think that's our answer," Luke said. "I hate to have to hurt you, but I can't let anyone harm my kid."

"Luke, seriously. He's building bombs. Do you think he'll stop?"

"He'll stop. And now it's time for you to stop."

His thumb moved and I instinctively ducked. Nothing happened. I glanced up and he stood there with confusion on his face. He hit the button again. Nothing.

I was not hanging around for a third try. I spun on my heel and ran as fast as I could away from him.

"No!" he shouted and started after me.

My heart pounded in my ears, blocking all sound but my own strangled breathing. Brush hit my face and arms as I tore through the woods. I was not going to look back like the girls in the movies who always got caught.

My red Keds covered the ground nicely as I tore past the Turtle Park sign and ran right into Officer Brown.

"Whoa," he said and grabbed me. "What's going on?"

I heard a sickening thunk of glass hitting stone and ducked as the blast wave rose up from the woods behind me.

"Holy Moses!" Officer Brown said as he ducked with me, putting his bulletproof vest between me and the explosion. He hit the radio on his shoulder. "Charlene, we need the fire department to Great Turtle Park ASAP. There's been some kind of an explosion."

"Roger," came Charlene's voice over the radio.

"Okay," Officer Brown said as he gently encouraged

me to sit. His bike was thrown to the ground nearby. He must have jumped off when he saw me running from the woods. "Are you okay?"

"Yes," I said, trembling all over. "It was Luke Archibald." I glanced at Charles, my eyes filled with the pain of knowing. "He had a bomb his son Sherman made. He was trying to kill me with it. He thought if he committed suicide, you all would not consider Sherman." Tears came to my eyes and I tried not to think about the sound of the blast. "He hit the detonator and it didn't go off so I ran."

"Good girl."

In the distance, the sound of the fire truck siren approached.

"Was anyone else with you?"

"No. Trent took my dog Mal to find the fire."

"There was a fire?"

"Yes. Sherman attacked us with screaming chickens. He thought it was funny. Trent caught him, but when I said I smelled fire, Sherman dared us to find it."

"I see."

"Trent took Mal to find the fire then Luke came out of the woods with the bomb."

"Okay. Okay. George is here with the ambulance. I'm going to leave you with him and go with the fire department to see what is going on in the park. Don't go back in there."

"You don't have to tell me twice." I shuddered at the sounds replaying in my head.

George got out of the ambulance and shared a silent look with Officer Brown. "Well," the handsome EMT said, "we have to quit meeting like this."

I lifted the corner of my mouth in a half smile. "I know, right?"

"Come on. Let's get you in the back of the ambulance so that I can check you out."

"I'm fine. Really," I said as he helped me up. My legs were wobbly.

"I know. You always are."

Chapter 25

It was close to nine PM when we gathered on the blankets Dad had put down to save our spot. Mom and Dad wore heavy, padded, flannel shirts and sat in folding chairs facing the lake. The air was cool and filled with the sounds of children laughing and screaming and fireworks popping. The scent of sparklers and smaller fireworks floated by, mixed with that of charcoal and hot dogs. Trent and Mal sat with me, triumphant from their arson hunt. Sherman had started a work shed on fire on the border of Harrisonville and the park. It was ironic that his fires would end where they'd started.

Luke had been found alive but badly burned and maimed from the shrapnel. He had been life-flighted to the Lower Peninsula. Rex had arrested Sherman, who didn't have any sense of regret over what happened, only a keen gleam in his eye to hear the details of his father's injuries and how the shed had been burnt to the ground before the fire was put out.

Jenn and Shane were with us. She sat comfortably

between Shane's legs, her back resting on his chest as he held his arms around her. She had brought the cat out in the carrier because she didn't want the poor baby to be alone in the house.

My mom had bought thunder shirts for both animals so they wouldn't panic over the noise of the fireworks.

Frances and Mr. Devaney sat with us tonight. They held hands. Liz and her father Angus sat with us, as well. She had gotten the entire scoop and had printed late-breaking news for the paper.

Finally, Sophie showed up right before the show started. "Is there room for one more?"

"A couple more." I patted the spot beside me on the blanket. "We're expecting Rex and Charles."

"Cool." She sat down next to me. "Nice to be one of the cool kids."

"We are the cool kids, aren't we?" I said with a smile. Then I saw Rex and Officer Brown enter the schoolyard. I waved them over.

"Who's the hunky guy in the police uniform?" Sophie asked, her gaze all over Charles.

My matchmaker eyes lit up. "That's Charles Brown. I'll introduce you."

Rex came over and grabbed a cold soda out of the cooler and took a seat in one of the empty chairs next to my dad. I waved Charles over and introduced him to Sophie. Chemistry was in the air beyond the fireworks that started in the sky above us. I gently pushed him down to sit beside Sophie on the blanket. Then I got two sodas and gave them to Charles. He was quick to take the hint and offered Sophie one. She happily took it, letting her fingers touch his in the exchange.

I sat down with a contented smile and put my head on Trent's shoulder. The fireworks bloomed in earnest and all conversation stopped as everyone admired their beauty. Mal curled up on my lap, happy to be with me. Halfway through the show, Sandy walked up with her grandmother. Trent got them chairs and my heart filled with happiness. My entire family was here, safe and sound and celebrating a Star Spangled Fourth.

This may have been the best Fourth of July ever.

Acknowledgments

It takes a team of people to make a book and I'd like to acknowledge just a few of those who help me with this fun project. I'd like to thank Kelsey Schnell, Mackinac Island State Park staff member, for answering my questions about forest fires on the island.

Next, I'd like to thank the staff at the Island Bookstore for supporting these books, as well as the great staff at Kensington Books, Michaela, Adeola, and everyone who helps make the books a success.

Please note that any errors about Mackinac Island are my own. I do my best to get details right, but I'm also a fiction writer and take liberties with the truth if it helps further the story.

Thanks to my family in Michigan and all the great bookstores who support me and allow me to write. Thanks to the many readers. Your support and encouragement means so much. Happy Reading!

Special bonus

In case you missed the delightful
first book in the Candy-Coated Mystery series
by Nancy Coco,
here's an excerpt from *All Fudged Up.*

Keep reading and enjoy . . .

Chapter 1

I figured that, after ninety-two years of living, Papa Liam probably had some skeletons in his closet. I had no idea they were real.

Not that Joe Jessop was a skeleton . . . yet. But the man was definitely dead and lying in my second-floor utility closet.

I don't think I screamed when I found him. You know how they always scream on television when they find a dead body. I was certainly startled when I turned on the light. I'll admit that. Who wouldn't be when they walked in on a person lying against the shelves with dried blood all over his face and looking, well, lifeless.

It took me a minute to figure out what to do. Should I rush to him and feel for a pulse and try to give him CPR? The idea made me gag since the guy was a funny color and puffier than the last time I saw him. Mostly I stood there thinking about what the right thing to do was. It was only for a few seconds. I was in shock. I'm certain.

My next thought was I should probably run out

screaming, but that seemed silly since I hadn't screamed at first glance and I was the only person in the building. I would have to run the length of the hall, down two flights of stairs, and out the building screaming and waving my hands. Yeah, I'm not really that kind of person.

I always thought of myself as more practical. After all, when Papa had died suddenly, I'd managed to step into his shoes with only a few bumps in the road.

After his funeral, it'd taken me two weeks to sublease my Chicago apartment, put my car in storage, and pack up my stuff. The plan all along had been for me to arrive on Mackinac Island in late April to help Papa Liam open the McMurphy Hotel and Fudge Shoppe for the season. This was to be the summer when my papa would give me all his best advice, see me through the day-to-day handling of the property, and turn over the keys to the family business.

Unfortunately, I was now on my own to figure out how to keep the family business going. Papa'd been at the senior center playing pinochle, drinking whiskey, and laughing when he'd suddenly fallen face-first into the table. Just like that. He was gone.

Sort of like Joe Jessop. One minute he was doing who-knows-what in my closet, and the next moment I was not screaming at the sight of his dead body. Life was a mystery that way.

I took my cell phone out of my pocket.

"9-1-1, this is Charlene, what is your emergency?"

"Um, I opened my closet and there's a guy on the floor. Well, not really on the floor, but mostly on the floor." I inhaled. "I think he's dead."

"Is this Sarah Jane? I'm not taking any more of your practical jokes, girl. You're wasting the taxpayer's money."

"Wait—" The phone went dead in my hand. Well, not as dead as Joe, but dead.

Joe stared at me accusingly. I noted that his eyes were bloodshot and his pupils pinpoints. Don't the crime shows say strangulation causes bloodshot eyes—or was that poison? I wasn't about to step farther into the scene and contaminate it to find out.

"9-1-1, this is Charlene, what is your emergency?"

"Hi, yes, Charlene." I tried to be reasonable. "This is Allie McMurphy over at the historic McMurphy Hotel and Fudge Shoppe."

"Pleased to make your acquaintance, Allie. I'm a big fan of your papa's fudge, but, you should know that this line is for emergencies only. If you want to talk to me, you need to call dispatch at 906.555.6600. Bye now."

"Wait!" Charlene hung up on me again. "I'm trying, Joe," I muttered to the dead guy. He didn't answer, but then I would have run screaming if he had . . . Which would take care of the whole "proper way to act when discovering a body" thing. For the third time, I punched numbers into my phone. This time I called the dispatch number. At least I hoped it was the dispatch number. I was a bit rattled and wouldn't be surprised if I accidently called my mother instead.

"Dispatch, this is Charlene, how can I help you?"

There was a moment of relief that it wasn't my mother on the line, although she might have been a bigger help. Except for the part where the cops ask why I didn't call 9-1-1.

"Yes, Charlene." I tried again. "This is Allie McMurphy."

"Hi Allie, how are you? I was sorry to hear about your Papa Liam passing suddenly like that. At least he went doing what he loved to do best."

Did she mean cheat at cards? I sighed and glanced at the dead guy. Did Joe wink? Okay, that thought creeped me out a little. I took a step back. "Thanks, Charlene, listen, I want to report a dead body in my utility closet. Well, at least I think he's dead."

There was a long moment of silence on the other end of the phone.

"Charlene?"

"Allie, why didn't you call 9-1-1? Everyone knows if they find someone hurt or, God help us, dead, they call 9-1-1. They don't waste time on the dispatch number."

Was it worth pointing out that I had called 9-1-1? No. "I promise to do that next time. Can you get someone over here?"

I turned my back on the "crime scene" out of respect for the old guy. I mean, he might have been Papa Liam's oldest rival, but that didn't mean his death didn't affect his family.

"I can indeed," Charlene said. "Stay on the line." I could hear her searching through drawers. "Hold on, one second. I need a pen."

A pen? Didn't they have some kind of computer database? Or was Mackinac Island that backward? I didn't think of the place as backward. Touristy maybe. Purposely laid-back in an island sort of way, certainly. But not backward.

"Found it." I heard Charlene click a pen. "Okay, now let's start with your name."

Really? "Charlene, it's Allie. Remember?"

"Yes, of course, I remember . . ." It sounded like she was writing something. "Allie McMurphy called at nine PM to report a possible DB. Allie, where are you?"

I glanced back at Joe. Was he laughing? Was I laughing? Someone was giggling like a crazy person.

"Allie," Charlene shouted. "Get ahold of yourself."

That straightened me up. If this call was being taped, I'm sure everyone would be wondering why I was laughing when faced with a dead man in my closet. "I'm sorry." I tried to breathe in and out and pretend I wasn't hysterical. "What did you ask? Oh, right. I'm at the McMurphy Hotel and Fudge Shoppe on the second floor in the utility closet."

"All right," Charlene said as her pen scratched away. "Stay on the line. I'll send Officer Manning over along with the EMTs."

I swallowed the laughter that threatened to spill out again. "Okay, um, should I go downstairs and let them in?"

"That's probably a good idea," Charlene said. "Unless the guy's not dead. Did you check for a pulse?"

That sobered me up. I turned to the puffy, blue/white, blood-encrusted face. "I, um, didn't touch anything."

Charlene made a sound very close to a snort. "Then how do you know he's dead? For goodness' sakes, you scared the devil out of me and all for no good reason."

"Oh, no, he's dead."

"How can you tell?" Her tone sounded impatient.

"He looks dead." Now I was getting impatient back.

"Have you ever seen a dead body before?"

I suppose that was a good question, but it didn't make me happy. I wanted to lie. I really did. "No." I tried not to sigh too loudly. Then a thought occurred to me. "Wait! I have seen a dead body." Papa Liam, of course.

She harrumphed. "One that wasn't prepped by the mortuary?"

Crap. "Give it up, Charlene. I'm not touching him. In fact, I'm going downstairs right now to wait at the door for the police."

"Fine." Charlene huffed. "But Officer Manning'll be pretty upset if this turns out to be a drunk asleep in your closet."

Wait, isn't that as bad or worse than a dead body? It would mean that some strange man was sleeping it off in my closet. There was a lock on my third-floor apartment door, but still. I'm the only one in the hotel before the season opens. I could have been attacked or worse. The dead body could have been me. That thought made shivers go down my spine as I scrambled down the stairs.

"Please tell me someone's really on their way over here." I'm afraid my voice was a tad breathless by the time I reached the bottom of the flower-patterned carpeted stairs.

There was a knock on the glass front door of the shop, and I screamed . . . a little.

Charlene snickered in my ear. "He's there," she said. "You can hang up now."

"Great." I practically ran to the door. "You've been a big help, Charlene. Thanks."

"You're welcome, dear."

So much for sarcasm, I thought as I answered the door.

The man outside had all the right gear on, a complete blue officer outfit. It was dark out, but I could see in the lamplight behind him the official police bicycle complete with flashing light and siren. I had a sudden thought that the local police ought to have a flashing light on the top of their hats. A giggle slipped out.

"Are you all right, Miss?" The officer narrowed what could only be described as pretty blue eyes. They were that soft baby blue and ringed with thick long eyelashes that curled. "Miss?"

"Right." I opened the door wide and waved for him to come inside. "I may be in a bit of shock. I'm Allie McMurphy."

He took off his hat and uncovered a wide bald pate that was attractive in that "tough-guy" way. "I'm Officer Rex Manning," he offered. "Charlene told me you might have a dead body situation."

Situation? I swallowed. "Um, upstairs, second-floor utility closet. Follow me."

He did, following me through the under-construction first-floor lobby to the twin staircases that led to the second floor.

"Is it okay if we take the stairs? The elevator repair guy is coming in the morning."

"That's fine," he said. I noted that his nice gaze took in the details of the building, including the renovations. "Is there anyone else in the building?"

"You mean besides the dead guy?" I climbed the stairs. My fingers brushed the cool, worn-smooth banister. The rubber of my athletic shoes snagged at the flowered carpet. "No, the crew working on the renovations left at six PM."

"It's a big building with lots of places to hide," he pointed out.

I stopped on the second-floor landing and drew my brows together. "Are you thinking the killer is still inside?" Suddenly there wasn't anything funny about the situation. I'd only been on Mackinac Island for a month, but it really didn't seem like the kind of place you had to keep your doors locked for fear of a serial killer. Not like Chicago, anyway.

I mean, on an island with five hundred to six hundred year-round residents, you could spot a serial killer a mile off. Couldn't you? Weren't they usually the quiet-keep-to-themselves-neighbor? Wait, was that me?

"All I'm thinking is that it's a big building," Officer Manning said with a nonchalant tone.

I pursed my lips. His words weren't encouraging. "All the rooms are locked." I lifted the master key I had in my hand. The hotels on island still had metal keys. It was quaint and fun. The keys were locked up in a key cabinet in Papa Liam's office. Once the renovations were done, they would hang from hooks behind the reservation desk. "I'm the only one with a key."

"Okay." The word was flat and monotone. I tried not to infer anything from it. "Where's the body?"

"Over here." I walked down the hall. Somewhere in the late seventies Papa had put down a green carpet with a raised flower pattern. It was a little worn now. Okay shabby, but I had it on my to-do list to replace. In the center of the hall was a set of elevator doors. Across the hall from there was the small utility closet where Joe Jessop died.

The door was still open, and the light shone into the dimmer hallway.

"Yep, that's a dead body." Officer Manning stood in the doorway, his expression serious as stone. My shock-crazed brain registered that he wore a bulletproof vest underneath his shirt, giving his pleasant girth stiffness. Even though we stood eye to eye, he looked strong.

I was glad of that because if there was a killer in my home, I wouldn't think twice about letting Officer Manning get between me and him. I mean, that's what they paid him to do, right?

He stepped carefully into the room. I knew he was a brave man because he knelt down and checked Joe for a pulse even though we both knew that ship had sailed hours ago. Officer Manning looked around, then reached up and made a call on the two-way radio that sat on his shoulder. "Charlene, get Doc Hamlin over here. We need a coroner on site. We have a DB."

"Yes, sir."

Sure, Charlene sounded completely professional when talking with the officer.

"Did you touch anything?" He stood and took pictures with his cell phone.

"I opened the door, turned on the light, and stepped inside." I hugged my waist, trying to quell the shivering that threatened to take over my body. "He was kind of hard to miss."

"He's a big guy," Officer Manning agreed absently as he took more pictures. "Did you touch him? Check for a pulse?"

"No."

All he did was nod at that. His cell phone clicked

away. My teeth chattered. I clamped down hard trying to stop them, but the sound caught the officer's attention.

"Sit down!" He said it sharp and tight, and I obeyed without thought; my knees gave way, dropping me to the hall floor. He moved lightning fast because the next thing I knew he was beside me. "Put your head down."

"Okay," I muttered as the shivering took over. I put my forehead on the floor. He must have grabbed a blanket off the shelf in the closet because he draped one over me. I tried not to think about it too much as I worked to hold myself together. The vibrations of more footsteps reached me or it could have been my teeth rattling my bones.

"What do we have?" a new male voice asked. A shot of adrenaline went through me. The sound I made would have been a scream except my throat closed up the instant I realized that I had not locked the door behind us when we came upstairs.

Chapter 2

"Was that a squeak?" the new male said. "Or a laugh?"

"She's in shock." I heard Officer Manning reply.

Could a person die of embarrassment? Maybe if I buried my face in the carpet and drew the pale blue blanket over my head, it would all go away.

The two hunkered down beside me. Someone put a hand on my back. It was a comforting gesture. I would have said something nice about it if I weren't afraid of biting my tongue with my stupid chattering teeth. Tears filled my eyes. I'm sure it was frustration. I mean, I don't cry easy.

"Miss, can you sit up?" the second voice said gently, causing more tears to track down my cheeks. Shoot. Don't be nice to me. Don't you know that nice is the worst thing you can be to a girl on the verge of losing it?

I sat up and wiped the tears off with the sleeve of my chamois work shirt.

The second voice belonged to a guy with deep brown eyes and the high cheekbones of a true local.

He wore a blue uniform as well, but this one said "EMT" on it. He was lean with broad shoulders and competent hands. My vision narrowed, and I saw stars.

Mr. EMT had me flat on my back with my feet higher than my head before I knew what was going on. Shoot, he hadn't even bought me a drink first.

"Thanks," I muttered through gritted teeth as he adjusted the blanket around me and then pulled out a blood pressure cuff. With silent movement, he pumped up the cuff, released it a little, and pumped it again as he listened. I have no idea what he heard as all I could hear was my heart pounding in my head. He put his fingers on my wrist and checked my pulse. I noted that his name tag said George Marron.

"I'm"—chatter—"fine"—chatter—"really."

"Take a deep breath. In through your nose and out through your mouth."

I did what he said and concentrated on his soulful eyes until I could talk. "Not used to finding"—breathe in, breathe out—"a dead person in my closet is all."

George's calm gaze watched me. It was kind of embarrassing getting all this attention when there was a dead man down the hall.

"Was I right?" Officer Manning asked as he stepped out of the crime scene.

The EMT nodded.

"Do you want to take her down to the clinic?" Officer Manning tipped his head and studied me as if I were a specimen in a zoo.

"No!" I tried to sit up, but George put his hands on my shoulder and kept me down.

"She'll be fine."

"See." I huddled under the blanket. "I'll be fine."

Officer Manning frowned. "Is there anyone you can call?"

"Um, why?" I had to ask. "It's only a little shock. I don't need a ba . . . ba . . . babysitter."

"You can't stay here tonight," he pointed out. "This is a crime scene."

"Oh." It was my turn to frown. "The whole hotel?" Distracted by this new development, I was able to use my elbows to hold myself up. The blanket pooled around my jean-covered lap.

"The season starts in four weeks. I'm in the middle of renovations." Not that I didn't have a backup plan. My hotel management degree had taught me how to be frugal and efficient. But I was stubborn and didn't want to use Plan B. That meant at least a three-week delay in opening, giving my competitors a significant advantage.

Wait . . . Was that why someone had killed Joe, to try to run me out of business?

I pushed the silly thought away. School had taught me that people would do the craziest things to see a competitor fail. But good sense told me most people drew the line at killing someone. What was the point of that? Right? Besides, it wouldn't take such a dramatic act to see a person fail. It was far too easy to lose money in any small business, more specifically the competitive fudge shop business here on island.

After all, Mackinac Island was known as the fudge capital of the world. Everyone here took their fudge very seriously—including my Papa Liam.

"Always have a backup plan," Papa Liam had

drilled into my head growing up. "Creative thinking helps."

"We'll need you out of the hotel at least for tonight while we work," Officer Manning said. "Longer if need-be."

"What? No. There's no need-be." I sat all the way up. George checked my blood pressure again. I waited patiently for him to be done before going on. "I have a business to run."

Well, get back up and running. Papa'd let the hotel wear down a bit the last two years while I was in culinary school. I'd been shocked at the shape of the place when I'd taken over.

It's why I'd started the renovations right after Papa's death. He'd already done most of the groundwork with the Mackinac Island historical society. I knew he wouldn't want me to put my dream of running the family business aside just because he'd gone toes up, or in Papa's case nose down, unexpectedly.

"At least let me continue with the renovations in the lobby." I tried not to beg. "If I have any delays, I'll lose my subcontractors."

I glanced at George, looking for support in my hour of need. He stood and crossed his arms over his chest, waiting, I assume, for Officer Manning to tell him what to do next.

Officer Manning narrowed his eyes. His mouth tightened slightly. "Subcontractors are the least of your worries, Ms. McMurphy. Is there someone you can call?"

"Frances Wentworth." She was a retired school teacher who'd spent the last twenty years working for

Papa Liam in the summers as front-desk clerk and reservation organizer.

"Call her," he ordered. "George, come with me." With that, both men took off down the hall and disappeared into the closet.

I lay back down and blew out a long breath as I stared at the hall ceiling. It needed painting. The white color was no longer eggshell, and in fact the plaster had cracked into the most interesting of shapes.

"Call her," Officer Manning said from down the hall. The man had stuck his head out to check on me.

"Yes, sir." I did my best interpretation of a salute and pulled my phone out of my pocket. "I could stay in a motel," I muttered; then I realized that I was on an island in the off-season and—the most important thing of all—the other hotels were also my competitors. Not that they had anything to worry about at this point.

I mean, I had a crumbling ceiling, half-completed renovations, and a dead body in my closet. Everyone would be taking bets I'd even open by the start of the season.